Leonardo Padura was born in 1955 in Havana and lives in Cuba. He has published a number of novels, short-story collections and literary essays. International fame came with the *Havana Quartet*, all featuring Inspector Mario Conde, of which *Havana Red* is the first to be available in English. The novel has won numerous prizes, including the Premio Café de Gijón and the Spanish Premio Hammett. It has sold widely in Spain, France, Italy, Germany and Portugal.

HAVANA RED

Leonardo Padura

Translated from the Spanish by Peter Bush

BITTER LEMON PRESS
LONDON

BITTER LEMON PRESS

First published in the United Kingdom in 2005 by
Bitter Lemon Press, 37 Arundel Gardens, London W11 2LW
Reprinted 2005, 2006, 2007

www.bitterlemonpress.com

First published in Spanish as *Máscaras* by
Tusquets Editores, S.A., Barcelona, 1997

Bitter Lemon Press gratefully acknowledges the financial assistance
of the Arts Council of England

A CIP record for this book is available from the British Library

ISBN 13: 978-1-904738-09-1
ISBN 10: 1-904738-09-5

Typeset by RefineCatch Limited, Broad Street, Bungay, Suffolk

Printed and bound by CPI Group (UK) Ltd, Croydon, CR0 4YY

ARTS COUNCIL
ENGLAND

Once again, and as it should be:
to you, Lucía

Author's Note

In this novel I have taken certain poetic liberties and quoted texts, some short, some long, by Virgilio Piñera, Severo Sarduy, Dashiell Hammett, Abilio Estévez, Antonin Artaud, Eliseo Diego, Dalia Acosta and Leonardo Padura, as well as some fairly officious documents and a few passages from the Gospels. On more than one occasion I have changed them, on others even improved them, and almost always omitted the quotation marks that were once used in such cases.

On the other hand, I'd like to thank the following friends for the time and talent they invested in reading and revising the drafts of this book: Lourdes Gómez, Ambrosio Fornet, Norberto Codina, Arturo Arango, Rodolfo Pérez Valero, Justo Vasco, Gisela González, Elena Nuñez and, of course, Lucía López Coll. Finally, as ever, I must point out that the characters and events in this book are the work of my imagination, even if they are pretty close to reality. Mario Conde is a metaphor, not a policeman, and his life, quite simply, unfolds in the possible space that is literature.

Summer 1989

PEDAGOGUE: (. . .) No, there's no possible solution.

ORESTES: There's always sophistry.

PEDAGOGUE: That's true. In a city as conceited as this, on the basis of feats yet to be performed, monuments never erected, virtues nobody practises, sophistry is the best weapon of all. If any of the wise women tells you she is a prolific writer of tragedies, don't dare contradict her; if a man declares he is an accomplished critic, encourage him to believe his lie. We have here, and don't you forget it, a city in which everybody wants to be deceived.

> Virgilio Piñera, *Electra Garrigó*, Act III

Above all, you have to accept that, like the plague, theatre is a delirium and is contagious.

> Antonin Artaud, *The Theatre and Its Double*

We all wear masks.

> Batman

The heat is a malign plague invading everything. The heat descends like a tight, stretchy cloak of red silk, wrapping itself round bodies, trees and things, to inject there the dark poison of despair and a slower, certain death. It is a punishment without appeal or relief that seems ready to ravage the visible universe, though its lethal vortex must fall on a heretic city, on a district condemned to hell. It tortures mangy, forlorn street dogs searching for a lake in the desert; old men dragging sticks that are more exhausted than their own legs, as they advance against the summer solstice in their daily struggle for survival; once majestic trees, now bent double by the fury of spiralling temperatures; dead dust piled against the sidewalks, longing for a rain that never comes or an indulgent wind, presences able to upset their becalmed fate and transform them into mud, abrasive clouds, storms or cataclysms. The heat crushes everything, tyrannizes the world, corrodes what could be saved and arouses only the most infernal wrath, rancours, envies, hatreds, as if it intended to provoke the end of time, history, humanity and memory . . . But how the fuck can it be so hot? he whispered as he removed his dark glasses to dry the sweat dirtying his face and spat into the street a minuscule gob of phlegm that rolled over the parched dust.

The sweat burned his eyes, and Lieutenant Mario Conde looked up at the sky to clamour for a cloud that would augur relief. And then the shouts of glee hit his

1

brain. The cacophony hurtled towards him, a rehearsed chorale expanding as if it had erupted from the earth and careered on the afternoon heat, rising up momentarily above the din of traffic and lorries rushing along the Calzada, gripping Conde's memory in a sullen embrace. But he saw them as soon as he reached the corner: while one lot celebrated, clapped and shouted, others argued, also at the top of their voices, and eyed each other up like real enemies, blaming each other for the same reason the others were so happy: vanquished and victors, he quickly concluded as he stopped to survey the scene. There were boys of various ages, between twelve and sixteen, of every colour and shape, and Conde thought how, if someone had stopped on that same corner, in that same district, twenty years ago on hearing a similar outcry, he'd have seen exactly what he could see now, boys of every colour and shape, except the guy celebrating or arguing most would have been him, the young Conde, grandson of Rufino Conde, or the Count as he was known to everyone. Suddenly he enjoyed the illusion that time didn't exist there, because it was that side-street which had served ever since as an area for playing baseball, though some seasons would see a sly, treacherous football appear, or a basketball hoop nailed to an electricity post. But soon baseball – with bat, hand, four bases, three rolling-a-fly or at the wall – would impose its rule not too acrimoniously, over those passing fads: baseball infected them, like a chronic passion, and the Count and his friends suffered virulent attacks.

Despite the heat, August afternoons had always been the best for playing baseball on the street corner. Holiday time meant everybody was in the neighbourhood all the time, and had nothing better to do, and the hyper-active summer sun allowed you to play on beyond eight o'clock at night when a game really deserved to be extended. Recently, however, the Count had seen few games of baseball on the street corner. The boys seemed to prefer other less energetic, more sweet-smelling diversions than running, hitting and shouting for several hours under a scorching summer sun, and he wondered what boys nowadays could possibly do on long summer afternoons. Not like them: they always played baseball, he recalled, and then recalled how few of them were left in the neighbourhood: while some went in and out of prison for lesser or greater crimes, others had moved on to such disparate destinations as Alamar, Hialeah, Santiago de las Vegas, Union City, Cojímar or Stockholm, and one had even collected a one-way ticket to the Colón Cemetery: poor Marquitos. Consequently, even if they'd wanted to and still had enough strength left in their legs and arms, the guys from that era could never organize another game of baseball on that street corner: because life had destroyed that option, along with so many others.

When the celebrations and arguments were over, the boys decided to play another game and the two obvious group leaders prepared to pick their sides with an eye to redistributing forces and continuing the war in more balanced conditions. Then the Count had an idea: he'd ask if he could play. He felt roasted by his eight hours that day in the Information Bureau at Police Headquarters, but it was only six in the afternoon and he'd rather not yet return to the solitary heat of his house. A much better idea would be to start playing baseball. If they'd let him.

He walked over to the group, which was around the plank chosen as home-plate, and hailed Black Felicio's son. Felicio was one of those he'd always played with and the Count reckoned he must be back inside as he'd not seen him for a long, long time. The boy was as black as his father and had also inherited that abrasive, acrid smell of sweat the Count knew by heart, for he always managed to catch it when out with Felicio.

"Rubén," he addressed the black kid, who looked at him slightly alarmed. "Reckon I could join the game for a bit?"

The boy kept staring as if he hadn't understood, and then looked at his friends. The Count thought an explanation was in order.

"I've not played for some time and suddenly felt like making a few catches . . ."

Then Rubén went over to the other players, so he wouldn't be the only one to bear the weight of the decision. Best to consult on everything in this country, thought the Count, as he waited on their verdict. Opinions seemed divided and agreement took longer than expected.

"All right," Rubén finally said, from his position as intermediary, but neither he nor the others seemed over-pleased by their concession.

As they discussed the make-up of the teams, the Count took off his shirt and rolled up his trouser bottoms twice. Luckily he hadn't taken his pistol to work today. He put his shirt on the wall of the house where Spaniard Enrique had lived – and also died, was it ten, twenty or a thousand years ago? – and eventually they told him he was in Rubén's team and an outfielder. But, when he found himself surrounded by boys, shirtless like them, the Count felt it all too contrived and ridiculous: his skin sensed the boys' sarcastic looks and he thought they perhaps saw him like the first missionary to reach a remote tribe: he was a foreigner, with a different language and customs, and wouldn't find it easy to integrate in that brotherhood which hadn't sought him out, which didn't want or understand him. Besides, all those boys must know he was a policeman and, in keeping with the neighbourhood's ancestral ethics, they wouldn't be particularly delighted if others saw them on such good terms with the Count, however close a friend he'd been of their parents or older brothers. OK, some things never changed on that street corner.

As the members of his team started to take up positions, the Count grabbed his shirt and went over to Rubén. He went to put his arm round his shoulders, but desisted when he felt his skin touch the layer of sweat covering the boy.

"Sorry, Rubén, I just remembered I'm expecting a phone call. I'll have a game another day," he told him.

And he went off towards the Calzada, feeling the red, merciless sun, already level with his eyes, burning body and soul. Above his head he could see the flaming sword indicating his irrevocable exit from that lost paradise that had once been his, but was no longer and would never be again. If that corner wasn't his, what did he own the title deeds to? A lacerating sensation that he was alien, foreign, different, hit him so strongly that the Count had to restrain himself and cling to his last ounce of pride to stop himself running away. And only then, when he realized it was too hot to be running around street corners, did he grasp the real reason they hadn't wanted to count him in: how come I didn't get it, those bastards were playing for money . . .

"What's the matter, wild man?"
  "I don't know. I think I'm tired."
  "It's hot, don't you reckon?"

5

"Fucking hot."

"Your face looks really shit awful."

"I can imagine," the Count agreed, as he coughed and spat out of the window in the direction of the yard. Skinny Carlos watched him from his wheelchair and shrugged his shoulders. He knew when his friend behaved that way it was best to ignore him. He'd always said the Count was a long-suffering bastard, a sucker for nostalgia, a total hypochondriac and the most difficult person to console in the world, and today he didn't feel he had time or stamina to relieve the fierce onslaught of melancholy his friend was suffering.

"Should I put some music on?" he asked.

"You feel like it?"

"Only asking. Just to pass the time, you know?"

The Count went over to the long row of cassettes on the top of the shelves. His eyes ran over titles and singers, and this time was hardly surprised by Skinny's eclectic taste in music.

"What do you fancy? The Beatles? Chicago? Formula V? Los Pasos? Credence?"

"Hey, Credence," they agreed again: they liked to hear Tom Foggerty's tight voice and the elemental guitars of Credence Clearwater Revival.

"Theirs is still the best version of Proud Mary."

"That's not even up for discussion."

"He sings like a black, or rather sings as if he were fucking God."

"Fucking right." And were surprised as they looked each other in the eye: both felt simultaneously the painful inevitability of the morbid replay they were engaged in. They'd repeated that same dialogue, the same words, on other occasions, often, over twenty years of friendship, and always in Skinny's room, and its periodical resurrection brought back the feeling

6

they were entering an enchanted realm of perpetual, cyclical time, where it was possible to imagine all was pristine and eternal. But so many visible signs, so much skulking behind shame, fear, rancour and even affection, gave notice that only the remastered voice of Tom Foggerty and the Credence guitars had any permanence. The baldness threatening the Count and not-so-skinny Skinny's sick flab, Mario's inveterate sadness and Carlos's intractable illness were all too conclusive proof, among a thousand others, of a wretched decline entirely in the ascendant.

"It's some time since you saw Red Candito?" Skinny asked when the song came to an end.

"No kidding."

"He was here the other afternoon and told me he'd given up his line in shoe-making."

"What's he into now?"

Skinny looked at the cassette player, as if suddenly something about the machine or song had distracted him.

"What's up, you sly bastard?"

"Nothing's up . . . He's got a *piloto* and he's selling beer . . ."

The Count nodded and smiled. He could smell his friend's intentions from several miles.

"And he asked me why we didn't go and pay him a visit one of these days . . ."

The Count nodded and smiled again.

"You know I can't go to that kind of place, Skinny. It's illegal and if something happens . . ."

"Mario, don't fuck around. In this heat, with your shit-awful face . . . and it's only a couple of minutes to Candito's place . . . A few beers. Come on, let's off."

"I can't, you bastard. Fucking remember I'm a policeman . . ." his weak-willed arms feebly hoisting flags proclaiming SOS . . . "Don't keep on, Skinny."

But Skinny did. "I'm damned desperate to go and I thought you'd jump at the chance. You know I never get out, I'm more bored than a toad under a rock . . . A few cold beers. Just for my birthday, right? And you're practically not a policeman any more . . ."

"But what kind of bastard have you turned into, Skinny? Your birthday's not until next week."

"All right. All right. If you don't want to, we won't . . ."

The Count brought the wheelchair to a halt outside the entrance to the building. He wiped the sweat away again, as he looked at a passageway lined with doors on both sides. His arms hung heavy after the effort of pushing his friend's two hundred and fifty pounds more than ten blocks, and the two hills he'd gone up and down. A light flickered in the dark at the end of the passage and the glare from television screens and voices of the characters in the latest soap emerged from every open door in the place. "Tell me, Mama, who's to blame for everything that's happened? Please tell me, Mama," asked someone who'd surely suffered terrible things in that life in daily episodes that craved to be the real thing. Then he put his handkerchief away and walked towards Candito's door, the only one still shut. As he pushed the wheelchair he tried to hide his face between his arms: I'm still a policeman, he thought, as the temptation from those clandestine beers drew nearer, with the cool, delectable oblivion their consumption would deliver.

He knocked and the door opened as if they were expected. Cuqui, the mulatta who now lived with Candito, had only to stretch out her arm to turn the door handle. Like all those living in the block, she too was watching the soap, and her face seemed to reveal the astonishment of the character finally discovering the whole truth. "I'm to blame," the Count thought of saying, but he restrained himself.

"Come in, come in," she insisted, but her voice retained something of the hesitancy of the character in the soap: she refused to believe, and perhaps that was why she shouted into the room, and kept her eyes trained on the newcomers: "Candito, you've got visitors."

Like in a puppet theatre, Red Candito's saffron-coloured head peered out from behind the curtains hiding the kitchen and the Count got the code: having visitors was different to having customers, and Candito should show himself cautiously. But as soon as he saw them, the mulatto broke into a smile and walked over.

"Fucking hell, Carlos, you persuaded him," he said, as he shook hands with his two old school friends.

"I told you I'd come and here I am, right?"

"You bet, come inside. I've still got some stuff left. Hey, Cuqui, get a nice snack for these mates of mine and forget the soap, go on. Whenever I look at it, they're spewing out the same bullshit . . ."

Candito sorted the furniture so Skinny's chair could cross the room, raised the curtain which hid the kitchen and opened the patio door: some six tables, all full, halted the Count in his tracks. Candito looked him in the eye and nodded: yes, he could go in. But for a moment from the kitchen the Count scrutinized the customers: they were almost all men, only three women, and he tried to identify the odd face. He instinctively touched his belt to check his pistol wasn't there, but calmed down when he didn't recognize anyone. Any of those characters could have had run-ins with him at Headquarters and the Count didn't like the idea of bumping into them in a place like this.

The cheap marble tables were round, iron legged and piled high with bottles. A cold bright light lit the space and a cassette recorder played at top volume the mournful songs of José Feliciano, whose voice did its best to drown out the drinkers' voices. By the sink, two metal tanks sweated ice against the heat. Candito walked over to a table in one corner, occupied by two awesome-looking specimens. He spoke quietly. The men agreed to give up their seats: one was huge, fair-haired, a good six feet tall with long, dangling arms, a face as cratered as the moon's surface; the other was smaller, his skin so black it was blue, and he just had to be a direct grandson and universal heir to Cro-Magnon man himself: Darwin's theory of evolution was reflected in the exaggerated jutting of his jaw and the narrow forehead where the eyes of a wild beast of the jungle glinted yellow. Red Candito gestured to the Count to push Carlos's chair nearer and to the men to bring three beers.

"What did you tell that pair of troglodytes?" the Count mumbled as they sat down.

"Calm down, Conde, calm it. You're anonymous here, right. Those guys are my business legs."

The Count turned to look at the big blond, who was now approaching the table with their beers; he placed them on the table and then, without a word, walked over to the tanks.

"They're your bodyguards, you mean?"

"They're my legs, Condesito, and they have a hundred uses."

"Hey, Candito," Skinny butted in. "What's a lager cost these days?"

"Depends how you get it, Carlos. Right now it's tricky and I sell it for three pesos. But yours is on the house, and no arguing, OK?" And he smiled as Cuqui appeared with a plateful of strips of ham, and cheese with biscuits. "All right, darling, carry on relaxing with that soap." And he stroked her backside farewell.

The ice-cold beer restored a degree of peace to the Count's over-heated spirit, and he regretted gulping down the first bottle almost in one go. Now he was only irritated by the aggressive volume of the music and the sensation of vulnerability he felt at turning his back on the other customers, but he realized it was Candito who had to survey the remaining tables and decided to stop worrying when the blond guy replaced the empty bottle with a full one. Efficiency was returning to the island.

"What are you up to, Conde?" Candito drank in small gulps. "I've not seen you in ages."

The Count tried the ham.

"I'm in the doghouse, because they suspended me after I had a row with an idiot there. They've put me on form-filling and won't let me as much as look into the street . . . But you've switched tack completely."

Candito took a long swig from his bottle.

"No choice, Conde, and you know it: you can't let yourself get burnt in any business. The shoes thing was half down the shoot and I had to change track. You know it's real hard in the street and, if you don't have a peso, you're no longer a player, you know."

"If you get caught, you'll be in dire straits. God won't spare you one hell of a fine . . . And if they catch me here, I'll be in the doghouse for the rest of my life."

"Don't get like that, Conde, I tell you there'll be no dire straits."

"You still go to church, I suppose?"

"Yes, sometimes. You've got to keep on good terms with some people . . . Like the police, for example."

"Stop talking shit, Candito."

"Leave off, gents," interrupted Skinny. "These beers are dead and gone. Tell them to pour me another, Red."

Candito lifted his arm and said: "Three more."

The fair-haired guy served them again. The melodious drunken voice of Vicentico Valdés was now playing on the cassette recorder – confessing he was sure he knew where to find the moon's missing earrings – and, as he downed his third beer, the Count felt he was relaxing. The fact that he'd been in the police for more than ten years had created tensions which pursued him. Only in a few places, like Skinny's, could he get rid of certain obsessions and enjoy the gut pleasures of old times, the times they were talking about now, when they were students at La Víbora high school and dreams of the future were possible and frequent, because Skinny was skinny then, walked on both legs and hadn't been injured in the war in Angola, Andrés wanted to be a great pitcher, Rabbit insisted on rewriting history, Candito showed off his effervescent, saffron Afro hair and the Count devoted himself to beating out his first tales as an aborted writer on an Underwood.

"Do you remember, Conde?" Candito asked, and Mario said of course he remembered that story, a story he hadn't even listened to just now.

Blondie brought a fourth round of beers, and Cuqui a second plate of titbits, which Skinny Carlos threw himself at. The Count was bending over to get a piece of ham, when Candito stood up, making his chair fall over.

"Bastard!" somebody shouted.

With no time to get up, the Count turned his head and saw a mulatto put his hands to his face and totter backwards, as if in flight from the big blond bruiser standing in front of him holding a bottle. Then the prehistoric black came up behind the guy, shouting bastard, bastard, stood firm on his simian fighting legs and delivered a quick flurry of hooks to the guy's kidneys that brought him to his knees. Big Blondie, meanwhile, had turned his back on his companion to look at the rest of the tables, hands on hips, threatening: The first to try it . . . But nobody else did.

The Count, now on his feet, saw Candito walk past him, reach the penitent mulatto and grab his shirt collar. Blood spurted from one of his eyebrows, as the small black, on the other side, gripped his hair and whacked him round the ears with a wash-brush.

"Let him be," shouted Candito, but the black kept on with the brush. "Let him be, for fuck's sake," he shouted and let go of the mulatto's shirt to grab the hand of the black, who only then loosened his grip. The Count observed with almost scientific interest the collapse of the macerated mulatto: he fell to his right and his head resounded on the cement like a dry coconut. No, he wouldn't have stood much more.

Blondie walked over to the cassette recorder and changed the music: Daniel Santos was the latest guest for the night. Then, in no great hurry, he went after the mulatto, held him up under the armpits, while the little black took his ankles. They went out though a door at the back of the yard which the Count hadn't noticed.

Candito looked at his other customers. For a moment only Daniel Santos's voice could be heard.

"Nothing happened, get it . . .?" he said finally. "If anyone wants another beer, then ask me, right?" and he lifted up the chair knocked over by his speed of take-off.

The Count had already sat down and Skinny was wiping away the sweat that had started to bathe every inch of his fat body.

"What happened, Red?" Skinny took a long, long swig.

"Don't worry. As they say: aggro that goes with the trade."

"The guy was after me, right?"

Now Candito gulped down his beer and took a piece of cheese without looking up.

"I don't know, Conde, but he was after somebody," he breathed loudly, still chewing.

"And how the fuck do you know, Red, if the guy didn't say a word?" Skinny couldn't get over his shock.

"You don't give them time to speak, Carlos, but he was after somebody."

"Fuck, they almost killed him."

Red smiled and wiped his forehead: "The real bitch is that's how it's got to be, my friend. Here it's the law of the jungle: respect is respect. Now neither that guy or any of the people here or anybody who hears the story of what happened will dare try it on."

"And what will they do with him now?" Curiosity gnawed at Skinny, who was sipping his drink nervously.

"They'll put him out to rest till he cools off. And after he pays for what he's drunk, we'll send him home because he needs to get some early shut-eye today, don't you reckon?"

Skinny shook his head, as if he'd understood nothing, and looked at the Count who was still silent, apparently absorbed in the bolero Daniel Santos was singing.

"Did you see that, you rascal?"

"You bet I did, you animal."

"And do you get it?"

"No. I swear by my mother every day I understand less . . . Hey, come on, Red, let's have another beer."

14

The worst thing was this sense of the void. As the alarm clock rang, it drilled into the Count's brain a quarter to seven, a quarter to seven, and his eyelids struggled against lethargy and the recent burden of beer, a quarter to seven, the void started to reclaim its space like an oil slick suddenly released and spreading over the sea of consciousness; but it was a colourless slick, because it was void and nothingness, the end which recommenced, day after day, with an unstinted capacity for self-renewal against which he lacked any defences or valid argument: a quarter to seven was all that was tangible in the depths of that void.

Recently he'd started to imagine death might be somewhat similar: waking to an absence of atmosphere, onerous yet painless, stripped of expectation and surprises because it was only this: a bottomless, empty void, a dark, padded cloud cushioning him definitively. He also tried to recall the time there hadn't been a sense of void or premonitions of death, when dawn rose like a curtain on a new performance, no matter whether imagined or improvised, at least it seemed right and appealed: a spontaneous desire to live another day. But it was like feeling sick and trying to think what it was like to be well, and he couldn't, since the ubiquitous quease prevented him from reviving other pleasant sensations.

When he went out into the street, on such mornings that came hot with the dawn, a solitary taste of coffee

15

lingering on his lips and no woman waving him farewell, no magnet drawing him into the future, the Count wondered what could be the latest incentive impelling him punctually to set his watch and alarm, given that time was the most objective manifestation of his void. And as he could find none – a sense of duty? responsibility? need to earn a living? movement by inertia? – he wondered yet again what the hell he was doing there, heading for a bus queue more crowded and violent by the day, smoking a cigarette that rotted his guts, seeing people who were less and less familiar, suffering a heat that got hotter by the minute, and he told himself it was his fast lane to hell. Then he touched his belt and realized, once again, that he'd left his pistol at home. He asked who was the last in the queue and lit his third cigarette of the day. If I'm going to die anyway . . .

"Major Rangel wants to see you."

And, with that declaration from the duty officer, the Count resurrected at least one lost expectation: yes, perhaps he might now down a good cup of coffee, purge the sweet, stewed taste of the brown liquid sloshing with unidentifiable particles he'd drunk in the shabby café where he'd stopped before reaching Headquarters. He took one look at the queue by the lift and made for the stairs. He couldn't imagine why the Boss wanted to see him, but his nasal memory was already enjoying the aroma of freshly brewed coffee, served in the shiny white cups his chief was so fond of. Three months ago, after his public punch-up with Lieutenant Fabricio, the Count had been tried by the Disciplinary Tribunal and sentenced to six months of card-filling and telex-sending in the Information

Bureau, until his case was reviewed and a decision taken that he could return to his detective work. He'd avoided meeting up with the Boss ever since: the Count's sentence was, as far the Major was concerned, a judgement against himself. Despite his eccentricities and increasingly apparent lack of rigour, the lieutenant had always been his best officer, and the Boss trusted him and more than once had shown him affection and respect, both publicly and privately. Consequently, to a degree, the Count felt he'd let him down. And, as the last straw, the Internal Inspection team now grilling the entire Headquarters kept Major Rangel in such a foul temper it was advisable to see him from a distance, he thought, when, that is, you had no option but to see him.

He pushed the glass-panelled door and entered the ante-room to the Boss's office. Another woman now sat behind the desk that had been occupied for several years by Maruchi, the woman in charge of the Major's office, someone in her fifties, uniformed, who wore a lieutenant's stripes and vaporized the cup of coffee the Count had dreamt of lifting to his lips. Mario walked over, saluted, told her who he was, and informed her that the Major was expecting him. The secretary pressed a button on the intercom and sent the message to her boss's office.

"Lieutenant Mario Conde."

"Tell him to come in," said the intercom, and the new secretary stood up to open the office door.

Major Antonio Rangel had got up behind his desk, and shook the Count by the hand. Such a gesture, unusual on the part of the Boss, was a warning to the lieutenant that things weren't looking good.

"How's it been downstairs, Mario?"

"So-so, Major."

"Take a seat."

The Count flopped down in one of the armchairs opposite the desk and could hold back no longer.

"What happened to Maruchi, Boss?"

The Major didn't look at him. He was searching in one of his desk drawers, and finally extracted a cigar. It didn't look good: too dark, veins too bulging, resistant to the flame from the lighter the Major brought to bear.

"It looks like a stick," he pronounced finally, after exhaling two or three puffs of smoke, as he looked incredulously at the brand and the Count awaited his verdict. "I can't believe it. Listen to this. '*Selectos*', made in Holguín. Who the fuck's ever heard of cigars made in Holguín? The country's gone mad . . . They transferred Maruchi. I still don't know where to, or why for. Anyway, don't ask me, I can't tell you anything, and if I could, I wouldn't . . . You get my drift?"

"Impossible not to, Major," the Count acquiesced, as he said goodbye to the coffee one could always extract from Maruchi. "And how come you've got no decent cigars?"

"I haven't, and what business is it of yours? To the point," said the Major as he slumped back in his chair. He seemed exhausted, as if he'd also fallen into the void, thought the Count, who'd always admired Major Rangel's youthful brio, so distant from his real age of fifty-eight, nurtured and refreshed by lengths in the pool and hours of knocking balls around a tennis court. "I called you because you're going out on a case."

The Count smiled wrily, and decided to exploit his minimal advantage.

"Any chance of a coffee?"

The Major's smile spread around the end of his cigar, slightly curled his upper lip.

"It's the seventh, and we're still waiting for this month's coffee ration . . . You made life really difficult. Well, the problem is I don't have enough detectives and I've got no option but to lift the sanction on you temporarily. I need you and Sergeant Manuel Palacios to get a hold on this case immediately: a trasvestite who's been killed in the Havana Woods."

"A transvestite."

"That's what the man said."

"No, you said a 'trass-vestite'. And it's 'trans-vestite'."

The Major shook his head.

"Will you never change, my boy? You still reckon life is a game?"

His voice had changed: the Major's voice could shift tone according to topic and agenda, or time and place, and currently it was sour and withering.

"Forgive me."

"I can't forgive you, Conde, no way can I forgive you. Can you imagine what my head's like? You think it's easy working with an army of Internal Inspectors here at Headquarters? You know how many questions I get asked every day? You know two detectives have been sacked for corruption and two more are about to get suspended for negligence? And do you realize all this stuff backfires on me? No, no way can I forgive you . . . And why are you in plainclothes? Didn't I tell you to come in uniform while you were downstairs?"

The Count stood up and looked through the big office window. A few buildings, scattered trees and such a calm sea, in the distance, setting the boundary on so many dreams, destinies and deceits.

"Who's got the low-down on the case?" he asked, and touched his belt again, where he sometimes wore his pistol.

"Nobody. He's just been found. I think Manolo's waiting for you in his cubicle. Now beat it."

The Count turned round and walked towards the door. Grabbed the door handle, and stopped. He felt strange, didn't know whether to feel flattered or manipulated, though he supposed the Boss must be feeling even stranger: as far as he knew, it was the first time the Boss had revoked a sentence imposed on a subordinate.

"It's a pity you won't forgive me and can't offer me a coffee. But as I'm really fond of you, if it's at all possible, I'll get you some decent cigars," he said, and left without waiting for a response or thanking the Major for giving him that assignment. He decided at the last moment it would have been in bad taste to thank him.

When the policeman lifted the canvas, the photographer took his chance to snap another picture, as if still needing to record that precise angle on the death of a carnivalesque creature who, according to his identity card, went by the name of Alexis Arayán Rodríguez. Now he was a red bundle, two pale protruding white legs, their muscles tensed, in violent contrast with the sun-scorched grass. A purple, puffy female face topped the body. A red silk sash of death was pulled tight round his neck.

The Count lowered his arm and the policeman, bored out of his mind, dropped the canvas. The Count took out a cigarette and Sergeant Manuel Palacios asked him for another. The Count gave him one reluctantly: Manuel Palacios said he didn't smoke but, really, what he never did was buy his own. The Count looked towards the river.

In the morning, under the leafy canopy of the Havana Woods, one lived the illusion that the city's luck was in and summer had lost its way. A pleasant breeze, carrying the dark odours of the river, rustled the branches of poplar trees and arrogant carobs, of almond trees that opened out like circus tents and of oleanders, laced with delicate lianas that criss-crossed to form hanging plaits. The Count remembered how, as a boy, he'd been to several birthday parties in the arbours in the woods that were hired out, on the other side of the bridge, and that once, aping a Tarzan hanging from the lianas in the oleanders, he'd scuffed on a stone new orthopaedic boots his mother had given him to wear to the party. The two accusing furrows on the black leather of his annual pair of new shoes earned him a week of punishment, no watching television, no listening to the episodes of the Guaytabó series, no playing baseball. The Count had never forgotten because it was precisely the week Guaytabó the Indian met old Apolinar Matías in Anatolio the Turk's tyre-repair shop and initiated their indestructible friendship as strugglers on behalf of justice against evil. And he'd missed that memorable encounter.

The Count looked towards the river and reflected how fortunate it was that people were still thieving, murdering, assaulting, embezzling in the city, ever more enthusiastically, for it was his personal salvation. Terrible, but true: that death by strangling the forensic doctor was now trying to explain to Detective Lieutenant Mario Conde and his aide, Sergeant Manuel Palacios, had enabled him to fight off the void and feel that his brain was working again, and that it had more to its existence than headaches from repeated hangovers.

"What do you reckon, Conde? Yes, it's a man.

Dressed and face-painted like a woman. Now we've got murdered transvestites, we're almost part of the developed world. At this rate we'll soon be making rockets and going to the moon . . ."

"Cut the crap and continue," said the Count, throwing his cigarette butt in the direction of the river. Sometimes he liked to speak like that and this forensic, for a reason as elusive as it was inevitable, always made him react curtly. Perhaps it was just his easy familiarity with death.

"I'll go on, but I'm not talking crap . . ." the forensic retorted and, as he listened, the Count tried to imagine the scene.

He saw Alexis Arayán, a woman without all the gifts of nature, tarted up in red, wearing a long, antiquated dress, her shoulders draped in a shawl that was also red, her waist emphasized by a silk sash, walking out with someone in the starry night of the Havana Woods. The Count reckoned a breeze was blowing, and the night must have been more appealing and welcoming than in the rest of the city. The footprints preserved from Alexis's sandals signalled the journey from road to woods. The other footprints belonged to her companion, a corpulent man, who must have leered at Arayán's face in eager anticipation: her finely drawn eyebrows, eyelids with pale purple highlights, mascara'd eyelashes and a mouth as gorgeously red as that strange dress which belonged to a vague, doubtless, distant past. Perhaps there were kisses, teasing gropes, caresses from Alexis Arayán Rodríguez's delicate fingers and varnished nails. Then they stopped by the battered trunk of a hundred-year-old blossoming flamboyant tree, and a tragedy of equivocal love was unleashed.

"You know something?" Conde interrupted the

forensic's narrative and looked over towards the covered corpse. "Yesterday was the sixth of August, wasn't it?"

"Yes, and so what?" the forensic now interjected.

"So you lot can see the benefits of going to catechism . . . August sixth is the Catholic celebration of the Transfiguration. According to the Bible, on that day Jesus was transformed before three of his disciples on Mount Tabor, and, from a cloud of light, God called on the apostles to listen to him for ever. Isn't it too much of a coincidence that this transvestite was murdered on August sixth?"

Sergeant Palacios folded his arms over his undernourished pigeon chest (he was only palatial by name) and looked at the Count. The lieutenant enjoyed that glance where a timid, squint-eyed hesitancy lurked: he knew he'd surprised his skeletal subordinate, and his subordinate liked him surprising him like that.

"And how the fuck do you remember that, Conde? As far as I know you've not been inside a church for thirty years or more."

"Less, Manolo, less. The truth is I always liked that story: in catechism classes I always imagined God in his cloud, illuminating everything, like a spotlight . . ."

"Hey there, Conde, and what if Alexis disguised himself day in day out?" asked the forensic, smiling triumphantly at his question and prompting the Count to think of other reasons for his aversion.

"Then end of mystery," the Count admitted. "But it would be a pity, wouldn't it? The transfiguration of Alexis Arayán . . . sounded good. Well, on with your story."

He saw them halt under the flamboyant tree. A glimmering moonbeam sweetly pierced the foliage, lending a silvery hue to the big man and fake woman, a

23

couple on whom the breeze rained down a shower of red petals. Perhaps they kissed, perchance they caressed, and Alexis kneeled, like a penitent, surely intending to satisfy his companion's urgent need with his nearest available orifice: the grass patches on his knees betrayed such genuflection. Then he plunged into the finale of the tragedy: at some moment the red silk sash went from Alexis's waist to his neck and the big man mercilessly terminated the breathing of the woman who wasn't, until her heavily made-up eyes bulged out of their sockets and every sphincter opened its floodgates, dislocation by strangulation.

"And this is what I can't square, Conde. The big guy killed him from in front, judging by the footprints, right? But it appears the transvestite didn't struggle, didn't scratch, didn't try to wriggle . . ."

"So there was no fight?"

"If there was, it was a battle of words. The dead man's nails don't carry any traces of anything, although I'll provide a conclusive report later . . . But now comes the second mystery: the murderer began dragging the corpse that way, look at the grass, do you see? As if to throw him in the river . . . But barely moved him two yards. Why didn't he throw him in the river if that was what first came to mind?"

The Count observed the grass where the forensic was pointing and the canvas which now covered Alexis Arayán's body and hid the patch of red cloth that had so alarmed the early morning jogger, who'd departed his daily route only to discover a corpse already crawling with ants which had rushed to the magnificent banquet.

"But the strangest of all is yet to come: after killing the transvestite, the big man pulled her knickers down and inspected her anus with his fingers . . . I know because he wiped himself clean on the gown afterwards. What do you make of that, lads? Well, that's as far as I can take my little tale. When they do the autopsy and finish the other tests in the laboratory, perhaps we'll have more to go on. Now I'll be off, downtown, as there's been another little murder in Old Havana . . ."

"Good luck to you, Flower of the Dead," replied the Count, turning his back on him.

He looked at the dirty river in the waters of which he'd once swum. In other waters, in fact, he thought, like Heraclitus: not as dirty, at least not up by La Chorrera bridge, where he and his friends used to catch *biajacas*, if not Chinese carp, when someone decided those red, exotic fish could grow and multiply in the island's rivers and reservoirs.

"All right, Manolo, try your hand at the questions Flower of the Dead left us. Why should anyone let himself be strangled and not fight back? Why didn't the murderer throw him into the water? And why the hell did he decide to inspect his anus?"

Sergeant Manuel Palacios folded two very rickety arms over an emaciated chest. In every case he was assigned to with the Count it was always the same: he had to be the first to get it wrong.

"I don't know, Conde," he said finally.

The Count looked at him, surprised by his wariness.

"But how come you don't know, you always know."

"But I don't today . . . Hey, Conde, what the hell's got into you today? You're evil, man . . ."

The Count returned his gaze, as he lit up. Manuel Palacios was right. What had got into him?

"No idea, Manolo, but it's something bad. Can you imagine, I cheered up when they said I was on a homicide case and could leave Headquarters! I'm fucked, my friend, now I get high when people are murdered. And this forensic gets at me bad, and big time."

Manuel Palacios nodded. He knew the Count too well to take those confessions of sinning seriously, and decided to be charitable for once.

"Well, how about a respectable married man with children, who suddenly picks up a woman, though he's not a flirt, and she's tall and beautiful, and he's so delighted with his catch he brings her to the Woods, they kiss, caress, the woman kneels down to suck him off, as the forensic said, and it's then the fellow discovers she's not a woman but quite the contrary. Or how about the big 'un also being quite the contrary, I mean as fruity as the dead guy, and he's taken revenge on Arayán because of some quarrel from queer street? Or how about if the big 'un's a pervert who likes going with transvestites so he can kill them afterwards, because he hates transvestites, as he's a transvestite himself, but frustrated by his size and girth? That's my best take ever, don't you reckon?"

The Count coughed, cigarette between his lips.

"You get more intelligent by the day, you really do ... This is fishy, Manolo. Nobody lets himself be strangled without scratching back. And you tell me, what can you hide in your rectum? Drugs? A jewel? And how come the other fellow knew he had to search there of all places? ... Well, because they obviously knew each other, right? But if the murderer decided against dumping him in the river it was because he was sure no one would connect him with this place or that transvestite. And what about the red dress, which must be from somewhere special? And why's such an elegant transvestite carrying his identity card? Don't you think it incongruous? I'll tell you something for nothing, Manolo. I don't like this case one little bit. It seems too mysterious, and in this country it's too hot and there are too many fuck-ups for us to handle mysteries as well. Besides, I've never liked pansies, just so you know. I'm prejudiced in that department . . ."

"You don't say," acknowledged the Sergeant.

"Piss off, Manolo."

The worst side of the dead is that they leave their living behind, thought the Count after the woman confirmed: "Yes, he's my son, what's happened now?" And as she seemed so strong and self-confident he told her without any soft-soaping: "The fact is he was murdered last night," and then the woman started to crumple, her body visibly shrinking on that nice leather sofa, and an inconclusive scream escaped from the hands she screwed up over her face . . .

The identity card Alexis Arayán was carrying indicated that the address was his permanent residence: a big two-storey house on Seventh Avenue in Miramar, with a well-trimmed garden, walls painted a bright white, panes of glass miraculously intact in a city of broken windows, and two cars in the drive. A Mercedes and a Toyota, pointed out Manuel Palacios, who knew all there is to know about cars and makes . . . It was the image of prosperity, as it should be, for according to his ID Alexis was the son of Faustino, *the* Faustino Arayán, Cuba's latest representative at UNICEF, a diplomat always away on long trips, a personage from the higher echelons, and of Matilde Rodríguez, that woman who was perhaps a well-preserved sixty-something, with hair a delicate shade of brown and well-kept hands, who suddenly seemed much older than sixty and to have lost the petulant confidence with which she'd welcomed the policemen.

When she cried out a black woman silently

emerged from somewhere in the mansion. She walked noiselessly, as if her feet didn't touch the ground. The Count noticed the bloodshot look in her bulging, shiny eyes. She didn't greet the policemen, but sat down next to Matilde and started whispering words of consolation accompanied by almost maternal gestures. Then she got up, went out the way she'd come, and returned with a glass of water and the tiniest pink pill, which she handed to Matilde. The Count's training enabled him to pick up a fleeting tremble in the black woman's hands as they neared the out-of-control hands of Alexis's mother. Still not acknowledging the Count or Manolo, the black woman said: "Her nerves have been very bad of late," and she helped Matilde stand up and led her towards the stairs.

The Count looked at Manuel Palacios and lit a cigarette. Manolo shrugged his shoulders as if to say: "Bloody hell," and they waited. The Count, meanwhile, decided to use a blue and white ashtray inscribed GRANADA. Everything seemed clean and perfect in that house where suddenly tragedy had unexpectedly intruded. The black woman came down ten minutes later and sat down opposite them. Finally she looked at them, her eyes still red and shiny, as if she were running a temperature.

"Her nerves have been very bad of late," she repeated, as if it were a set phrase or the best her vocabulary could muster.

"And comrade Faustino Arayán?"

"He's at the Foreign Ministry, he left early," she said, joining her hands together and pressing them between her legs, as if praying to an image nailed to the floor.

"You work here?" interjected Manolo.

"Yes."

"Been here long?"

"Over thirty years."

"Do you know if Alexis went out from here yesterday?"

"No."

"Didn't he live here?"

"No."

"But this was his home, wasn't it?"

"Yes."

"Yes what: was it or wasn't it, did he go out or don't you know?"

"Yes, it was his home, but he didn't live here and so he didn't leave here. For months . . . Poor Alexis."

"So where did he live then?"

The black woman looked towards the staircase that led to the bedrooms. She hesitated. Should she ask permission? Now she did seem nervous, as she lowered her bloodshot gaze and bit her lips.

"In somebody else's house . . . Alberto Marqués's."

"And who might he be?" continued Manuel Palacios, perching his sparse buttocks on the edge of the chair.

The black woman looked back at the staircase and the Count felt that anonymous sensation for which a girlfriend of his, for want of a better word, had invented the term *liporis*: embarrassment at somebody making a spectacle of themselves. That woman, in the year 1989, still harboured the atavistic instinct of deference: she was a servant and, what was worse, thought like a servant, wrapped perhaps in the invisible but tightly clinging veils of genetics moulded by numerous enslaved, repressed generations. Physical discomfort then replaced *liporis*, and the Count felt the desire to flee that world of glitter and veneer.

The black woman looked back at Sergeant Palacios and said: "I think he's a friend of Alexis . . . A friend he lived with. Poor Alexis, oh God . . ."

When he found that the almost impossible address really existed, the Count shut the notebook where he'd transcribed various data from the stout file on Alberto Marqués Basterrechea and tucked it into his back pocket. He contemplated the miraculously cheerful bougainvillea in the garden under that anti-social two p.m. sun. Magenta, purple, yellow, like enchanted butterflies, their flowers entangled the small clump of leaves, thorns and branches which seemed capable of surviving any local or universal cataclysm. The sylvan shadow in the garden, dominated by the arrogant plumes of several palms, lent a dark patina to the house rising up a few yards behind, exhibiting its number 7, on calle Milagros, between Delicias and Buenaventura. Could that number and the names of the three streets – Miracles, Delights and Good Fortune – be an invention of Alberto Marqués in order to locate his house in a corner of Earthly Paradise, in perfect arcadian bliss? Yes, it had to be one of the devil's infinite stratagems, since, according to the information the Count had recorded in his notebook, extracted from the aged but ever healthy file he'd been handed with a broad grin by the security specialist who dealt with the Ministry of Culture, anything was possible if it involved that very particular, diabolical Alberto Marqués: a hugely experienced, predatory homosexual, politically apathetic and ideologically deviant, a provocative, conflictive individual, lover of the foreign, hermetic, obscurantist, potential consumer of marijuana and other substances, protector of derailed queers, a man of dubious philosophical affiliations, steeped in class-based, petty-bourgeois prejudice, all annotated and classified with the precious help of a Muscovite manual of social-realist techniques and procedures . . . That impressive curriculum vitae was the result of reports written, collated and précised by diverse police informers, successive presidents of the Committee for the Defence of the Revolution, cadres of the long-gone National Council for Culture and the present Ministry of Culture, the political attaché's office in the Cuban Embassy in Paris and even by a Franciscan Father who'd been his confessor in a prehistoric era and a pair of perverse lovers who'd been interrogated for strictly criminal reasons. What the hell have I got myself into? Trying futilely to cleanse his mind of prejudices – the fact is I love prejudice and can't stand pansies – the Count crossed the garden and walked up the four steps to the front door in order to press the bell that stuck out like a nipple under the number 7. He stroked it twice and repeated the operation, for no sound of a bell reached him, and when he was about to touch it again, hesitating over whether to try the knocker, he felt assailed by the darkness beyond the slowly opening door, which surrounded the pale face of Alberto Marqués, dramatist and theatre director.

"What's the charge this time?" asked the man, his deep voice heavy with irony. The Count tried to suppress his surprise at the door, which apparently opened by itself, at the remarkable pallor of his host's face and the question he fired at him, and opted to smile.

"I'm looking for Alberto Marqués."

"Yours truly, Mr Policeman," the man replied, opening the door a few inches more, with a distinctly theatrical touch, so that the Count had the forbidden pleasure of seeing him full length: colourless rather than pale, thin to the point of emaciation, his head barely adorned by a drooping, lank lock. He was covered from neck to ankles by a Chinese dressing gown that might have belonged to the Han dynasty: yes, thought the policeman, no less than two thousand years of anguish must have passed through that silk, its colours as faded as the man's face, worn and rough as if it were no longer silk, prominently marked by testimonies to many a battle, by what could be coffee, banana, iodine or even blood stains, endowing what masqueraded as the attire of historic emperors with a dismal, out-of-sorts leitmotif . . . The Count forced a smile, remembered the awful reports stuck to his buttock, and dared ask: "How do you know I'm police? Were you expecting us?"

Alberto Marqués blinked several times and tried to organize his dank strands of hair.

"You don't have to be a Sherlock Holmes . . . In this heat, at this time of day, with that face and in this house, who is going to pay a visit if not the police? Besides, I've heard what happened to poor Alexis . . ."

The Count concurred. It was the second time recently he'd been told he had a policeman's face and he was on the verge of believing it was true. If there were bus drivers who looked like bus drivers, doctors like doctors and tailors like tailors, it can't be difficult to have a policeman's mug after ten years in the job.

"Can I come in?"

"Can I not let you come in? . . . Enter," he added finally, opening the door into the pitch black.

It wasn't hot inside, although all the windows were shut and he couldn't hear the hum of any refreshing fan. In the cool half-dark, the Count imagined a distant high ceiling and glimpsed several pieces of furniture as dark as the ambience, scattered without rhyme or reason across a spacious room divided in two by a pair of columns that were possibly Doric in their upper reaches. At the back, some five yards away, the wall receded towards an equally sombre corridor. Without closing the door, Alberto Marqués went over to one of the room's walls and opened a french window that spread the obscene light of August on the room's chequered floor, to create an aggressive, decidedly unreal luminosity: as if from a spotlight turned on a stage. Then the Count got it: he'd been dropped into the middle of the set for *The Price*, a work by Arthur Miller that thirty years earlier Alberto Marqués had staged with a success that still resonated (that was also on his file) and which he himself had seen some ten years ago in a version staged by one of the dramatist's more orthodox disciples. He'd stepped into the production – too many stages! – like one of the characters and . . . of course, that was it. But could it possibly be?

"Sit down, please, Mr Policeman," said Alberto Marqués, reluctantly pointing to a mahogany armchair darkened by fossilized sweat and grime, and only then did he close the door.

The Count used those seconds to get a better look: between the floor and the dressing gown he saw two rickety, starved ankles, as translucent as the face, extended by two unshod ostrich feet that ended in funny fat toes, splayed out, their nails like jagged hooks. The fingers of the hands were, on the contrary, slender and spatula'd like a practising pianist's. And the smell. His sense of smell ravaged by twenty years of vigorous smoking, the Count tried to distinguish the odours of damp, fumes from reheated oil and a whiff he recognized but found difficult to pin down, as he observed the man in his Chinese silk dressing gown settling down in another armchair, parting his legs and carefully positioning his skeletal hands on the wooden arms, as if he wanted to embrace them entirely, to possess them, as in a final gesture he folded his oh-so-delicate fingers over the front edges of the wood.

"Well, I'm all ears."

"What do you know about what happened to Alexis Arayán?"

"Poor ... That they killed him in the Havana Woods."

"And how did you find out?"

"I got a call this morning. A friend got wind."

"Which friend?"

"One who lives round there and saw all the bother. He enquired, found out and phoned me."

"But who is he?"

Alberto Marqués sighed ostentatiously, blinked a bit more, but kept his hands on the arms of the chair.

"Dionisio Carmona is his name, if you must know. Are you happy now?" And tried to make it evident he found the revelation troubling.

The Count thought of asking permission, but decided not to. If Alberto Marqués could be ironic, he, Conde, could be rude. How dare that pansy try it on with him, a policeman? He lit his cigarette and puffed the smoke in the direction of his interlocutor.

"You may drop your ash on the floor, Mr Policeman."

"Lieutenant Mario Conde."

"You may drop your ash on the floor, Mr Policeman Lieutenant Mario Conde," the man said, and the Count demurred. You'll get it from me, you wanking pansy, he thought.

"And what else do you know?"

Alberto Marqués shrugged his shoulders, as he shut his eyes and released another sonorous sigh.

"Well ... that he was strung up. Ah, my God, the poor dearie."

34

Perhaps the man was really upset, thought the Count, before going on the offensive.

"No, technically, he was strangled. His neck was pressed tight till the oxygen was cut off. With a red silk sash. And you know he was dressed like a woman, all in red, with a shawl and the whole works?"

Alberto Marqués had let go of the chair arms and his right hand rubbed his face from cheek to chin. *Touché*, concluded the Count.

"Dressed like a woman? In a red dress? One as long as an old bathrobe?"

"Yes," replied the Count, "what can you tell me about that? Because I already know it was this house he left yesterday."

"Yes, he left here at about seven, but I swear I saw him just before and he wasn't dressed like Electra Garrigó."

The feast in Paris is never over, and everyone who has lived there retains distinct memories ... And it's so true, though Hemingway said it first, and he was the century's most egocentric, narcissistic writer. My memories of Paris are a nostalgia in blue I've not managed to throw off in twenty years. Because when I arrived in Paris, in April 1969, a painfully beautiful spring had just begun and it made you want to do something to be happier, if happiness exists, to be more intelligent and all-encompassing, or be freer, if freedom exists, or could ever exist. And I remember feeling the magic of an affectionate, almost velvety sun bathing the Champs-Elysées, the grand Napoleonic palaces, the frivolous cafés, and I better understood what had happened the year before. I still feel the afternoon light on the rose-window of Notre-Dame's façade like a caress on my skin, and hear the dark, historic sound of the Seine by the Cité, and that black organ-grinder in front of the Louvre making his little African monkey dance to the tune of a Viennese waltz. I also remember the Rolling Stones concert when they tried to out-rebel the Beatles, and they were only two hundred yards away from me, under a cold sky of a Paris spring, among shrieking, liberated French blondes, daughters who'd aborted and mothers newly born of the revolution that might have been and was not, although after that month of May the world would never be the same again, because the revolution had been made: the revolution in customs and morality, the twentieth-century's permanent revolution that Lev Davidovich Bronstein, alias Leon Trotsky, never imagined. I remember each day, each minute, each conversation with Jean-Paul Sartre and the inevitable Simone de Beauvoir, dinners with George Plimpton while he interviewed me for the *Paris Review*, researching the life, sensitive madness and papers of Antonin Artaud for an edition under contract of *The Theatre and Its Double*, the nostalgia I acquired upon the death of a Camus whom I never met yet always knew so well, the re-encounter, guided by the eyes and footsteps of Néstor Almendros, with the real sets of so much French cinema, and the pursuit, on the arm of my friend Cortázar, of the archaeological sites of pre-war jazz, cherished in bars like miraculous grottoes . . . I remember it all because it would be my last trip to Paris, if not my last tango, and memory anticipated history and sage memory knowingly manufactured its own self-defence and tucked away each happy moment of my last trip to Paris as if it knew it would be my last.

That's why I also remember that day of multiple coincidences charged with encouraging magnetic attractions, when Muscles, the Other Boy and I floated over to Montparnasse on the last sigh of the afternoon, in search of a Greek restaurant that just had to be called the Odyssey, and was renowned for its mountain goat. We were enjoying our leisure and freedom, advanced arm in arm, an invincible army, when Muscles saw him, or rather her, to be more exact. She was a tall, engagingly elegant woman, as prepossessing as the owner of Edith Piaf's voice, if Edith hadn't been a mere alcoholic sparrow: a woman who towered alarmingly, projected her breasts pugnaciously and sported a metallic flower of a mouth. I felt her pride tingle my skin: she was dressed in red, strident and so serene, and I found her image bore the tragic dignity which I'd recurrently seen in Electra: she was a revelation, or premonition, dressed in red.

"She's a transvestite," Muscles piped up.

And I (and the Other Boy as well, whose name I must not and do not want to recall, for it would be politically and ideologically gauche to reveal his old friendship with Muscles and myself, in that phantas-magoric Paris where everything was possible, even walking the streets with him) felt like a pillar of salt: petrified and speechless.

"My God, how can it be?" asked the Other, even allowing himself a mention of God in Paris, that distant bastion of liberty, when in his Havana conversations he would publicly defend historical, dialectical materialist ideology and his conviction that religion was the opium, marijuana, if not the Marlboro of the people . . .

"She's perfection," I said, for I already knew about pushy Parisian transvestites who went into the street to mingle and exhibit themselves, but I'd never imagined such a spectacle: that woman could have bowled any man over because she was more perfect than any woman, I'd almost go as far as to say she was *Woman* incarnate, and in fact I did.

"No, a transves*tite* doesn't imitate women," Muscles commented, as if dictating a lecture, with that know-all voice and way with words of his. He always used long, spiralling baroque sentences, as if caricaturing our poor paradisiacal Fat Lezama. As far as he was concerned, *à la limite* there is no woman, because he knows (and his greatest tragedy is this knowledge he can never cast off) that he, that's to say, she, is an appearance, her fetishistic realm and power concealing an irredeemable defect created by an otherwise wise nature . . .

And he explained to us that the transves*tite*'s cosmetic erection (Muscles always gave it the emphasis transves*tite*), the resplendent aggression of her metallic eyelids trembling like the wings of voracious insects, her voice displaced as if it belonged to someone else, a constant voice-over, the imitation mouth drawn over her hidden mouth, and her own sex, ever more castrated, ever more present, is entirely appearance, a perfect theatrical masquerade, he said, and looked at me, as if he must look at me, as if he had no choice.

It was when he uttered the word *appearance* that I understood everything, that my discovery rushed like iron filings to his magnet and I swung round in alarm to look for the transvestite. But she'd already disappeared into Paris's magical penumbra, like a fleeting sparkler . . . An appearance. A masquerade. That had always been the very essence of performance, ever since ritual dances were transformed into theatre, when awareness of artistic creation was born: the transvestite as artist enacting herself . . . But she was no longer there, and I beheld the Other Boy, in an epiphany, refusing to budge, smitten by that possibility of what he'd always longed to be – or do – and never dared . . .

From the Greek restaurant, through a glazed window, the Moulin Rouge glowed scarlet. The Other, who had been sent to Paris by the National Council for Culture because he'd just published a successful bad book programmed to fit the Latin Americanist third-world fashion of the time – always hunting for opportunities – had caught the blood-red glow full in the face and it made him seem more aroused, while Muscles, who had galloped off on his hobby-horse, was writing a few paragraphs for a future essay at the top of his voice.

"King" – he sometimes addressed me thus, promoting me up the noble hierarchy – "the human transves*tite* is an imaginary apparition where three mimetic possibilities converge" – and he paused to drink a glass of rough Balkan wine, served in beautiful imitations of ancient Greek amphoras. "First, cross-dressing properly speaking, stamped on that unfettered impulse towards metamorphosis, in that transformation which is not restricted to the imitation of a real, precise model, but rushes to pursue an infinite reality (and from the start of the 'game' is accepted as such). It is an unreality which becomes more and more elusive, beyond reach (becoming more and more womanly, till the boundary is transgressed and womanness is transcended) . . .

"Secondly, camouflage, for nothing guarantees that the cosmetic (or surgical) conversion of man into woman doesn't have, as its hidden final goal, a kind of disappearance, of invisibility, of *effacement* and erasure of the macho himself from the aggressive tribe, from the brutal macho horde. And finally," Muscles continued, "comes intimidation, for the frequent disarray or excessive make-up, the visibility of the artifice, the variegated mask, paralyse or terrify, as happens with certain animals who use their appearance to defend themselves or hunt, or to compensate for natural defects or virtues they don't have: courage or cunning, right?"

The Other – always so vulgar, "camouflaged" behind a culture he didn't possess, sonorously sucking the goat cutlets he was devouring – Muscles was paying – looked out of the window, as if he were searching for something.

"But, at the end of the day," he asked, "are they queens or aren't they?"

The truth is I never discovered why Muscles insisted on bringing him with us on our sentimental, culinary tours of Paris. Because the Other Boy – as everybody knows – only wants queens, and the more public-lavatory and over-the-top the better. And if Muscles needed someone to cross swords with, there were thousands in Paris, and he had five-star choices, so beautiful and sweet . . .

"Cubanly speaking I would say, 'Yes, they are queens,' " Muscles finally declared, a man who also had his off-the-rails longing for queens. "Like you," and he smiled, pointing at the Other, "but more daring, you know? And while we're about it, do you want to go tomorrow, Saturday, to a cabaret where some transves*tites* will perform?"

I was so struck by the invitation that I furiously downed the contents of one of those amphoras, something I'd never done and will never do again as long as I live. But everything was possible in Paris: even drinking without getting drunk . . . We walked home through the city, and it was that night, in Muscles' studio, that I began to etch some lines on cardboard, and by dawn I'd designed the red dress my Electra Garrigó would wear in that luminous, tragically aborted performance which showed Virgilio Piñera his work was more inspired than he could ever warrant.

The Count thought: this pansy and a half is getting on my wick, just as he realized he couldn't repress his desire to urinate. This story of Parisian transvestites the Marquess (as his coteries entitled him) had narrated, searching for the red dress of his dear little friend who'd been murdered, was too much like a fable rehearsed and staged to snare the unwary, catch them in a spider's web and swallow them, perhaps intellectually, maybe physically when, for example, they said they needed to urinate. He crossed his legs and it got worse: the pressure grew on a bladder overwhelmed by liquids he'd ingested to mitigate the heat and he realized he had two options in this emergency: to withdraw or to ask the dramatist if he could use his lavatory. The first solution was as hopeless as the second, for he didn't want to establish any kind of relationship with that character, but nor could he abandon him now, when he presented himself as the best way into the more scabrous mysteries in the double life of Alexis Arayán. The Marquess, fallen on hard times, was his main witness, perhaps even the murderer of the masked man, although, he thought, while he felt he was about to urinate and reviewed yet again his host's physical disposition, how could such premature baby arms have strangled anyone? But the Count had always thought urinating in a stranger's house was the first step to a revealing intimacy: seeing what's in a bathroom is like seeing into people's souls: dirty pants, an unflushed toilet or perfumed bath gel are usually as revealing as a confession to a priest.

"I need to go to the bathroom," he said, without first instructing his brain.

He supposed the Marquess would smile and he did, and he glanced down at the Count in a way that made him feel his privates had been weighed, measured and fondled.

"Just through there, third door on the left. Oh, and to flush you must hold the handle down till the water swills out all your emanations, get me?"

"Thanks," replied the Count, standing up and accepting that his bladder had let him down badly. He made for the dark passage and walked through two rooms: as he was in the Marquess's line of vision, he hardly looked to one side or the other, but he saw one was a bedroom and the second a study, with books piled high to a remote ceiling. Then he discovered the origin of the odour he hadn't been able to identify initially: it was the oppressive, alluring scent of old, damp, dusty paper that came from that equally dark precinct, where was to be found what must be Alberto Marqués's library, surely inhabited by authors and works banned by certain codes and exotic publishing wonders, unimaginable to the ordinary reader, that the Count tried to conjure up using residues of intellect not preoccupied by doubt as to whether or not he'd reach the lavatory in time.

He opened the door and looked at the bathroom: unlike the rest of the house, it seemed clean and organized, but he didn't stop to scrutinize. He stood in front of the bowl, brought his desperate penis into the light of day and began urinating, feeling the whole world was relieved by the jet hitting the glaze. And it ran on and on as he looked towards the door and thought he saw a shadow through the panes of murky glass which had been badly patched up. Could he be looking at him? The Count put his hand over his penis and stopped urinating as he peered at the door. This is all I needed, he thought, as he shook himself, and welcomed the incontrollable shiver that accompanied the end of micturition. He rapidly popped his diminished extremity into his trousers and flushed the toilet, following the instructions given. Goodbye, effluvia.

When he went into the corridor he saw the Marquess in the sitting room, seated in his armchair. He walked over to him and sat down again.

"How lovely to urinate when you feel like it, don't you agree?" commented the dramatist, and the Count was certain he'd been observed. Fuck your mother, he said to himself, this is too much, but he tried to get back on to the offensive.

"And what has all this Paris story got to do with Alexis Arayán?"

The Marquess smiled, then tittered.

"Forgive me," he said. "Well, it has to do with the dress they found him in and the fact he wasn't a transvestite. Rather he wasn't what you'd call practising, although he sometimes played at it. He donned disguises and created various personae. As much feminine as masculine, though he'd never have been capable of going on stage, you understand? He was too shy and cerebral for that and very inhibited, do you see? . . . But he always liked that dress, the one I designed on that night in Paris for my version of *Electra Garrigó* to be premièred in the Théâtre des Nations in Paris in 1971. And although Alexis was homosexual, as you must have gathered, I never imagined he'd have the daring necessary to be a transvestite and, as far as I know, he never did go into the street dressed as a woman."

"So why did he do so yesterday?"

"I don't know, you should find out . . . That is what you're paid for, aren't you?"

"Apparently," replied the Count. "By the way, was Alexis Catholic?"

"Yes, of course. And half mystic."

"And did he ever mention the day of the Transfiguration?"

"Of the transfiguration? What transfiguration?"

"Christ's . . . the one celebrated yesterday, on August sixth."

"No, he didn't mention that . . . You know, he left yesterday without saying goodbye, but I wasn't too worried, because he was like that: half neurotic, and sometimes very introverted. I heard him go out into the passage, and that's why I know it was around seven. . . . Besides, for your information: Alexis and I were just friends. He had problems at home, his parents were threatening to kick him out every day, so he asked me to let him live here. But that was all there was to it, right? Every sheep has her mate and I'm too old to wolf it . . ."

The Count lit up another cigarette and again wondered: what the fuck have I got into? This world was too remote and exotic for him and he felt totally bewildered, with a thousand questions the answers to which he had no access to. For example: did that old queer like queers or men? And is a man who goes with queers also queer? Can two queers be friends, even live together without having it off with each other? But he said: "Of course, I understand . . . And how did you and Alexis get to know each other? When did it happen?"

The Marquess smiled again and patted his dressing-gown lapels.

44

"You really don't know? ... You know, eighteen years ago, the year of Our Lord 1971, I was parameterized, and, naturally, didn't possess the parameters they were after. Can you imagine – parameterizing an artist as if he were a pedigree dog? It would be almost comic if it weren't tragic. And, on the other hand, it's such an ugly word ... To parameterize. Well, that whole business of parameterizing artists began and they expelled me from the theatre group and association of theatrical artistes, and after finding out I couldn't work in a factory, as I should have done if I wanted to purify myself by contact with the working class, though nobody ever asked me if I wanted to be pure or the working class whether it was ready to accept such a detox challenge, they put me to work in a tiny library in Marianao, cataloguing books. I'll confess something to you for which I hope you won't put me inside, lieutenant sir: it was a mistake. You can't put an artist too near fine books he doesn't own, because he'll steal them ... Though he doesn't have the soul of a thief, he'll steal them ... Just imagine: that library had an edition of *Paradise Lost* illustrated by Doré. You know the one I mean? Well, I can show you, if you like ...."

"That won't be necessary," interjected the Count.

"Well, I was working there and Alexis went to study in the library, as it was near the school where he was enrolled. And the fact is he knew who I was and obviously admired me. The poor kid, he didn't dare speak to me, because he'd heard so many things about me ... but you'll be familiar with all that, I guess? Until one day he dared, and confessed he'd read two of my works and that he'd been present at a rehearsal of *Electra Garrigó*, and it had been the deepest emotional experience of his life ... The poor child adored me, and no artist can resist the adoration of a young apprentice. So, we became friends."

"Just one last question for now," said the Count, looking at his watch. That last story seemed the most extraordinary of all he'd heard and read, and he tried to imagine what a man so acclaimed and loved by the critics could have felt in the anonymous silence of a municipal library, where his expectations were reduced to the theft of the odd desirable book. No, it wasn't so easy. "Did Alexis have problems with anyone?"

Alberto Marqués didn't smile or blink this time. He merely shifted the very long fingers which he'd draped over the end of the chair arm.

"I'm not sure if he had what people call problems. He was a sensitive soul, to put it one way. He craved peace and affection and at home they treated him like a leper, were ashamed of him, and that turned him into someone obsessed, who saw ghosts on every street corner. Besides, he knew he'd never become an artist, which had been his lifelong dream, but he courage-ously recognized his lack of talent, something not everyone's capable of doing, right?"

The Count thought: right. And wondered: could that be a dart aimed at me? No, no way, he doesn't know me and I am really talented. A real fucking talent.

"The people at the Centre for Cultural Heritage loved him, especially the artists, because he always defended them against the filthy sniffing bureaucrats leeching on talent. And I think he really enjoyed a fairly stable relationship with a painter, one Salvador K., whom I don't know personally. Will that do for now? Do you want to go to the bathroom again?" And now he did manage a smile.

The Count stood up: he'd met an awesome verbal adversary, he thought, and stretched out a hand to receive the emaciated, poorly articulated bones of the famous Alberto Marqués. It was a frog's hand.

"I don't want to go to the bathroom, but I'm not done. Besides, you owe me the end of the transvestite story."

"True, my prince," said the Marquess, unable to restrain himself, and added: "Forgive me, but I've got a real thing about titles of nobility, you know? Well whenever you fancy, Sir Policeman Count, but wait a minute: to force you to come back I'm going to lend you the book Muscles wrote on transvestites. It's dedicated to me, you know? . . . You'll see what madness human beings are capable of." And he smiled, rising up to a string of uncontrollable grunts and blinks.

The Count looked at the book's front cover: a butterfly was emerging from a chrysalis with a grotesquely divided human face: a woman's eyes and a man's mouth, female hair and male chin. It was entitled *The Face and the Mask*; and was quite uncryptically dedicated to "The last active member of the Cuban nobility". He felt an urge to return home and start reading this book, which might perhaps supply a few keys to what had happened or, at least, teach him something about the dark world of homosexuality. In his mystic dissertation the Marquess had mentioned three possible attitudes among the changelings: metamorphosis as a way to overcome the model, camouflage as a form of disappearance, and disguise as a means of intimidation. Which could have pushed Alexis Arayán into dressing up like Electra Garrigó the very night of the day of the Transfiguration? He was coming round to liking that story, but if he wanted to understand anything he had to know a little more. At least one thing was definite: Alberto Marqués couldn't be the physical murderer of Alexis Arayán. It would have taken those arms two hours to strangle the youth, while he held his nose between two fingers. But he was also sure Alberto Marqués was deeply implicated in that death dressed in red.

When he saw Manuel Palacios leaning on the car's bumper, in the shade of the first flamboyant trees in Santa Catalina, the Count realized how much he was sweating. He'd barely walked four blocks and the sweat was already drenching his shirt, but, bewildered by the rush of information, his brain hadn't yet processed the feeling of heat he now found in that moisture. It was almost 4 p.m. and the temperature had leapt several degrees.

"What happened?" asked the sergeant, as the Count mopped himself with his handkerchief.

"A very peculiar fellow who's fucked up my whole day. He's queerer than a Sunday afternoon," he said smiling, because the metaphor wasn't his: it bore the copyright of his old acquaintance Baby Face Miki. "And you know I can't stand queers . . . Well, this guy's different . . . The bastard got me thinking . . . And what did you find out?"

As the car drove up Santa Catalina en route to Headquarters, Manuel Palacios recounted the first surprising result from the autopsy: "According to your friend Flower of the Dead, they didn't take anything from the guy's arse, Conde: on the contrary, they inserted . . . Two one-peso coins. What do you reckon? Have you ever heard anything like it?"

The Count shook his head. But the sergeant didn't give him time to process his shock at the unexpected revelation: "The man who killed him is white, blood group AB, and between forty and sixty. Possibly right-handed. In other words, we've already a million and a half suspects . . ."

48

The Count declined to laugh at the joke and Sergeant Manuel Palacios finished his story: the murder had been by strangling, and the murderer had pulled the sash tight while facing the transvestite, and yet there was only the smallest speck of someone else's skin on Alexis's nails. The man's footprints indicated he weighed some one hundred and eighty to two hundred pounds, that his shoe size was number nine, that he walked normally and probably wore blue jeans, for they'd found a multi-coloured thread that had snagged on a shrub. The possible fellatio was ruled out, for there was no trace of semen in the dead man's mouth. There was not a single finger-print and the silk sash provided no useful informa-tion. Nothing of special interest was found at the location of the crime: the usual rubbish you come across in such places: a bottle, a used condom, a rusty key, cigar butts with and without their labels – Rey del Mundo, Montecristo, Coronas – and a plastic comb missing six teeth, not to mention a wisdom tooth . . .

"Then it's obvious there was no struggle," the Count commented as Manolo wound up his inventory. "And as for the coins . . ."

"It's a real bastard, isn't it? But I reckon the strangest thing is that he didn't throw him in the river. You can imagine if he'd appeared in the sea we wouldn't have known where he was from, or the fish might have eaten him and, if we'd found him, we wouldn't have identified him. Should we go to Headquarters?"

"No, no," said the Count, who paused to glance self-pityingly towards the house of Tamara, the most con-stant of his lost loves, a woman whose skin always smelled of strong eau-de-cologne, whom he'd dreamed about for the last two thousand years of his life. "Better carry on to Vedado, a friend just came to mind and I want to talk to him."

"But what the hell you doing here, you motherfucker?" And almost reluctantly he scoured the other tables, scenting possible reactions to the Count's arrival. "Look, if this lot realize you're a policeman and you start whispering to me, I'll get a bucket of shit chucked over me . . ."

"You're the whisperer," said the Count at the top of his voice, as he grabbed the glass of rum from the table and despatched it in one gulp.

Baby Face Miki didn't dare stop him or take another look around; the Count smiled. He'd known him for almost twenty years and he'd not changed: a load of bollocks. When they were at school, Miki'd become a famous flirt and used to say he'd set the definitive record for girlfriends in one year – naturally, kissing always included – thanks to his immaculate features and clean complexion, on which the years had wrought a vicious toll: with more wrinkles than to be expected at thirty-eight, traces of late pimples and poorly distributed body fat, Miki – never again to be called Baby Face – tried to hide behind a luxuriant beard that contrasted with the scant hair over his forehead, equally mortal remains of what had once been arrogant blond locks. The passage from adolescence to adulthood had been, for Miki de Jeva, a devastating mutation. Nevertheless, despite everything and against all odds, Miki had turned out to be the only accepted writer from among his school friends keen on writing: a wretched novel and two books of particularly opportune stories had granted him that undeserved standing. He knew – as did the Count – that his literary fruits were sentenced irrevocably to deepest oblivion, after their premeditated moment, much vaunted by certain critics and publishers for his writing about peasants and the need for cooperatives when every newspaper spoke of peasants and the need for cooperatives, and about anti-patriotic scum and emigrated filth, when such epithets echoed down the country's streets in the summer of 1980 . . . Nevertheless, his Writers' Union card said just that, writer, and every afternoon Miki took refuge in the Union bar to drink a few rums which, thought the Count, didn't strictly belong to him.

"Would you like us to speak elsewhere?" the lieutenant suggested, pained by the despair of this would-be author.

"No, don't worry, nobody knows you here and the rum's running out. Do you want a double?"

The Count looked at the bar, where they were serving white Bocoy rum. Irritated, he acted as if he weren't sure, perhaps wanting to bolster his confidence.

"Yes, I think that's just what I need."

"Give me four pesos," Miki said, holding out a hand.

The Count smiled: of course, you shit-head, he thought, and gave him a ten-peso note.

"A triple for me and a double for you."

While he waited for Miki, the Count lit a cigarette and tried to listen to the conversation of his nearest neighbours. There were three of them: a young but very greying mulatto, who talked non-stop, a fat bearded half-caste with a hump like a jerry-built camel; and a tall guy, with a bugger's face which would have astounded Lombroso himself. Oh image of literature! They were enthusiastically slandering another writer whose recent novel had apparently enjoyed a lot of success and who wrote very popular articles in the newspapers, and were calling him a fucking populist.

51

Yes, they said, secreting bile on the bar floor, just imagine, he writes crime novels, interviews crooners and mooners, and writes stories about pimps and the history of rum: I tell you, he's a fucking populist, and that's why he wins so many prizes, and they changed topic in order to talk about themselves, writers really preoccupied by aesthetic values and reflections on social contradictions, when Miki returned with two glasses of rum.

"I didn't tell you . . . we got the last drops from the bottle. It puts me really on edge. Every day it happens earlier."

"You like coming here, don't you, Miki?"

The writer tried his rum, as he extracted a cigarette from the Count's packet.

"Yes, why not. There's rum, you can talk a pile of shit and now and then lay some woman who's gone overboard for poetry. Right now I'm expecting one who's got more cash than the National Bank. I don't know where the hell she gets it. So if my poetess turns up, you vanish, right?"

The Count nodded, thinking he'd ask him who his neighbours were and whom they were dissecting now, but was afraid they'd hear him. He'd like to have read the history of rum, he thought, as he downed a gulp of incestuous, ahistorical alcohol, the molecules of which carried too much undistilled water.

"Miki, what do you know about a painter called Salvador K.?"

Miki smiled and took another sip of rum.

"He's a piece of shit."

"Fuck, everyone here is shit, opportunist, populist or queer, right?"

"Right first time. What did you expect? Parnassus? That when you came in they'd whisper in your ear,

"Sing, my muse, the glory of Pelida Achilles," or something as stupid? No, no chance, and for your information: that cock is all four things at once. The guy paints garish paintings which sell very well, but it's the purest shit . . . You know, I think he lives around here, between N and Seventeenth, his wife's house. And what's there between you and this fellow?"

"Nothing, somebody mentioned him the other day. And you say he's married?"

"No, I said he lives in his wife's house."

"I get you. Hey, Miki, as you know the downside on everybody's life, what can you tell me about Alberto Marqués?"

If you were to stand out in the entrance to the Union and shout, "Who is Alberto Marqués?" two hundred guys would rush up, kneel on the ground, bow down and chant: He's God, he's God, and if you leave them for a while, they'll organize a homage to him and chorus his praises, you bet your bottom dollar . . . But if you'd shouted that fifteen years ago, the same two hundred you see now would have rushed up and shouted, fists aloft, veins bursting in the neck like the fat guy's: he's the Devil, the class enemy, the apostate, the apostate of the prostate, not a bad metaphor, do you think? . . . Because that's how it is, Count: before it was better not to mention him, and now he's a living monument to ethical and aesthetic resistance, it's a load of bullshit . . . Every minute someone's recounting how he went to his place and talked to him, and you should hear them: you'd think they'd been to Mecca . . . The motherfuckers. Just imagine, now they say he's the father of creole postmodernism, that with Grotowski and Artaud he's one of the three geniuses of twentieth-century theatre, that Virgilio Piñera, Roberto Blanco and Vicente Revuelta owe everything they are to him, and even his queerness is a virtue because it allows him to voice another sensibility. That's right. Do you understand what's going on? Well, I do: when betrayal was the name of the game, they betrayed him, and now it's not dangerous, and it's even in good taste to weep over those who fell in old ideological skirmishes, you know, they worship him. And what are we left with? A guy who's really fucked up, with more hate inside him than if he'd been spawned by a Nazi, and now converted into a big cheese, and not because of what he did, but because of what he might have done, because they rubbished him and, when he was offered a second chance the guy refused, for he didn't want to do more theatre or publish anything, and he retired. A bloody hero is what he is now . . . And worst of all, the guy had to suffer a ten-year sentence of silence and solitude. Perhaps of the two hundred worshippers he has now, four or five carried on seeing him after he was destroyed, with all that stuff about queers, ideological deviants and idealists and foreignizers and the trip on socialist realism and art as ideological weapon in the political struggle . . . They took the guy out of circulation and sent him to run some bookshop or other, I'm not sure. Bloody hell: a stack of years without a single line of his published in the paltriest magazine, critics were banned from mentioning him when they wrote about the theatre, he disappeared from anthologies and even from dictionaries of writers. Straight: he no longer existed. He crumpled in the air, whooosh! not because he'd died or left the country, which amounts to the same thing. No. But because he was forced to change his routines. He became famous in the queue for bananas, and the queue for bread, at the Policlinic and milk stand ... It's terrible, right? But almost nobody talks about the kind of queer he was and still is. Do you know the story about the rent-a-blacks? Well, you know, it's amazing. The gist is he was talking to a black bugger and saying he'd pay him to fuck him, but on one condition: he'd have to take him by surprise, so it would be more exciting. And he told the big black guy to enter his house and rape him one day that week. Then he'd settle down to read, every day at that time, until lo! one day the black came and he started to run around the house and the black chased after him, and he shouted and hid and the black finally grabbed him, took his clothes off and bang! gave it him from behind. You heard of anything more poofy? And the stories about when he went beautiful boy-hunting in the street ... and a thousand similar stories. He was a queer and a half! But do you want me to tell you what's truer than all this, truer than all his queer business, his being annihilated, his betrayal by his old girlies, or the way they worship him now? Do you want me to? Well, the truth is that that queer who shits himself when anyone shouts after him has got balls down to his ankles. He took it like a man and stayed here, because he knew if he'd left the island he'd have died for sure, so he didn't play anybody's game: he shut his gob and bolted himself in at home ... I wish I'd got half the spunk that queen's got ... Fuck, get on your way, you motherfucker, my poetess is coming round the corner. You know what this crazy woman calls me? Mickey Rourke, hey, that's neat! I'll be fucked, not a drop of rum left. This lousy place!

The Count plunged into Seventeenth Street with a bad taste in his mouth – and it wasn't the rum's fault – prow pointing seawards and hull battened down so as not to be over-awed by the galling sumptuousness, apparently oblivious to the test of time and other erosions, of those palaces which had one day expressed the pride of a class at the height of its creative splendour and given the street the nickname from time immemorial of Millionaires' Row. The success of those extremely rich men – who couldn't get over their shock at being so flush, by merely hitting the three buttons of political, financial or even smuggling bravado – needed visual confirmation so badly that they insisted on giving their fortunes eternal form, and hired all the necessary talents to perpetuate the triumphs they glorified in stone, wrought iron and glass, throwing up the most dazzling mansions in the whole city. Immersed in the afternoon reveries of an aimlessly wandering mariner, he didn't even ponder how it was possible to live in a forty-roomed house or what one might feel seeing the dawn through the panes of glass that went into that stained-glass window of St George and the dragon or the tropical glade on a gigantic skylight, bearing all the possible fruits of nature and the imagination. What he was thinking, as he walked down the avenue, recycled three decades ago and now occupied by offices, businesses and a few citadels packed with the citizenry, was that when he was exactly sixteen years old and writing his first story, Alberto Marqués had already been condemned to forget glory and plaudits. His pathetic tale went by the title of "Sundays" and was selected to appear in issue zero of *La Viboreña*, the magazine of the school's literary workshop. The story told was a simple one, which the Count knew well: the unforgettable experience when he woke every Sunday morning and his mother forced him to go to the local parish church while the rest of his friends enjoyed their only free morning playing baseball at the corner of the house. The Count wanted thus to speak about the repression he'd experienced, or at least the kind he'd suffered in the most remote years of his sentimental education, although while writing he didn't formulate the theme in exactly those terms. What was frustrating, however, was the repression unleashed on that magazine which never reached issue number one – and thus also on his story. Whenever he remembers it, the Count relives a distant but indelible sense of shame, all his own, which invades him physically. He feels a malevolent torpor, a choking desire to shout out what he didn't shout the day they gathered them together to shut down the magazine and workshop, accusing them of writing idealist stories, escapist poems, unacceptable criticism, stories hostile to the country's present needs, now that it has embarked on the construction of a new man and a new society (thus spake their headteacher, the very same guy who one year later would be expelled because of countless frauds committed in his drive to be known as the best headteacher of the best high school in the city, the country, the world, even when his headship was based on fraud: all that mattered was that everyone should think him the best head and recognize him as such, and endow him with all the privileges such recognition might engender . . .). How did his story relate to all they were told? he wondered again, as he floated down the street, the wind in his sails. Yes, when it happened he was sixteen and Alberto Marqués was almost fifty, it was his first story and he thought he'd die, but Alberto Marqués was already used to living among plaudits, praise and congratulations suddenly denied him one black day because he and his works didn't meet particular parameters that were suddenly considered vital. What must he have felt, that man who looked so diabolical, whose tongue was so barbed, when he found himself separated from what he loved, knew and could do, when he saw himself condemned to suffer a silence for a period that might be perpetual? The Count tried to imagine, as he'd tried on other occasions to imagine dawn rising over those palaces, and couldn't: he didn't have the experience, but he remembered his old shame, his elemental rage at the age of sixteen, and thought he should multiply it by a hundred. Thus he might perhaps approach the dimensions of that Frustration trapped in a municipal library. Was he so harmful that he deserved such brutal punishment and a castrating exercise of re-education so that ten years on they could tell him they were strategic errors, misunderstandings by extremists who now had neither name nor office? Could the new ideology, the education of the new masses, the brain of the new man, be infected and even destroyed by enterprises such as those undertaken by Alberto Marqués? Or wasn't it more damaging to write the kind of opportunist literature cultivated by his ex-comrade Baby Face Miki, who was always ready to prostitute his writing and vomit his frustrations on anyone really talented who wrote, painted or danced? No, there was no comparison, and the world, though it was grey, could never be the way Miki – never again to be called Baby Face – coloured it. Then the Count sensed that the whole business was softening him, that he was getting softer by the day, and also that Alberto Marqués's queerness was beginning to worry him less and a furtive rebel solidarity was beginning to draw him to the dramatist, and he even began to regret any evidence that might implicate him in the assassination and take him, all his queerness, frustration and dignity, not to mention that ugly face, to a prison where his buttocks would become a flowerpot, and the service plied by buggers, though not surprising, would be free, that was for sure . . . At last he had reached the sea.

Kick his guts out, hit him hard, gouge his eyes, he'd ordered Manolo after explaining who Salvador K. was and allotting him the first interview with the painter. And when he saw him, the Count's expectations were replete with prejudice: the guy was just over forty and weighed some two hundred pounds, had two enormous feet – could he be a size nine? – and flexed a weight-trainer's arms, just right for tightening a silk sash to strangle a man while ensuring he didn't fight back.

Seated in the living room to the flat, the policemen rejected his assiduous offers of water, tea and even coffee, keeping to the plan they had agreed. No, not even water.

Salvador K. seemed nervous and was trying to ingratiate himself.

"It's an investigation, I suppose?"

"No, on the contrary," said Manuel Palacios, sitting on the edge of his armchair. The Count liked his skeletal friend's hostile manner. "It's something much more serious and you know it. Shall we speak here or should we go elsewhere?"

The painter smiled in trepidation. He's shitting himself, the Count's experience told him.

"But what about . . .?"

"Then we'll talk here. What was your relationship with Alexis Arayán?"

As he didn't like him, the Count was pleased to see

Salvador K.'s last hopes fade and the smile abandon his lips.

"I know him," he said, trying to fake a degree of offended dignity, "from the Centre for Cultural Heritage. Why?"

"Two reasons. First, because Alexis Arayán was murdered yesterday. Second, because we've heard you two were very close."

The painter tried to stand up, but desisted. It was obvious he had no plan of attack, or perhaps they had really taken him by surprise.

"Was murdered?"

"Last night, in the Havana Woods. Strangled."

The painter looked into his house, as if fearing some unexpected presence. The Count stood up while Salvador stared and formulated a question, but decided to wait.

"You really want to talk here?" persisted Manolo.

"Yes, of course, why not? . . . So he was murdered. But where do I come in?"

Manuel Palacios smirked.

"Well, Salvador, this is very delicate, but some people claim your friendship was a touch more than friendship."

Then he did get up, very offended, his muscular arms tensed.

"What are you implying?"

"What you just heard. Do I need to spell it out? People are saying you and he sustained a homosexual relationship."

Still on his feet, the painter tried to look disaster in the face: "I will not allow you . . ."

"That's fine, don't allow us, but go into the street and shout it out publicly and see what people say."

Salvador appeared to contemplate the possibility and

reject it. His muscles began to lose momentum and he sank into the lower reaches of his chair.

"They're jealous. Gossips, slanderers, envious . . ."

"Of course, you're right . . . But the fact is Alexis was killed dressed as a woman," said Manuel Palacios and, not giving Salvador time, he manoeuvred round a bend in the conversation: "When was the last time you saw him?"

"Yesterday morning at the Centre. I took some paintings to sell. Was he really dressed as a woman?"

"What did you talk about? Try to remember."

"About the paintings. He wasn't too keen on them. He was like that, meddling in other people's business. I expect that's why someone murdered him."

"And what can you tell me about the relationship you had with him?"

"That's pure slander. Just try to get someone to come and say to my face that he saw me . . ."

"That would be more difficult, you're right. So you deny it?"

"Of course I do," he said, and seemed to gain in confidence.

"What's your blood group, Salvador?"

His confidence evaporated again. The Count looked daggers at Sergeant Palacios. He'd never have asked him that question at that point, but the one buzzing round his head. Manuel Palacios was definitely better.

"I really don't know," he said, and he did really seem not to.

"Don't worry. We can find out in the Policlinic. Which one do you go to?"

"On the corner of Seventeenth and J."

"And you didn't see him last night?"

"I told you I didn't. But what's my blood group got to do with it?"

"And where were you last night between eight and midnight?"

"Painting in the studio I've got on Twenty-First and Eighteenth. Hey, I don't know anything . . ."

"Oh . . . And who saw you there?"

Salvador looked at the floor, as if searching a point of support that continually eluded him. His fear and embarrassment were as prominent as his muscles.

"I don't know, who might have seen me? I don't know, I work alone there, but I arrived at around six and worked until around midnight."

"And nobody saw you. What bad luck!"

"It's a garage," he tried to explain. "It's outside the building and if nobody's parking nearby . . ."

"Twenty-First and Eighteenth are very near the Havana Woods, right?"

The man didn't reply.

"Hey, Salvador," the Count then intervened. He thought it a good time to move the direction of the dialogue on a little . . . "What does the K mean?"

"Oh, my surname is Kindelán, that's why I sign K."

"Predictable. Something else I've been wanting to ask you for some time. I only see reproductions of famous paintings, but no works by you. Don't you think that strange?"

The painter smiled, at last. He seemed back on firm ground and breathed loudly.

"Have you never heard the anecdote about the friends of Picasso who go to his place to eat and don't see a single work by him? And one of them asks, intrigued: 'Maestro, why don't you have any of your work here?' And Picasso replies: 'I can't afford the luxury. Picassos are too expensive . . .'"

The Count faked a smile, to accompany Salvador's.

"I get you, I get you, and the other day, did he mention the day of the Transfiguration to you?"

The painter looked down, making it clear he was making an effort to remember. The Count saw that he was deciding what would be the best reply.

"I don't know, it doesn't ring a bell. But I do remember he had a Bible on his desk yesterday ... And so what?"

"Nothing, police curiosity pure and simple ... By the way, Salvador, why do you think Alexis dressed up as a woman last night?"

"How should I know ... I told you, it's just gossip ..."

"Of course, there's no reason why you should know. Well, that's enough for today," the Count added, as if tired, and his sergeant was the man most surprised by this dénouement. The Count sighed exhaustedly as he stood up, and looked the painter in the eye. "But we'll be back, Salvador, and get this into your head: try to be straight, for I can see you've got a few numbers that might win you the jackpot. Good evening."

As the painter voiced his final protests, they went into the street and got into their car. Sergeant Manuel Palacios turned the first corner tightly.

"So the Transfiguration ... Why did we leave, Conde? Didn't you see how I'd got him?"

The Count lit a cigarette and lowered the window.

"Softly, softly," he urged his sergeant, and added, "What did you expect, that the man would say yes, he's a bugger who took advantage of the other guy to sell his work and that last night he killed him because Alexis said his paintings were a load of shit? Don't fuck around, Manolo, you extracted what there was to extract and he had nothing else ... Let them check his blood group and investigate him at the Centre and in the studio he's got on Twenty-First and Eighteenth, and see if anyone saw him last night. Tell Headquarters to give you a couple of guys, better still if they're Crespo and El Greco, and let me stay at home, for I've got a book I have to read. You get an early night, tomorrow we'll go and see Faustino Arayán and ten other people . . . I'll tell you this: you're a much better policeman than I am . . . Pity you're so skinny and sometimes go squint-eyed."

The Count realized that while reading he couldn't get out of his mind the image of the mask behind which Alexis Arayán hid, the closest he'd ever come to a transvestite. And that he was searching not only for explanations to a mystery, but to something definite: his desire to return to talk to Alberto Marqués. Each paragraph in his book became a weapon for a possible verbal duel with the Marquess, an idea with which to scale his heights and level the dialogue. It gave him a knowledge of the subject that would let him close in on that sordid business which had finally begun to attract him the way he preferred: as a challenge to his apathy and prejudice. Mario Conde the policeman was a bad case of *idées fixes* and the pursuit, in each case, of his own obsessions. And the story of that dead transvestite (perhaps symbolically transfigured into ephemeral significance) contained all the ingredients to fascinate him and lead him to its resolution. Consequently Alexis Arayán's fake female face appeared at every moment as a graphic complement to the treatise on metamorphosis and bodily self-creation penned by Muscles, thanks to which various things were becoming clearer to the Count: cross-dressing was more vital and biological than the simple perverted exhibitionism of going into the street dressed as a woman, as he'd always viewed it viscerally as a red-neck macho. Though he'd never been completely convinced, it was true, by the primary attitude of the transvestite who changes his physical appearance in order to enhance his pick-up rate. Pick up who? Heterosexual real men, with hairy chests and stinking armpits, would never knowingly tangle with a transvestite: they'd bed a female, but not that limited vision of woman, whose most desirable entry-point had been blocked off for good by the capricious lottery of nature. A passive homosexual, for his part, preferred one of those real men, because that was why they were homosexual and passive, for heaven's sake. And an active homosexual, hidden behind his appearance of a real man – crudely put: a bugger, cultured archaic version: *bougre* – didn't require that often obscene exaggeration to feel his sodomizing instincts aroused and penetrate *per angostam viam.*

The book attempted a philosophical explanation of that contradiction: the problem, as the Count thought he saw it, wasn't being, but appearance; wasn't the act, but the performance; it wasn't even an end, but the means as its own end: the mask for the pleasure of the mask itself, concealment as supreme truth. That's why he thought it logical to identify human cross-dressing and animal camouflage, not for the purposes of hunting or self-defence, but to fulfil one of the dreams eternally pursued by man: disappearance. Because it wasn't likely, all in all, that the only meaning of such morphological transformation was capture of male prey, as with certain insects which vary their looks in order to simulate the aspect of attractive flowers loved by others who then fall bewildered into the lethal trap; nor was the disguise about deception, as with certain insects whose aggressive physique scares off possible assailants. It was, on the contrary, the will to be masked and mistaken, to negate the negation and join the common tribe of women, which perhaps guided a transformism that could so often prove to be grotesque.

But if erasure were the ultimate goal of cross-dressing, the practical results of the exercise had its equivalents in the animal world which one could compare – through a series of case-studies – with the sad destinies of those transvestites who were always found out despite all their efforts: the inevitable Adam's apple, hands that had grown by natural design, a narrow pelvis, alien to any sign of maternity . . . The book quoted a study, carried out over forty-seven years, which demonstrated how birds' stomachs contained as many camouflaged as non-camouflaged victims, according to the statistics recorded in the region. Was disguise then futile, vulnerable and without guaran-tees of safety? And Muscles concluded, quoting some-one who must have known more than he did, that transvestites confirm only that "a law of pure disguise exists in the living world, a practice which consists in passing oneself off as somebody else, and that's clearly documented, beyond debate, and cannot be reduced to a biological necessity derived from rivalry between the species or natural selection". So then, what the hell was the big deal? All that simply to conclude that it was a simple game of appearances. No, that clearly could not be the case. But could it be entirely chance for a Catholic transvestite who moreover wasn't a transvestite to transform himself on the day the liturgical calendar set as the date of the Transfiguration? It couldn't be so, it must be a coincidence, it's too *recherché*, thought the Count as he shut the book and looked through the window from which he could see the old English castle, all white stone and red tiles brought from Chicago, which had risen up opposite the quarries, on the neighbourhood's most prominent hill.

He'd suddenly remembered poor Luisito the Indian, the only self-confessed little queer of his generation, there in his neighbourhood. He remembered how Luisito was treated as a kind of plague-carrier by the boys playing baseball, marbles and leapfrog among whom the Count grew up. Nobody liked him, nobody accepted him, and, more than once, several of them threw stones at Luisito until his mother, Domitila the mulatta, came out, broom in hand, to rescue him, cursing the mothers, the fathers and the whole lineage of his aggressors. Theirs were cruel attitudes and successive nicknames – Luisita, the first and longest-lasting; Luisito the Duck; Rubber Bum (because of his abundant buttocks, already predestined for certain uses and abuses); and Cinnamon Flower, because of his Indian skin-colour – constant insults and a historical marginalization culturally decreed for all time: it's his fault if he's such a pansy, they said, as did the other mothers, who taught their children not to walk with that different, inverted, perverted boy, infected with the most abominable illness one could imagine. Nevertheless, the Count discovered that some of the stone-throwers who cursed him in public on certain propitious nights climbed the second rung of their sexual initiation via Luisito's promiscuous arse; after experimenting with she-goats and sows, they tried Luisito's dark hole, in the darkest tunnels of the quarry. And as none of them would ever admit to ancillary kisses and caresses to raise the temperature (you know, that's really poofish, they'd argue when talking about these incidents), for all who made it, the relationship with Luisito was forwarded as proof of virility reached at penis point . . . Luisito was; they weren't: as if homosexuality were only defined by the acceptance of the flesh of others in female fashion. Later, when they started to have girlfriends and stopped playing baseball and leapfrogging on the street corners in the neighbourhood, they forgot Luisito and Luisito forgot them: then the boy began to cruise La Rampa and El Prado, in the company of other youthful inverts like himself, in flocks which sidled slowly and tetchily, like La Florida Park ducks, in search of welcoming lakes in which to splash, until in 1980, thanks to his undeniable homosexual condition, and hence as an anti-social, expendable dreg, he was allowed peacefully to board a launch in the port of Mariel and leave for the United States. The last news the Count had received of Luisito the Indian were two photographs which circulated in the neighbourhood, describing a before and an after, like Charles Atlas: in one he was sitting on a shiny sofa – both Luisito and the pearl pink sofa were most pansyish, Luisito with his high-lighted eyebrows and bouffant hair; in the other, on the same sofa, sat a rather fat, uglyish mulatta, who was none other than Louise Indira, a woman surgically transformed, the only recognized queer of his generation, there in the neighbourhood. And the Count wondered if Luisito the Indian had ever had any philosophical or psycho-natural principles first to sustain his homosexuality, and second to carry through his irreversible transfigur-ation. Or could it simply be that from childhood he'd felt an irrepressible desire to dress up in lace and play with dolls, which would later lead to an obsession for slotting things in his backside?

The Count moved away from the window and his memories as he felt the jungle call of his entrails galvanized by so much inactivity. The evening was drawing to a close and apart from two dark, evil-looking fish, which had absconded to the back of his fridge, he had no other edible products on the home front. He looked at his watch: seven forty-five, and dialled a telephone number.

"It's me, Jose."

"Of course it's you, Condesito."

"I'm really hungry."

"Why you're ringing me so late? You never change . . . But you're in luck, because I got into a state looking for stuff here and there, and started late. Let's see what I can rustle up."

"Anything will do."

"Shut up, I'm thinking. I've got red beans on the stove and I was choosing the rice . . . Come round then, I've had an idea."

"It's *paisa* mix," Josefina announced, and her eyes shone with pride and satisfaction the way Archimedes must have looked just before he got out of his bath.

Skinny Carlos and the Count, like two rather dim-witted pupils, were listening to the woman's explanation. Feigning surprise was part of the ritual: the impossible would become possible, dreams reality, and then their Cuban longing for food would suddenly transgress any frontier of reality measured by quotas, ration-books and irremediable shortages, thanks to a magical trick only Josefina was capable of performing.

"My uncle Marcelo, who you know was once a sailor, fell in love in Cartagena de las Indias and lived in Colombia for several years. But the woman was *paisa*, as they call people from Medellín, and she taught him to prepare *paisa* mix, as Marcelo calls, or called it, may he rest in peace, the poor guy, for it's a typically *paisa*

69

platter. Then, as I had some red beans on the boil when you called, I started thinking and had this idea: of course, *paisa* mix, and, right there, when the beans started to soften, I threw in half a pound of minced meat, so the meat cookcd in the juice, you follow me? Then I cooked crackling from really big pigs, with some of their meat, ripe plantains, eggs for you two, for at this time of night eggs don't suit me because of my gall-bladder, a beef steak, with plenty of garlic and onion, and I cooked the rice with extra lard so it separates out right. You can eat the beans separately or put them on the top of the rice. How do you prefer them?"

"Both ways," they chorused, and the Count sat behind Carlos's wheelchair. They followed in the footsteps of Carlos's mother to the dining-room, with the solemnity one adopts when visiting the holiest of holy places. Jose, Conde told the woman while downing spoonfuls of beans and meat, you've saved my life.

"Jose," said Carlos, stretching out a hand to caress his mother's, "you beat your record. This is out of this world . . . I'm going to go *paisa*, I swear I am."

As they ate, the Count must have related the temporary lifting of his punishment and the new case he was working on. It was another of the policeman's necessary rituals to tell Skinny and Josefina his stories, unfolding a plot in daily chapters, till the grand finale came.

"But that's all very nasty, Condesito."

"So the guy, I mean the gal, didn't kick out, lash out or anything? Hey, you know I can't really believe that."

"And that painter, with a wife and all. These things never happened in my day . . . What I don't understand one bit is why you had to mix poor Jesus Christ up in all this."

The Count smiled and licked his fingers, streaming

70

in grease from the crackling. He wiped himself with a handkerchief and lit a cigarette, after swigging some of his second beer.

"Hey, Skinny," he finally spoke, "you still got that copy of *La Viboreña*?"

"Of course."

"You've got to lend it to me."

"Fine, but read it here."

"Don't arse around, let me take it."

"Not even if I'd gone crazy. You were the one who threw it away and I kept it."

"I swear on your mother I'll look after it," the Count promised, smiling and making a sign of the cross with his fingers, and Josefina smiled as well, because the visible happiness of her son, an invalid for ten years, and of the other tormented, ever ravenous man who was also like her son, constituted the only scraps of happiness left in this world where bladders went on strike and you saw so much squalor. Happiness seemed a thing of the past, the time when her son and the Count shut themselves in of an afternoon to study and listen to music, and she was sure one day the house would be full of grandchildren and Carlos would hang his engineering diploma on the wall and the Count would present her with his first book and all would be sweetness and light, as life ought to be. But the know-ledge she'd got it wrong didn't stop her smiling when she said: "I'll make some coffee," and departed.

"Hey, Conde, Andrés called me this afternoon. He asked after you."

"And what's he up to?"

"He's say's he's got problems in the hospital, but he'll come by tomorrow to talk."

"Then tell him from me to buy a bottle and drop in to see us one of these nights, OK?"

The policeman had just downed his second beer and was peering into the darkness beyond the window. His stomach, body and mind were sighing in relief and he felt his muscles and brain distend, lose electricity, that he was on the verge of one of those moments of confidences and emotion he would share with Skinny Carlos, right there in his house. All the shields, armour and even masks he walked the world with – like any hunted insect – would tumble to the floor, and a necessary, much longed-for spiritual levity would replace the fears, wariness and lies he employed daily, as frequently as his blue jeans that daily clamoured for an emergency wash. And then he said: "I can't get the story of the Transfiguration out of my head . . . Do you know, I still remember when I heard it for the first time? What's more, Skinny, I think I'm getting the writing bug."

"Fuck!" exclaimed Carlos, hitting the table with one of his heavyweight's fists. "What's happened? You fallen in love again?"

"If only!"

"If only!" repeated the other, who then looked incredulously at his bottle of beer: how the fuck had it emptied? And the Count waited calmly for the inevitable suggestion to come. "Hey, you bastard, go and buy a bottle of rum. This calls for a celebration."

"Twenty-eight years ago," the Count calculated.

He said it out loud so it seemed more credible, used his fingers to reckon up yet again the obscenely inflated figure, which represented so many, many years, and he began to accept it must be so when he felt the anxiety stirred by what had gone forever to be in denial. Then time changed into an irritating, identifiable feeling, like a pain spreading from his stomach and starting to oppress his chest; his mother was next to him, a tiny white headscarf on her jet-black hair and that linen – linen? – dress that crackled because of the macerated yucca juices in which she'd soaked it before subjecting it to trial by iron, and he fingered the bluish, gentle spume of prickly starch and the final severity of the now ironed cloth, as he felt it minutes before they went into church, and his mother gave her son that hug he would never forget. You're going to be a saint, she told him, you are my handsome boy, she told him, and the white purity of the material wrapped round them that Sunday morning passed through his pores and reached his soul: I am pure, he thought, as he walked towards the front row of pews to listen to the mass Father Mendoza would intone and receive at last that memorable wafer with an ancient flavour that should change his life: when it fell on his tongue, he would join a privileged clan: those with a right to salvation, he thought, and he looked at her again, and she smiled back at him, so beautiful in her headscarf and white dress, twenty-eight years ago.

Father Mendoza jumped from the altar of memory to the real door where the Count had knocked twice. Although their spiritual relationship had never been renewed after that distant Sunday of purity he'd never revisited, the priest and the dissident had always maintained an affable relationship, in which the cleric insisted on calling the Count a mystic without faith and the latter on dubbing Father Mendoza a cunning old devil, capable of doing anything to win – or bring back – a believer to the fold. Nevertheless in subsequent years their dialogues had always taken place in the middle of the street, the result of casual encounters, for the Count had never gone back inside the local church or the adjoining house where the priest lived and where he'd received the necessary instruction in catechism in order to accede to communion with the holy and eternal.

"My Lord, can this be a miracle?" exclaimed Father Mendoza when his eyes, still bloodshot from sleep and clouded by the passage of time, allowed him mentally to locate the image of his morning visitor.

"Miracles are a thing of the past, Father. How are you?"

The priest smiled as he led him into his sitting room.

"Miracles still happen. And I'm a real ruin, or are you blind to boot?"

"As I can see, but you're not that bad. We're both growing old at a similar pace."

"But I've got a forty-year lead. How can I help? Have you finally come to confess your multiple sins?"

The Count sat on the wood and straw sofa, for he hadn't forgotten how the high-backed rocking-chair was the only earthly property the priest defended like a vehement, haggling merchant. As usual, Father Mendoza settled down in his armchair and began swaying furiously.

"Don't keep on, Father: that decision was for ever."

"This is your greatest sin, Condesito: pride. And the other, I know for certain, is that you are afraid of yourself . . . Do you realize that one day you'll fall . . ."

"Don't be so sure, Father. Do you know when I was last here?"

"Twenty-eight years ago," replied the priest, as if he didn't have to think twice, and the Count suspected he'd thrown out a figure and only by chance hit on the right number.

"Exactly twenty-eight years, but don't play at cheap miracles."

The priest smiled again.

"Don't worry, it's not because of you that I remember . . . My father died on the day of your communion. I found out ten minutes before saying mass. It was the worst mass of my life, or the best, I don't know. And it was also the last time I doubted the goodness of God."

"And why did you talk to us about the Transfiguration that day?"

The priest almost shut his eyes, as if needing to look within himself.

"So I'm not the only one who remembers that day, am I?"

"No," the Count admitted.

"Wait, would you like a coffee? I can tell you I don't offer everybody coffee. Just imagine, twenty people come and see me every day, and I've still not worked the miracle of multiplying the little envelopes of coffee they give me in my ration book . . ."

Father Mendoza leapt from his chair as if propelled by the rocking and the Count's heart felt the vitality the old parish priest exuded. He looked round the sitting room, at the wooden walls with scenes of the stations of the cross – all the fallen women were present – and the resplendent statue of Archangel Raphael, an exact replica of the one in the church, under which – twenty-eight years ago – the children taking part in the catechism had sat and listened to the lessons from Miss Merced and Father Mendoza. Just the fucking job, he thought when the priest returned with a cup of coffee, which his stomach, ravaged by alcohol and lack of sleep, was piously grateful for.

"Do you still smoke?" he asked the Count, who nodded. "Well, give me one. That's one pleasure I'll allow myself today."

The Count took two cigarettes out of the packet and then lit the priest's and his. They both exhaled at the same time and were enveloped by the same cloud of smoke.

"I want to talk to you about the Transfiguration. Something has happened which reminded me of that passage, but I failed Bible History."

The priest, who'd recovered his rocking speed, contemplated his cigarette before speaking.

"I knew you wanted to get something out of me . . . Do you know why I used the passage on the Transfiguration that day?"

His eyes tired of following the pendulum marked by the priest's face, the Count looked towards the painting which represented the arrival at Mount Calvary.

"You really want me to guess?"

"I'm sorry, I'm becoming old and stupid, and ask stupid questions . . . I did so because I felt very sick, and in that passage, when God appears before the apostles, Jesus understands the human soul more than

76

ever and tells his disciples: 'Arise, be not afraid' . . .
And not everyone can understand the dimensions fear
can have. And that day, you understand, I went in great
fear of death."

"And after six days, Jesus taketh Peter, James and John
his brother and bringeth them up into a high mountain
apart. And was transfigured before them: and his face
did shine as the sun and his raiment was white as the
light. And, behold, there appeared unto them Moses
and Elias talking with him. Then answered Peter and
said unto Jesus: Lord, it is good for us to be here: if
thou wilt, let us make here three tabernacles, one for
thee, one for Moses and another for Elias. While he yet
spake, a bright cloud overshadowed them: and
behold a voice out of the cloud which said, This is my
beloved son in whom I am well pleased: hear ye him.
And when the disciples heard it, they fell on their
face, and were sore afraid. And Jesus came and
touched them, and said: Arise, be not afraid. And
when they had lifted up their eyes, they saw no man,
save Jesus only.
   "And as they came down from the mountain, Jesus
charged them, saying, Tell the vision to no man, until
the Son of man be risen again from the dead.
   "This is chapter seventeen according to St Matthew.
Mark and Luke also relate the Transfiguration, and,
listen to this interesting detail, Mark saw it thus: 'And
his raiment became shining, exceeding white as snow;
so as no fuller on earth can white them.'
   "Conde, you know, the scholars say that this
happened on Mount Tabor, some forty miles from
Caesarea. It's a strange mountain, because it stands a
thousand feet above the plain of Esdrelon, and reigns

in solitude, as if it had sprung from the ground or fallen from heaven. On the mountain meseta the Byzantines raised a basilica with two chapels that the Crusaders rebuilt several centuries later and entrusted to the Benedictines. After the Crusades, the Muslims transformed it into a fortress in the year 1212. The latest news I have is that the present basilica was consecrated in 1924 and has a central façade flanked by two towers.

"But what is important in all this is that it was on Mount Tabor that Jesus's divine character was publicly revealed for the first time, that he was recognized by his father and introduced as the Messiah. Hence the disciples saw the appearance of Jesus, who must have been really dirty after such a long journey over the sea and desert, profoundly transformed: his clothes, skin and hair shone, but in reality everything was the result of an inner brilliance necessary to receive the revelation from his father. It is then the greatness of Jesus is made manifest: being who he is, introduced as a divine being, he doesn't lose his humanity and understands the fear of his followers, who have witnessed something that transcends them infinitely. And do you know why? Because I think Jesus predicted his own fear when he talks to them about how his work will be carried through: his glory will be in a resurrection, but first he must endure the suffering and sacrifice which await him on the cross, that was the necessary test for this greater miracle to take place. Beautiful and heart-rending, don't you think? And if He was afraid and understood what fear is, why should we deny ourselves such a human sentiment? Perhaps the most human of all, Conde."

Quite the contrary, thought the Count, already set on forgetting biblical transfigurations too remote from sordid, earthly transvesting, as he took another look at Faustino Arayán's house and compared it to the dark, damp cavern inhabited by Alberto Marqués, whence the transvestite Alexis had emerged on his last night-time excursion. An unbridgeable, impossible abyss existed between those two vital spaces, of established strata, self-interest, merits forgotten and recognized, favours lost and opportunities grasped or not, which distinguished them and set them apart, like light and shadow, poverty and opulence, sorrow and happiness. Nevertheless, in life and death, Alexis Arayán had fused the extremes of his origins and destiny, and created an unlikely link.

From the moment his car turned into Seventh Avenue in Miramar, under the still benevolent sun of that August morning, the Count felt he was entering another world, its face more pleasant and better washed than that of the other city – the same city – they'd just crossed. And now, in front of Faustino Arayán's house, he brought his idea full circle: quite the contrary, when he thought how the original owners of that preening mansion with its window-panes still intact had no doubt also tried to delineate a drastic difference between two worlds, the best of which – naturally for them – they had intended to magnify by building that house: oh, those good old bourgeois pretensions to permanence ... At this moment, perhaps in Miami, Union City or wherever the hell they were, thirty years on, they must still miss the precise beauty of that construction where they'd invested fistfuls of dreams and money, thinking it was eternal. But people usually get it wrong, the Count told himself, penetrating the maze of his mind as it raced on and thinking that, if he'd lived in a house like that, he'd like to have owned at least three dogs running around the garden. And who'd pick up the shit? he wondered, lifting a foot in his imagination to avoid doggy deposits, and decided to do without his pack of hounds and devote his time – and this was beyond debate – to cherishing the library he'd have on the second floor, overlooking the garden.

On his journey the Count had also gleaned from the lips of Sergeant Palacios two choice items of disturbing news: Salvador K.'s blood, like the murderer's, was AB, and nobody in the vicinity of the studio on Twenty-First and Eighteenth had seen him on the night of the crime, although they'd seen him go in more than once with Alexis Arayán. According to the Count's calculations, those two tickets meant he was sure to win the raffle he'd bought into.

Manuel Palacios rang the bell and the maid opened the door.

"Come in," she said, without saying good-day, and pointed them to the armchairs in the sitting room. "I'll tell Faustino right away." And she disappeared on ghostly tiptoe.

The Count and Manolo looked at each other, laughed and prepared to wait. Ten minutes later, Faustino Arayán appeared.

He was wearing a *guayabera* that was so white and elegant the Count wouldn't have dared to wear it for a minute: it was resplendent rather than white, with tenuous tucks, a shiny thread and the maker's name discreetly but visibly embroidered on the top right-hand pocket. The grey pin-stripe trousers displayed the precise crease of an expert iron, while his dark patent leather moccasins seemed light and comfortable.

"Good-day," he said, holding out a hand; a strong, solid, pink hand, like its owner, whose only sign of being in his sixties was an almost totally bald pate which distinguished the equally shiny roundness, noted the Count, of his enormous head.

"I'm really sorry to trouble you today, *compañero* Arayán. We know you had a bad day yesterday, but . . ."

"Not to worry, not to worry . . ."

"Lieutenant Mario Conde," he introduced himself, and pointing to his colleague, he said, "and Sergeant Manuel Palacios."

"I told you, Lieutenant, not to worry. You're doing your job, and I have to do mine today, because life goes on . . ."

"Thanks," said the Count and observed the ashtray from Granada, as clean as ever, as if it had never been used.

"Just a moment, I'll get us a drop of coffee, if you'd like one?" asked Faustino Arayán, and without waiting for a reply, he whispered: "María Antonia."

The black woman appeared like a flash, with a tray of three cups of coffee, as if she'd been waiting for the gun from behind a starting line. The damn bitch floats, the Count was convinced, and he was the first to be served. When she'd passed the cups around, she left the tray on the table and flitted back into the inner recesses of the house.

"May I smoke?"

"Yes, of course. Would you like a cigar? I have some excellent Montecristos."

The Count thought about it: no, he shouldn't, but he dared. "What the hell," he told himself.

"I'd be glad to accept one, to smoke later."

"Yes, of course," answered his host, and from the lower drawer of the table in the centre of the room he offered the Count a cedar-wood box where a dozen Montecristos lay in perfect formation, finely scented and pale-hued.

"Thanks," the Count reiterated, and put the cigar in his shirt pocket.

"Well, Lieutenant, what can I do for you?"

Only then did the Count become aware that he had nothing to say or had forgotten what he'd intended to say: he'd been dazzled by so much glitter and couldn't clearly see the route he should follow. He had returned simply to comply with police routines in that perfectly ordered house, with its gleaming *guayaberas* and bald pates, black maids with wings on their ankles and ashtrays from Granada without a speck of dust, which seemed quite unrelated to the eschatological story of a queer who'd been strangled with two coins up his backside, after exhibiting himself through the city streets in a theatrical garment which would end up stained by major and minor effluvia – as Alberto Marqués might have said.

"How's your wife?" he asked, looking for a way to broach the matter.

Faustino nodded repeatedly.

"In very bad shape. Yesterday, when we got back from the funeral, Dr Pérez Flores, well, I'll tell you his name because everybody knows who Jorge is, prescribed sedatives and tension-reducers. She's asleep now. The poor woman can't accept it. But I knew one day that boy would give us a big upset, and now look what's happened." He paused, and the Count decided not to interrupt. "Who knows what business he'd been mixed up in? From adolescence Alexis has been a constant headache. Not only because of his . . . problem, but because of his character. Sometimes, I've even thought he hated both me and his mother, and he was particularly despotic with her. He always blamed us for the fact that we spent so much time outside Cuba and that he had to stay here with María Antonia and my mother-in-law. He refused to understand that my work forced me down that path. He couldn't come with us, where would he have studied? Six months in London, three in Brussels, a year in New York, then back to Cuba . . . Can you imagine? I'd have preferred to give him a more stable life, for us to have brought him up here, and I can tell you I'd have kept him like that, under my thumb, but my work has always assigned me very important duties and my wife and I always made sure he had all he needed: the house, his grand-mother, and María Antonia, who loved him as if she were his real mother, school, the home comforts he wanted . . . everything. If this seems like a punishment . . . I'll confess something, so you see where I'm com-ing from: my son and I never got on. I think I was really to blame, I never made concessions to him, though to begin with I did speak to him and try to help. Now I think mine was the worst approach possible. And look what has happened, how it's all turned out. I feel guilty, I don't deny that, but he also behaved very badly towards me and his mother, right from adolescence. And afterwards, when he befriended that scoundrel, the Alberto Marqués guy, it was impossible to see eye to eye. That man brainwashed him, injected his head with poison, changed him for ever in every way: it isn't that he started to write or waste paper trying to be a painter. No, it was worse than that. It was his moral, even political behaviour, and I couldn't allow that, no way, now do you understand me? No one, not Alexis nor anybody, was going to defile the status I'd won from so many years of struggle, work and sacrifice, so I dictated my rules of the game very clearly: if he wanted to live under this roof and enjoy all the comforts that gradually one had been able to accrue, one couldn't think certain ideas about this country, or be criticizing it all the time or eat shit in church or associate with an envy-ridden guy like Alberto Marqués . . . It had to be all or nothing, and that's what I told him one day, because he was no longer a child, and he got furious, I wish you could have seen him, and heard the things he said, that I was a dogmatist, an extremist and a troglodyte and a good few things besides . . . And that was when he said he was leaving home. I know he always came back to see his mother and María Antonia, after his grandmother died, and if I arrived, he left, and I was almost pleased, because I didn't want any more arguments with him. These conflicts upset me a lot, you know? . . . I regret that now, perhaps I could have done more for Alexis, forced him to keep going to the doctor, been more strict with him, whatever, but he never gave me that option," he said, and bent down to the cigar-box. He took one, but rejected it immediately, as if suddenly the possibility of lighting one of those beautiful Montecristos seemed inappropriate.

"Faustino, do you or your wife have any idea about what might have happened the other night?"

The owner of the house looked at his hands as if he'd find a truth there, and looked the Count in the eye.

"What can I say, Lieutenant? It was all the result of a wrong choice . . . Alexis chose his path and look where it led. What I can say, it's like a punishment . . . The very thought of it fills me with shame. Disguised as a woman . . . Can I tell you something?" The Count nodded, like an eager pupil. "Neither his mother nor I deserved to suffer this. All I hope is that time passes so

84

we see if we can wake up from this nightmare. Of course you do understand me . . ."

"Of course," the Count affirmed and looked at his own hands, searching, perhaps, for another possible truth.

"It's really shaming," Faustino repeated, and the Count looked him in the eye for the first time in the whole conversation: he found two damp eyes, where he thought he spotted real grief, and tears which perhaps his sense of manliness prevented him from shedding. Although it was difficult, given he was such a powerful, self-confident man, the policeman was surprised to find he could feel pity for him.

"Faustino, you may know nothing about this. Because of your relationship with Alexis, I mean . . . But perhaps your wife, I don't know . . . Please ask her if she heard Alexis mention at all the day of the Transfiguration. I'm following this line of thought, though I can't tell you why. It's an idea I can't get out of my head . . ."

Mario Conde began to feel a degree of relief when the car took to the tunnel under the river and ran along the Malecón, towards the city centre. The sea had a pacifying effect, and absorbed him in a state of all-consuming fascination. And that morning the sea was an invitation to quiet and calm: tranquil and blue, like the breeze blowing in through the windows.

"What do you reckon, Manolo?" he finally asked the sergeant, and lit a cigarette.

Sergeant Manuel Palacios drove down the right lane and reduced speed slightly.

"It's difficult for him. It must be the talk of at least the diplomatic service, right? But I can tell you one thing. I reckon he's pleased from one point of view. It's like when someone dies of cancer: if there's no cure, the sooner it's over, the better."

"Maybe," the Count agreed, not knowing exactly what it was that might be.

"Where do we go now?" Manuel Palacios asked, preparing to accelerate.

"I'm not sure . . . Salvador K. looks to be top of the list, right? But it's also true we have nothing definite against him . . . I'm pissed off," he said, throwing his cigarette into the street.

"Conde, Conde," Manolo shook his head, as if he couldn't believe it. "Here you are and you still get like that. Don't gripe like that; if we need to invent something to implicate the painter, we will, won't we?"

"Don't suggest such a thing. At least not today."

"Why not?"

"Because I'm very worried. Did you manage to find out what happened to Maruchi?"

The sergeant reduced speed slightly.

"No, I haven't got anything on that . . . But this morning I didn't tell you something else that happened yesterday. I've got an appointment at three this afternoon with the Internal Investigation people."

"And what do they want from you?"

Manuel Palacios shook his head, and the Count noticed he was wiping the sweat from his hands on to his trousers.

"I don't know. I really don't."

The Count looked into the street, more and more potholes, dustbins overflowing with rubbish, houses eroded by salt water and neglect.

"If you don't have problems, nothing to worry about, but watch what you say, OK? You're no idiot, Manolo, so think out your replies carefully . . . But don't get too worked up, I expect it's something quite trivial."

"All right, Conde. It's really hot, isn't it?"

The fishermen congregated on the Malecón at that early hour with little hope that fate would place a fine specimen on their hooks and bring justifiable cheer to the family table. When the Count saw those silhouettes over the calm sea, he was filled with envy. He knew life was healthier there, with a piece of string in the water and one's mind thinking only about a possible catch and the dinner of one's dreams, and not about a series of stories of deaths, thefts, frauds, rapes, lesser or greater forms of assault – that could also help save him from boredom – or, the last straw, about the enquiries of the Internal Investigations team bent on throwing light on business the Count hadn't even imagined and that had already cost two of his colleagues their positions at work. Will they find something on me? he wondered, and tried to recall any heinous act in his career. Who knows . . . And what about Maruchi, what the hell had happened to her?

"What shit, right." And he added, "Turn down there, I want to revisit the Havana Woods."

Without patrol cars, ambulances pretending to be in a rush, the obscene line of bystanders, the photographers, forensics and police summoned by death, that forest of fantasies, in the middle of the city, by the dirty river, radiated a harmony which the Count's every pore tried to inhale, in an urgent, greedy act of appropriation. He felt that violence and that place now seemed so alien that even his own presence in the area was an incongruous irritant, and, as usual, he meditated on death's insalubrious ability to change everything. The grass so green, the indefatigable sound of the river, the generous shade from the trees, had been but a few hours earlier the scenario framing a macabre murder, the pre- and post-histories of which the policeman was now trying to grasp, with his unprofessionally manic tendency to feel he too was an accomplice. That was why he now stood there, in that anonymous space – nobody would ever erect a pretentious funeral monument to the first Cuban transvestite killed in sexual combat – where Alexis Arayán's life had ended and Mario Conde's eschatological labours had begun. Death was thus transformed into a social event, ceased to be a drastic biological fact which no exact, medical, natural or supernatural science could revoke: its only importance now lay in the crime and possible punishment for the transgressor of a law, already established by the Bible and Talmud, and the Count knew his mission in the world would conclude with the Pyrrhic victory of a conviction that was predictable and necessary, but could not restore what was gone for ever.

"What you thinking about?" Manuel Palacios pulled up a blade of grass and put it in his mouth.

"About woods and wild animals," the lieutenant replied as he headed towards the river. "That transvestite didn't get dressed to go on parade or hunt, Manolo. He was seeking something more difficult to find. Peace of mind, perhaps. Or revenge, how do I know . . . What was he seeking here, looking the complete transvestite, if he wasn't one, and right on the evening of the day of the Transfiguration? It gets stranger by the minute . . ."

"I don't see why you have to over-complicate things all the time. Why do you always want to imagine what nobody else can? . . . Something strange is happening to you, Conde. I'll tell you one thing: I sometimes think you're not interested in being a policeman any more."

"Manolo, you are a genius."

The policemen followed the path down to the bed of a river, a slow, decidedly sickly serpent. The Count got close to the edge and lamented the advanced stage of agony he contemplated there: patches of oil, acidic foam, dead animals, countless bits of detritus flowing in the slow waters of the Almendares, the city's only real river. And then he had a premonition: "Of course, hell, didn't Alexis own a Bible?"

"Oh, you're back already, Mr Police Lieutenant Mario Conde. Tell me right away, because I bet you know who did it. I sometimes see these series where the police get their man straight away, you know? The police are so good at . . ."

The Count ignored the barbed wit and went into a living room as dark and cool as on the previous day, and sat back in his armchair while Alberto Marqués sat in his. He felt they both moved with the premeditation of actors conscious of their movements on stage.

"Would you like a cup of tea? I can give it to you ice cold, ice cubes included. . . ."

"Yes, I think I could do with that," the Count nodded, and the Marquess disappeared down a corridor at the back of the peculiar stage set arranged in that dark room. Now, as he watched him walk, the policeman noticed that the dramatist had the unlikely springy step of a young lad tiptoeing at an impressive rate, like a rabbit or crane in a hurry. He doesn't seem that old, thought the Count, but his mind wandered off to the interview awaiting Sergeant Palacios that afternoon. What the hell were they after? A slight but disconcerting feeling of fear lodged in his stomach. Experience screamed at him that an incisive investigation would light on annoying evidence, delicate truths, improbable but definitive clues, and that was why he'd begun to wonder what the hell they were after, while he'd opted to return to the Marquess's house, driven by a need to find out more: he must log Alexis's belongings, search for pointers. Meanwhile, Manolo had to carry on research at the Centre for Cultural Heritage on the transvestite and his pathetic friend Salvador K., and look for the Bible the painter had mentioned. But what the hell are they after? he wondered again as the Marquess tiptoed back like a young crane, a cup in each hand. He gave one to the Count and returned to his armchair.

"Should I open the window?"

"If it's no bother . . ."

The dramatist put his cup on the floor and opened the window behind him. All the very high windows in the room had grills, and the Count was curious to discover how the rented lovers Miki had mentioned went about taking the house by assault. As the Marquess sat back in his chair, the Count understood how it had all been prepared afresh: the sun, perfectly arranged, only allowed him sight of the man's silhouette. He was expecting me, he thought.

"Well, don't prolong the torture . . . Are you on to something?" And he blinked insistently.

"Very little, in fact . . . But this case has its curious features. Alexis was strangled but didn't put up a fight."

"For God's sake," the old dramatist exclaimed softly, touching his neck as if to beat off a strangler's approaching hands.

"And after he was dead, the assassin stuck two coins up his anus."

"Ay, ay, ay," repeated the dramatist, closing his legs as if to avoid possible monetary penetration.

"Have you ever heard of anything like it?"

"No, never . . . It's like something out of a mafia film."

"Yes, you could say that . . . The other thing I did was to read a bit of the book you lent me and I learned several things about transvestites."

"Of interest, I hope?"

"Yes, but a touch too conceptual. Is it really true transvestites go in for all this philosophy of mimetics and erasure?"

In spite of the intense background glare, the Count thought he saw the Marquess smile.

No other city in the world – not even Havana – can offer the miraculous harmonies of Paris. In Paris evening and night fuse in a tentative symphony, dawn seems a necessary consequence, shy yet inevitable, and if the spirit of man can penetrate by osmosis the sensibility in the breeze, stones, smells and colours of Paris, life in the city can be a gift from the gods: and that's how I felt, that spring.

Washed and perfumed, we got into the taxi and my hands sweated profusely on the drive, as my eyes twice saw the illuminated shape of the Eiffel Tower, the edifice of the Opéra, the cheerfully lit Café de la Paix, until we turned down narrow, cobble-stoned side streets – cobbles that had become famous the previous year, when love, intelligence and ideology spawned revolutionary copulations behind barricades made from the very same cobbles – the sinuous streets of the Quartier Latin, and we stopped in front of a neon-lit joint advertising LES FEMMES, a gateway to a dive we anxiously desired. Muscles paid and said something to the taxi-driver – a Moroccan, who handed him a small envelope – while the Other Boy and I contemplated the shabbiness of the place; then the padded door creaked noisily open to give us our first vision of the cabaret: a blue glow.

Muscles came over to us and for the first time that spring on my last visit to Paris I saw his round peasant face, still slightly uncouth, beam with happiness. A few days earlier, when I'd arrived in Paris, he'd told me about the end of his relationship with Julien, the young anthropologist he'd lived with over the last two years on a permanent honeymoon – as Muscles reported it, a man at other times so exquisite in his poetic images – and who'd humiliated him by leaving him for a woman: no more, no less than a Russian dancer – and corps de ballet, not even a soloist – who'd defected from the Bolshoi. As ideology had interfered in matters of love, I commented and queried: "Did the dancer carry the plague in her armpits and have a shot-putter's face like most of our Soviet sisters?" Women, what filth, we chorused, and Muscles could only laugh . . . But now, near that blue, yellow-lettered cabaret, Muscles seemed to rediscover his desire to live.

"Come on," he said, and took us by the arm (my left, the Other Boy's right), and dragged us into the blue glow . . . Light shone from the floor and drew volutes of smoke, over-sweet even for Virginian cigarettes, which mixed its hypnotic emanations with the waft of acrid sweat and the heavy perfume of Arab essences that are sold wholesale in Paris's apocryphal Persian markets. Their ears, in the meantime, were hit by the wild rhythms unleashed by the voice of Miriam Makeba (a Third World invasion), projected from a cubbyhole built in the wall. I felt strangely afraid to find myself at the vortex of that attack on all the senses, but Muscles and the Other seemed to have entered familiar territory where they moved completely naturally. Then I started to see fake Valkyries performing their ancient function as pourers of beer. They seemed to float on the blue, like phosphorescent, newly hatched chrysalises, parading the starched organdy and anorexic pleated skirts they modelled as the last word in retro chic. Each Valkyrie carried a tray of glasses in one hand and yellow (yellow?) flowers in the other. I was looking at those hands, too large even for a Valkyrie, even for such a genuinely Scandinavian item, when one exemplar brushed her tunic's abrasive edge against me and I felt I'd been touched by a prehistoric insect.

I was bewildered and grateful that Muscles pushed me towards a table, where the Other Boy was already seated, drinking an amber liquid I soon discovered wasn't beer. How did he manage it, that innate ability of his always to get there first? Then the disc jockey switched from Makeba to Doris Day and I discovered that, like any good cabaret, Les Femmes had a stage where seven perfect – if not more than perfect – versions of Doris Day had settled – they must have settled – singing along to the recording to the delight of an enraptured audience, where I began to see men and women whose affiliations I doubted: too many opulent, peroxide blondes in best Marilyn Monroe style, dark-skinned beauties from post-war Italian cinema, black women with large, acromegalic hands and metallic robo-comic lips which regaled their colleagues around the table with kisses as intense and syncopated as Doris Day's ballad.

I was still nonplussed when Muscles invited me to go to the bathroom and waved the envelope the taxi-driver gave him. He knew I wouldn't go, and so didn't insist, but the Other Boy did go . . . It isn't that I was a puritan. On the contrary, I must have been pretty daring in my life, I've tried everything, but my instinctive lucidity has always proved more useful, and that day, it was certainly having a party out there, expectant, wanting to digest everything my eyes could take in. And thanks to that lucidity I realized I'd come upon a giant happening, all transmutation and masks, that was less famous but more real and intense than a Venetian carnival. The idea of the chrysalis and the feeling that a huge insect had brushed against me held the key to what I was living and seeing: a party for insects. I remember thinking, among those transvestites, the movement's cutting-edge pioneers, that man can create, paint, invent or re-create colours and forms he finds around himself and impose them on material, what is beyond his body, but is unable or powerless when it comes to modifying his own organism. Only a transvestite can transform it radically and, like a butterfly, paint himself, make his body the subject for his master work, convert his sexual emanations into colour, through the bewildering arabesques and incandescent hues of physical adornment. It is a vital plastic surgery of the self, though those infinitely repeated replicas – seven Doris Days, four Marilyn Monroes, three Anna Magnanis in twenty square yards – could not avoid, at best, a coldly nostalgic perfection. What was most disturbing was to understand that this was the apotheosis self-conscious theatre people have dreamed about from the days of Pericles: the mask become character, the character carved out of an actor's physique and soul, life as visceral performance of the dreamt . . . It was like an epiphany which had been waiting, crouched in that dirty corner of Paris, and in a few minutes I'd

94

planned and staged the solution I'd been looking for my version of *Electra Garrigó* . . . What I could never imagine was that my genial idea would be the beginning of my last act as a theatre director. The end as a beginning without means . . .

Then, when I went to tell Muscles about my illumination, I found he and the Other Boy had disappeared with one of those perverted insects. A delightful touch came the day after when they accused me of vanishing on the arm of a Sara Montiel. Anyway, I told Muscles what I'd felt there, and the ungrateful creature didn't give me any credit for it in his book on transvestites, and I still think I could put between quotation marks whole paragraphs I dictated on the occasion . . . And certainly, as I didn't have enough money, I had to walk home, but I'd never have gone with a Sarita Montiel, because the fact is, I never could stand *la Saritísima.*

"This is by Salvador K., isn't it?"

"Yes, that's his signature, SK. Such bad taste . . . Looks like a kind of medicine, don't you think?"

"Or beer."

The Marquess had taken him into Alexis Arayán's bedroom, which turned out to be the old servants' quarters. It had its own small, separate bathroom, and you could reach the room without entering the main house. Everything appeared meticulously ordered, as if its owner had arranged it with particular care before departing two days ago: shelves tidy, pictures dusted, clothing clean and hanging up in the small wardrobe, two pairs of underpants dry on the bathroom window, ashtrays without cigarette ends. The Count concentrated on the books, letting an envious finger run across various sizes and textures of spine where several appealing titles caught his eye.

"Did Alexis smoke?"

"No, he loathed tobacco. Particularly cigars."

"What do you make of this drawing by Salvador K.?"

The drawing, framed and behind glass, represented a kind of woman's head beneath a parasol. The angles were sharp, the colours aggressive.

"He's employing an ancient technique of wetting paper and making human figures like that. It's like an etching on paper, or kind of collage, although he boasted that he'd discovered the warm water technique. And that drawing is a piece of shit, to put it Cubanly, as Muscles would say. The expressionists and cubists did this kind of portrait sixty years ago, when it really meant something, but now . . ."

"And are you sure they had a relationship?"

Now the Count could see the Marquess was smiling.

"The walls of this room are paper-thin. If you like, go out, and I'll whimper, and you tell me . . ."

"That won't be necessary . . ." The Count tried to frighten off the image of what the Marquess was suggesting. "Alexis kept this all very clean . . ."

"He was scrupulous, as I was saying. And even worse, he tried to convert me, but always failed. Besides, María Antonia used to come here once a week, a woman who works as a maid in his parents' house, and she helped him wash and clean, and sometimes prepared us meals for several days at a time. Do you know what? She'd steal tasty morsels from Alexis's house and bring them here: some Spanish chorizo, smoked salmon, a couple of lobster claws, the things one can only imagine or find in the dollar-stores, you get me?"

"What else can you tell me about María Antonia? She's a woman with a certain . . ."

96

The Marquess's fingers tried in vain to comb the remnants of his hair.

"You must forgive me, but yesterday I lied . . . It was María Antonia who called to tell me about Alexis. Please forgive me? She also warned me you'd be paying a visit."

The Count preferred to skip over any kind of reproach.

"What did Alexis tell you about María Antonia and his family?"

The Marquess sat on the edge of the perfectly made bed and smoothed the folds of his Chinese dressing gown over his legs.

"Ever since his grandmother died, he'd been thinking of leaving. Alexis really loved her a lot, because she and María Antonia brought him up . . . And what I'm about to tell you may seem incredible, but it's a hundred per cent true: you know Alexis was a specialist in Italian Pre-Renaissance art? Well, María Antonia knows as much as he did. That's right. Alexis studied with her, lent her his books, and taught her what he was learning. If you are interested, talk to her some time about Italian Madonnas and especially Giotto, and expect a weighty dissertation . . . The person Alexis really couldn't stand was his father, for a thousand reasons, but I think in particular because once, when he was some seven years old, he almost drowned on the beach, and someone else rescued him from the sea, because his father was drunk. And Alexis never forgave him and even said his father had left him to drown . . . I don't know which damn Greek gave a name to that complex . . . Besides, his father hated him because he was, well, queer. Whenever he could, he made it clear he hated him . . . Just imagine, it was the worst disgrace imaginable for such a respectable man

. . . But God must have shamed him as a punishment. You know what I mean: men who have sons who are going to turn out like them, strong, fond of skirt, tyrannical, and suddenly he turns out homosexual. But Alexis suffered a lot, suffered every way possible, and if they hadn't killed him, I'd have said he'd committed suicide."

"Did Alexis talk to you about suicide?"

The Marquess stood up and pointed at one of the bookshelves.

"Look for yourself: Mishima, Zweig, Hemingway, my poor friend Calvert Casey, Pavese . . . He was fascinated by suicides and those who committed suicide, a morbid fascination, to be sure. He kept saying everything in his life was a mistake: his sex, his intellect, his family, the times he lived in, and he would say that if one was conscious of such mistakes, suicide might be the solution: that way perhaps he would have a second opportunity. I think this mysticism was one of the things that turned him into a Catholic."

"Did he go to church?"

"Yes, a lot."

"What about yourself?" asked the Count, led on by his spirit of curiosity.

"Me?" smiled the Marquess, blinking. "Can you imagine me praying on a hassock? . . . No, you must be kidding. I'm too perverse to get on with those gentlemen . . . Though I prefer them to you lot . . ."

The Count observed the Marquess's duly perverse smile, and decided to cultivate it, because in some way the invitation was there. He checked his parachute and launched himself into the Sea of Sarcasm.

"Do you hate the police?"

The Marquess's laugh was genuine and unexpected. His parchment body suddenly seemed a smooth kite ready to fly out of the nearest window, launched by the guffaws now convulsing it.

"No, in no way. You guys aren't the worst. Look, police do police work, they interrogate and imprison people, and even do it well, if the truth be told. It's a cruel, repressive vocation, for which certain aptitudes are necessary, do forgive me. Like, for example, being ready to beat someone else into submission, or destroy their personality through fear and threats . . . But they are socially and sadly necessary."

"So who then?"

"The real bastards are the others: the self-appointed police, volunteer commissars, improvised persecutors, unpaid informers, amateur judges, all those who think they own the life, destiny and even the moral, cultural and historical purity of a country . . . They were the people who tried to finish off people like me, or poor Virgilio, and they succeeded, you know. Remember how in the last ten years of his life Virgilio never saw a single book of his published, nor a play performed, nor a study on his work published in any of those six magical provinces which suddenly became fourteen with a special municipality. And I was transformed into a ghost guilty because of my talent, my work, my tastes and my words. I was one huge malign tumour that had to be extirpated for the social, economic and political good of this beautiful, pre-eminent island. You see what I mean? And as it was so easy to parameterize me: whenever they measured me, whatever the angle, the result always came out the same: he's no use, no use, no use . . ."

The Count recalled yet again the meeting in his headteacher's office at school, when they were informed that *La Viboreña* was an inappropriate, inopportune and unacceptable magazine and they had to recant ideologically and literary-wise.

"How did you find all that out?" he decided to ask, with a degree of historicist sadism, opening himself up to a flurry of darts poisoned with ironic resentment.

"I've worked at it and for a few years even enjoyed telling the story. And now it barely hurts, you know? But before ... And why are you so interested in all this?"

"Curiosity pure and simple," suggested the Count, unable to admit his real reasons. "I'd like to hear your version, right?"

"Well, I'll tell you. They'd already suspended the works we were performing that had been advertised while I was rehearsing *Electra Garrigó*, when they called us to a meeting in the theatre one day. Everybody went, except me. I wasn't prepared to go and listen to what I knew I'd have to listen to. But afterwards they told me how they got the people together in the entrance hall and called them in, one at a time, like at the dentist's. You know what it's like waiting for three or four hours in a dentist's waiting room, hearing the drill and the cries of the people going in? Inside they'd put a table on the stage, where there was still part of the set for *Yerma*, with its mournful atmosphere, draped in black ... There were four of them, a kind of inquisitional tribunal, and they'd put one of those enormous tape recorders on the table and told people how they'd sinned and asked them if they were ready to change their attitudes in the future, if they'd agree to engage in a process of rehabilitation, to work in places where they'd be sent. And almost everyone admitted to sinning, even added sins their accusers hadn't mentioned, and bowed to the need for that purifying purge to cleanse their past and spirit of pseudo-intellectual, pseudo-critical tendencies ... And I understood them, I really did, because many thought it was right such accusations were made and even felt guilty for not doing the things that they were told they ought to have done, and became the most vicious critics . . . of themselves. They called a kind of mass meeting afterwards: the protagonists were still behind the table on the stage with the people in the stalls. All the lights were on . . . You ever been to a theatre with the lights on? Have you seen how it loses all its magic and the whole world of artifice seems fake and meaningless? Then they talked about me, as the main person responsible for the theatre's aesthetic policy. The first accusation made was that I was a homosexual who flaunted his condition, and they added that in their view homosexuality had a clearly anti-social, pathological character and that the accords negotiated to reject such manifestations of milksop softness or its propagation in a society like ours should be even more draconian. They were in a position to prevent 'artistic quality' (people insisted the guy talking opened and closed the quotation marks, as he smiled) being used as an excuse to cir-culate certain ideas and fashions which were corrupt-ing our selfless youth. (It has to be said that the guy doing all the talking was a mediocrity who'd tried to make it as an actor but was never more than a pos-eur, and his reputation was down to the fact his was tiny and he was nicknamed Titch.) Nor would well-known homosexuals like me be allowed to influence the training of our youth, and for that reason they would assess (he said 'carefully', this time the quota-tion marks are mine) the involvement of homo-sexuals in cultural bodies, and relocate all those banned from having contact with the young, and they wouldn't be allowed to leave the country in delegations representing Cuban art, because we were

101

not and never could be true representatives of Cuban art."

The Marquess sighed, as if releasing a great wave of exhaustion, and Mario Conde felt he was awaking from a long dream: through the dramatist's words he'd entered a theatre of cruelty and heard the words of the protagonists wrapped in dense, real tragedy where destinies and lives were decided with a chilling sang-froid.

"I never imagined it being like that. I thought—"

"Don't think anything yet," the Marquess snapped, his verbal hostility taking the policeman by surprise. "You wanted to hear the story? Well, let me go on, for the best is yet to come . . . Yes, because the aesthetic judgement came next: they said my work and productions attempted to transform elitism, extravagance, homosexuality and other social aberrations into a single aesthetic subject, for I had deviated from the path of purest aspirations through that philosophy of cruelty, the absurd and total theatre, and they wouldn't allow me my 'haughty arrogance' (his quotation marks again, because it was a very useful textual quote) in apportioning myself the role of exclusive critic of Cuban history and society, at the same time as I abandoned the stage of real struggles and used the peoples of Latin America as themes for creations that turned them into the ones preferred by bourgeois theatres and imperialist publishing houses . . . I really don't know what it all meant, but that's what he said word for word, and he also said my person, my example and work were, as everybody acknowledged, incompatible with the new reality . . . And finally they took a vote. They asked everyone to raise their hands if they agreed that artists should join the struggle by criticizing harshly the horrors of the past and thus contribute with their work to the eradication of the traces of the old society still surviving into the period of the construction of socialism. The vote was unanimous. There was a vote against manifestations of elitism, namby-pambyism, hyper-criticism, escapism and petty-bourgeois remnants in art, which was also carried unanimously. They voted on everything you could possibly vote on, almost always with complete unanimity, until it came to the vote on whether I should stay in the theatre group, the same group I had founded, named and devoted my whole life to, and of the twenty-six present, twenty-four raised their hands, called for my expulsion, and two, only two, couldn't stomach any more and left the theatre. Then they voted on whether those two should stay in, and they were expelled by twenty-four in favour with none against . . . Followed by the final speech read out by the man chairing the session, who hadn't said a word till then. As you can imagine, he barely said anything new: he repeated that it was a vital struggle against the past, against imperialism and the lackeys of the bourgeoisie, for a better future in a society where it was no longer dog eat dog. To sum up: a bad finale to the show and a historical performance that afternoon in 1971, which was even greeted by applause and cries of joy . . . And they let the curtain fall on my neck . . ."

That last sentence from the Marquess made the policeman feel an urgent need for a dose of nicotine. He touched his packet of cigarettes and observed yet again how clean the place was, and decided to fight off the anxiety of abstinence: he wanted to visit the depths of that open wound Alberto Marqués had decided to expose to him. Could it all have happened in the same country where they both lived?

"How did you find out?"

The Marquess smiled and sighed again, exhausted.

"First, from the two who overcame their own fears and stood out against the penultimate vote. Then, within a few months, one after another, the twenty-four who'd stayed till the end ... Even ten years after, I heard it all again from one of the people on stage who asked me to forgive him for what he'd done. But I didn't, because he'd been so vile, I couldn't ... Of course, I've just learned that the one who made the closing speech is now the guy most in favour of *perestroika* and a proponent of the social necessity of *glasnost*. What do you make of that change of mask?"

The Count looked him in the eye and again felt he was in the theatre, among the accused, full of fear and guilt, and wondered if he'd have voted against the Marquess. And he told himself that now it was very easy to think he wouldn't have and stand on his dignity. But on that day of all days?

"If you believed in God, you could forgive, couldn't you?"

"That's probably why I don't want to believe, Mr Policeman."

The Count sensed that he couldn't resist his need to light up a second more. It annoyed him to do so in a place so clean and tidy, and the last occupant would certainly have been upset, but he couldn't resist and decided to use his own hand as an ashtray.

"But even you say things changed later, that they invited you to go and work back in the theatre, didn't you?"

The Marquess tidied the three awkward wisps on his skull. He wasn't smiling now.

"Yes, it's true, but the first thing to happen was that several people who'd been expelled from groups

104

decided to mount a legal challenge against what they'd suffered and, so strange and just is justice in my country, they won their case in the High Court Chamber for Constitutional Guarantees and were restored to their groups, paid a wage, but it was a long time before they worked again, because obviously a director must be able to choose freely whom he wants to work with, you must agree? I didn't pursue that line, I didn't want a trial, then, later or now. Because it wasn't a legal problem: it was a judgement of history, and I didn't accept the pay-off either. I preferred to be a librarian than enjoy a stipend that could buy my right to take decisions. So, when asked to go back, I refused, because they couldn't force me. Something which couldn't be mended had been broken. If I went back, it would be for reasons of vanity or revenge, rather than from the need to make statements, which always muddies the waters of art. Ten years are a lot of years and I got used to the silence, almost learned to enjoy it, with people whispering about me, and pointing at me from afar. Besides, nobody could guarantee that what happened in '71 might not happen again, you know? . . . I wouldn't have had the strength to suffer a second sentence after returning to the stage and the limelight."

Mario Conde thought he'd listened to an otiose declaration. He'd have preferred to preserve the image of pride and courage Miki had created or the one of provocative, amoral petulance that emerged from the bulky reports he'd been given two days earlier on a man who had to be condemned for being a rebel. He even preferred the sense of hostile, sarcastic irony he'd taken from his first meeting with the Alberto Marqués now confessing to his real motive: fear.

"And wouldn't it be better to forget all this?"

The old dramatist smiled and looked up at the ceiling, as if he expected something to fall on him from heaven.

"You know, it's very easy to say that, because memory loss is one of this country's psychological qualities. It's a self-defence mechanism employed by many people . . . Everybody forgets everything and they always say you can start afresh, this very minute: the past has been exorcized. If memory doesn't exist, there's no blame, and if there's no blame, no need to forgive, you see the logic? And I understand, of course I understand, because this island's historical mission is always to be starting afresh, to make a new beginning every thirty or forty years, and oblivion is usually the ointment for all the wounds which are still open . . . And it isn't that I must forgive or want to blame anyone: no, the fact is I don't want to forget. I don't want to. Time passes, people pass on, histories change, and I think too many things, both good and bad, have been forgotten. But my things are mine and no way do I want to forget them. You understand?"

"Yes, I understand," the Count replied and went into the yard to ditch the cigarette butt and the ash accumulated on his hand. He also wanted to quit that shadowy detour in the conversation and return to his hunch. "Do you know where Alexis put his Bible?"

The Marquess looked at him with a bored shrug, as if the policeman's persistence seemed sick, if not lunatic.

"No. Did you take a good look at his bookshelves?"

"It's not there, that's why I asked."

"Well, search me if you like," he suggested, and raised his arms and brought the Count to the edge of the abyss: his dressing gown almost reached knee level while the buttons were struggling to come undone . . .

"No, no need for that. I think it's time for me to

go. I've still got work to do," the Count responded hurriedly, and, seeing the Marquess still in the position of a prisoner waiting to be frisked, he couldn't restrain his laughter. "But I'd like to talk to you again."

"Whenever, my prince," the Marquess replied, and only then did he lower his arms.

"One last question, and forgive me if I'm being indiscreet . . . What were your feelings towards Alexis Arayán?"

The Marquess looked towards the empty room.

"Pity. Yes. He was too fragile to live in this cruel world. I also loved him."

"And why do you think he dressed in Electra Garrigó's costume?"

The Marquess seemed to ponder a moment, and the Count hoped to hear something that might clear up that whole business at a single stroke.

"Because it was a very pretty dress, and Alexis was queer. Do you need any other reason?"

"But he wasn't a transvestite . . ."

The Marquess smiled, as if he'd given up.

"Ay, you've understood nothing."

"That's my lot recently: I never understand anything."

"Look, don't think I'm interfering, because I know who I can interfere with . . . But as I see the subject interests you so . . . Why not accompany me to a party tonight where you might see some transvestites and other most fascinating people? . . ."

High on nostalgia, the Count surveyed the unchanging landscape spread before him from his office window: crests of trees, a church belfry, the top floors of several tower-blocks, and the eternal, challenging promise of the sea, always in the background, always beyond reach, like the damned presence of water everywhere which the Marquess's poet friend talked about so much. He appreciated the bucolic, solicitous landscape framed by the window, now diffused with the flat, harsh August light, because it allowed him to think and, above all, remember, and wasn't he just one hell of a rememberer. And he recalled how much he'd wanted to devote himself to literature and be a real writer, in the ever more distant days of school and the first years of his unfinished university degree. He felt that Alberto Marqués, possessed by certain Mephistophelian powers, had stirred that occasional ambition, which he used to think he'd definitively left behind but which, at the slightest provocation, returned to obsess him like a recurring virus he'd never really been cured of. Mario Conde felt that that premature pang, which had stung him, perhaps only worked as a wily move on the part of his consciousness to unload in someone else's port a guilt that was only his: he'd never seriously applied himself, perhaps because the only real truth was that he was unable to write anything (that was both squalid and moving). He'd always thought he'd wanted to write stories about ordinary people, without grand passions or terrific adventures, small lives that pass through the world without leaving a single trace on the earth's face but who carry on their backs the fantastic burden of living from day to day. When he thought of his literary preferences, and read Salinger, Hemingway's stories, a few nineteenth-century novels, and books by Sartre and Camus, he still thought yes, it was possible, it might be possible. Was it an exhibitionist urge? he wondered, when he didn't know whether he should regret an impulse to sincerity that had made him confess to the dramatist his eternally deferred artistic instincts, so inappropriate in someone professionally dedicated to repression and not creation, to sordid truths, not sublime fantasies ... Smiles and sniggers, the only response he got from the Marquess, who'd carried on sniffing the non-existent scent from a bougainvillea, now riled him like a poor joke. Nevertheless, the stories that man kept teasing him with went beyond the limits of any prejudice, and he could no longer see him simply as that shitty queer he'd gone to meet barely twenty-four hours earlier. I'll be fucked, he told himself, as he heard the door opening to allow the awaited figure of Sergeant Manuel Palacios to become a tangible reality.

"Why did you take so long, man?"

Sergeant Palacios flopped down in his chair and the Count was afraid it would come apart. Who the hell ever accepted him in the force? It must have been the same lunatic who recruited me.

"Let me get my breath. The lift's broken down again."

The Count glanced back at his landscape with sea, and bid farewell, until they next met.

"Well, what happened?"

"Nothing, Conde, I had to wait for Alexis's boss. And I think I was right to because the waters are muddying."

Sergeant Palacios took a deep breath before he spoke.

"Alexis was no longer with Salvador K. His boss at the Centre, one Alejandro Fleites, who also looks like one great queer, says Alexis and Salvador had cooled off recently and that he twice saw Alexis with a mulatto who works at the Film Institute, a guy called Rigofredo López. You can imagine the kind of hulk ... And he says someone told him, you know what they're like, that Rigofredo and Salvador K. had a row in Alexis's office. Fleites's conclusion: jealousy. Then I went to the Film Institute and discovered Rigofredo's been in Venezuela for the last ten days . . . What do you make of this can of worms?"

The Count sat back in his chair and only then asked:

"So what did he tell you about Alexis?"

"Little that's new . . . That he was a hard worker, that he got on with painters very well, that he was very cultured and that he couldn't imagine him dressed in red in the Havana Woods. Also that he was very shy and screwed up . . ."

"What about the Bible?"

"The Bible? Hell, yes, the Bible . . ." He paused for a long time as if his thoughts were elsewhere and then said, "Here it is," and searched in the briefcase he'd put on the floor.

"Give it me, give it me," demanded the Count, looking for the Gospels on the contents page.

St Matthew started on page 971 and, according to Father Mendoza, the Transfiguration episode was in chapter 17. He skimmed the tops of the pages till he reached chapter 16 and then 19, in a fatal leap which caught him by surprise like a cry for help. He then looked among the pages and discovered what was missing: the sheet with pages 989 and 990, where chapters 17 and 18 of Matthew ought to be.

"I knew it, for fuck's sake, Alexis was thinking about the Transfiguration . . . Look at this, the page where it happens isn't there. Let me see if it's missing in the others."

The Count slowly embarked on his quest for the verses in Mark and Luke, discovering that both had all their pages, and he found the story of the Transfiguration in Mark, chapter 9: "And his raiment became shining, exceeding white as snow; so as no fuller on earth can white them." And also in Luke 9: "And as he prayed, the fashion of his countenance was altered, and his raiment was white and glistering."

"Where was the Bible, Manolo?"

"In Alexis's desk. In the unlocked bottom drawer."

"And people knew it was there?"

"Well, his boss says he didn't know . . . You didn't tell me . . ."

"Not to worry. The problem is someone tore out the missing page. And look at this: he did it very carefully, you don't notice the tear, do you? It was probably Alexis himself . . . Can you imagine what this means?"

"That there was something written there."

"Something that annoyed or endangered someone, and that someone tore the page out. Or, if not, it meant something special for this boy and that's why he decided to take it out himself. And if that was the case, it clarifies a lot for us, Manolo: the bastard was mad and transfigured himself in order to enter his own Calvary. I'll bet my buttocks on it."

"Hey, I'd bet something else if I were you. I think certain influences aren't good for you . . . But remember Salvador knew the Bible was there."

"You think it was him?"

"I don't know, but I'd bring him in and tighten his 'K' into a 'Q' ."

"I'm not so sure, Manolo . . . If it was him, why would he mention the Bible? No, I don't think Salvador is so stupid as to appear guilty of something so serious and be that guilty person into the bargain. What do you reckon? . . . Now I've got to talk to the Boss. Wait here."

"I'm always waiting for you, Count."

The lieutenant ignored the irony and went out into the passage. He climbed two flights of stairs, to the top floor. Walked along another corridor and entered the anteroom to Major Rangel's office. Behind Maruchi's desk – she always had a flower in a small vase that was no longer there, perhaps she took it with her – there was the lieutenant who'd surprised him the day before. The Count saluted her and asked to see the Major.

"He told me to make sure nobody bothered him," the lieutenant warned.

"Tell him it's urgent," the Count retorted. "Do me a favour . . ."

She hummed sonorously – how this guy likes to hassle, she must have been thinking – but she pressed the intercom button and told the Major that Lieutenant Conde was there and said it was urgent. "Tell him to come in," said the Boss's voice on the intercom.

The Count opened the door and saw him, cigar in his mouth. It was the same kind of smoke as the previous day's wretched Holguín specimen.

"What's up, Mario?" asked the Boss, and his voice was slow and opaque.

"I've brought you this, that's why it was urgent." And he took out of his pocket the long, resplendent Montecristo with which Faustino Arayán had regaled him.

"Where did you get this from, my boy?"

"I promised you one, didn't I?"

"Fuck, this is a fine piece of work," he said, and almost without looking threw his Holguín weed out of the window and started to smell the Montecristo. "It's a little on the dry side, isn't it?"

"You can sort that . . ."

"And what else do you want? I know you too well . . ."

The Count sat down and lit one of his cigarettes.

"They've called Manolo in. What's his problem?"

The Major didn't reply. He sniffed his new cigar again and carefully put it away in a drawer.

"For after lunch . . ."

"Are you going to tell me?" persisted the Count.

"They want him because of you," replied the Boss as he stood up.

"Because of me?"

"Yes, it's logical enough. You're officially suspended and that's why you are of interest to Internal Investigations—"

"I'll fuck the—"

"Hey," Rangel bellowed, switching his tired voice to a gruff, authoritarian tone that culminated in the fingertip he flourished at the lieutenant. "You don't need to worry . . . If you do, say, comment or think anything about this and I find out, I'll get your balls sliced off, get that? This is red-hot and I don't want any more problems. They're going to question Manolo about you, and what will he say? Nothing . . . That you had a set-to with Fabricio because you can't stand each other and there's nothing else to go on . . . Nothing!"

The Count put out his cigarette and suddenly wanted to be well out of there. It was already complicated enough looking for rapists, thieves, swindlers and murderers of mystical transvestites without becoming the subject of suspicion oneself.

"Talk to Manolo and tell him what's at stake. But talk to him away from here. OK? If anyone finds out I told you this, I'll be the one who'll get it in the balls. OK?"

The Count didn't reply.

"OK, Conde?" the Major persisted.

"OK, Boss . . . I'm off . . ." And he stood up.

"Just a minute. How's the case going?"

The Count shrugged his shoulders. Suddenly he wasn't overly interested in his case.

"So so . . . I've got a dead man who occasionally had visions of God, and a suspect who's too suspicious, but no proof against him."

"So what next?"

"I'll carry on searching."

"What the fuck," said the Boss as he opened the drawer and took out the Montecristo. He broke off the end with his teeth in the traditional manner and briefly chewed on it. He spat the end in the basket and then, when he went to put the lighter-flame next to the end of his cigar, something stopped him and he shook his head. "It's too good to light now. This at least deserves a cup of real coffee." And he put it back in the drawer. "There's one more thing I've got to tell you, Conde. Someone phoned me and asked me for discretion in everything around this case. He told me something I didn't know: the dead man was old Arayán's son and you know what that means. They want everything to stay a problem unconnected to the family so links can't be made between them and that mess of tranvestites and queers their son was mixed up with. So now you know: first I said trasvestites because that's what came to me, and don't hassle the family much and try to resolve this quickly, without creating too much of a stir, get it?"

"Yes, Siree, as they say," the Count riposted and left the office, without saying goodbye to the Major. Now he wanted to abandon everything even more. And he thought: what a load of shit. They don't even have a decent cup of coffee to go with a decent cigar.

"What do you reckon?"

The Count smiled, looking at the faded, parched pages of what had aspired to be the school literary review, and thought how all that might as well belong to another life, one too distant to be the one he was still living: his story on the back of the title page with the print of the Jesus del Monte church, and the pompous title of *La Viboreña*, which hid so many expectations and longings severed by the brutal chop from the hatchet of intolerance and incomprehension.

"Naive and without depth. I remembered it as being more squalid and more moving," he said, and reclined back on Carlos's bed. "Far too many 'thats' and far too few commas . . ."

"And why did you want to read it?"

The Count poured more rum into his glass and moved the bottle towards Skinny's glass.

"I didn't know if I wanted to remember what the story said or what they said to me about the story."

Carlos downed some rum and grimaced far too dramatically for the owner of a throat burnt by the slow fire of a sustained daily habit.

"Who remembers any of that now, Conde . . ."

"I do," he rasped and took a long, possibly excessive gulp.

"Hey, hold on, man . . . What the fuck's up with you today? You were perfectly fine yesterday, and today . . ."

The Count looked at his friend: an ever more amorphous mass in his wheelchair. He closed his eyes, like the character in his story and thought, like him: if only it weren't true. He would have liked Skinny still to be skinny, and not that fat type keeling over, like a sinking boat, taking with it in the wreck Mario Conde's last chance of happiness. He wanted to play on the street corner again, for all his old friends to be there and nobody to exclude him from a place which so much belonged to him. At the same time he wanted to forget everything, for good.

"Won't you tell me what's wrong?" Carlos insisted,

moving his chair to the edge of the bed where his friend had flopped down.

"I'm fucked, Skinny. They don't even want me as a policeman any more . . . Today they're going to talk to Manolo about me. They'll probably retire me. What do you reckon? Retired at thirty-five . . ."

"Are you serious?"

"As serious as Desiderio's arse."

Skinny laughed. The bastard couldn't help it.

"You're done for, man."

"That's what they say. Pour me some more rum. I'm running shit-scared."

"Why, you idiot? Are there real problems?"

"I don't know, but I can't stop being scared . . . More rum."

"You've got to forget all this, man . . . Conde, you're well fucked, but you're a good man. I know you've done no wrong, so quit being scared, right?"

"All right," the other agreed, not overly convinced.

"Did I tell you Andrés came to see me this morning?"

"Yesterday you told me he was going to come. What did that lunatic want?"

Carlos poured himself out more rum, downed a murderous gulp and pulled his wheelchair over until he was in front of his friend.

"Dulcita's coming," he said.

"Dulcita?" Conde was taken aback. "Dulcita?"

Dulcita had left for the United States more than ten years ago, and the Count remembered how often he and Skinny had spoken about the departure of the girl who'd been Carlos's girlfriend for two years at school. Intelligent Dulcita, perfect Dulcita, the great laugh, who'd then left, leaving them to wonder why, oh why did it have to be her. And now she was coming back: "How come?"

"She's coming to see her grandmother, who is apparently dying. Andrés knows because they talked to him in order to get the medical certificate the Red Cross requires to negotiate the travel permit."

"Fantastic, right?" the Count went on, getting over his shock.

Skinny finished his rum and put his hands on the Count's knees, which felt the moist, red-hot heat of those voluminous extremities.

"More than fantastic, it's brilliant. Do you know what Dulcita's sister said to Andrés? That if we weren't angry and it wouldn't hurt, she'd like to see us. But above all she wanted to see me."

The Count started to smile, moved by an inevitable feeling of happiness that immediately languished and killed the stillborn smile.

"You tell me, Conde, do you think it right for Dulcita to see me like this?" He used his obese hands to indicate his body overflowing the wheelchair.

Mario Conde stood up, went over to the window and spat venomously. It wasn't right, he thought, remembering that photo featuring Pancho, Tamara, Dulcita, Skinny and himself, coming down the stairs at school the day they'd put in for their university courses. Skinny, who was very thin in those days and walked on two legs, was in the centre, arms open wide and head to one side, as if awaiting crucifixion: Carlos and Dulcita had been a beautiful, lovely couple, eager for sex, life, happiness and love . . . No, it wasn't right, he kept thinking, but he said:

"Hey, if she comes to see you and you want to see her, let her: you are you and always will be, and the person who loved you must still love you, or should go to hell."

"Don't talk shit, Conde, things aren't like that."

"Aren't they? Well, they are as far as I'm concerned,

because you're my brother and it has to be like that
. . . But if you don't want to see her, well, don't, and
forget it."

"That's the fucking point, Conde, I do want to see
her. But whatever way, it's not exactly going to be a
party for her to see me like this. Get me?"

The Count lit a cigarette and went back to the bed.
He pulled the wheelchair even nearer, and Carlos's
face was only an inch or two from his.

"Skinny: don't be such a pansy," he said. "Don't give
up, for Christ's sake, because if you do, we're all
fucked. Do it for yourself, for me and old Josefina;
don't let anything fuck you up: a bullet, the past, the
war, or this damned wheelchair," he declared breath-
lessly, and, against his usual custom of thinking everything through, he took Carlos's face between his hands
and kissed him on a cheek. "Don't give up, brother."

"But what the fuck is this!"

Of course. It just had to be the hottest summer he'd
ever experienced, he concluded while undressing
before getting in the shower. For several days now the
Count had been pinching memory and flesh to try to
remember other August temperatures like this cruel
year's, but the wall-scorching sun, the haze from the
ceiling, the moisture wrapping round him in bed and
the deep depression, able to sap his will and his
muscles, told him it was impossible to recall a similar
muggy heat. Or did the heat come from his body
rather than the infernal atmosphere possessing the
island? He looked at his watch: yes, it was still early for
Sergeant Palacios to call him and he still didn't know
whether he'd dare call the Marquess.

When he got out of the bath, streaming water, the

towel round his shoulders like a defeated boxer, the Count decided to finish drying himself on the ecstatic gusts from the fan. He flopped on to his hot bed and for a moment enjoyed the minimal privilege of solitude, felt the draught massage his drooping testicles and hit his anus particularly deliciously. He closed his legs slightly. Then, to help the draught, and impelled by a straightforward burst of onanism, he started lifting up his wet penis, sliding his fingers to the head that had been surgically uncapped, only to let it drop in a free fall that gradually became an upward tilt transmitting a warm, erect hardness to his fingers. He hesitated for a moment over whether to masturbate or not: and decided he had no reason not to try. No woman was out there waiting for that spare ejaculation, and as he stroked himself, even the heat in the air seemed to have abated. But his decision hit fresh doubts: whose turn was it? Still grasping his member but reducing the rubbing rhythm, the Count opened his much-fingered book of erotic memories and began to flick through the pages of women he'd loved by remote control when seeking to protect himself against the successive departures, deceits and disappearances they'd inflicted on him: on the last page – he always began at the back when he read an issue of the magazine *Bohemia* – he found Karina, naked, sucking a dazzling saxophone whose intense music caressed her nipples as it moved between her open legs, but he let her go, humiliated her with mental indifference, a form of revenge on a woman too painfully close to be called upon, and the fact is he could still feel her scent of ripened fruit, between a mango and velvety plums, which mingled with the deep, animal dampness from her desire-swollen sex: "No, not you."

He likewise abandoned Haydée, trying not to

remember shared alcoholic belches, miserable wretched bouts of drinking, rums poured on mouths, breasts and a doubly moist pubis, and that was why he fled, he tried not even to brush against her – though he failed to resist that painful temptation – because she'd been his best lover, so hard-working in bed the Count's productivity couldn't keep up with her and she'd replaced him with an Olympic-class fornicator (whose anus was she now kissing with her drilling, eschatological, reptilian tongue?); but he did pass without major upset on the memory of Maritza, his first wife, too distant and faded to be of use even for a summery masturbation, that pink scent from her virgin skin hardly perceptible now, always washed to face sex, at once clean and apprehensive; he breathed, more nostalgic than horny, the essential feminine fragance that nurse gave off, a nymphomaniac on the thin side, whose name he'd now forgotten but whom he always remembered because she'd initiated him in the pleasure of the other's hand which strokes, rubs, allowing one to discover the value of another's skin, giving the act of masturbation an unexpected dimension, only because it comes from other hands, from another skin; and, when her turn came, he almost stayed with Tamara, felt her on his fingertips, on the wrinkled sac of his testicles, as he revisited her rumba-dancer's butt and black nipples, the dark depths of her curly patches of down, and breathed in the strong aromas from her male colognes – Canoe is my favourite, she'd confess, allergic to other subtle, feminine perfumes – and then his hand stopped on the album – and on a glans gorged and ready to spit – to reach a final conclusion: none of them ... He stretched a hand out from the position he found himself in, slipped it under his bed and extracted the *Penthouse* that Peyi had lent Skinny and Skinny had lent him and went on an immediate search for that shameless blonde – lots of hair upstairs, next to none down – who in the same position as he – in bed, legs open to the breeze or other possibilities – made her professional nakedness stand out against red, photographer-ready sheets: if there was a breeze in the photo – and there had to be – it must smell of moist, ploughed earth, and the woman must surely have exuded the same fertile, primary fragance. Better you than one concocted from deceit and memories, he told the blonde, as he leaned forward and continued to rub until he could no longer see the woman and felt his life being drained by those white drops spilling without rhyme or reason on the dusty tiles of his room, which now emanated, like a disturbing perfume born of his painful solitude, the sweetness of ejaculation . . .

But sexual relief didn't relieve the heat: his body and brain burned, and he understood all had been in vain: there was only one remedy against that specific heat and that was a real woman, not one made from memories, scents recalled, or glossy paper, but a tangible female, able to smash the desperate abandon burning him cell by cell, without recourse to more or less individualist soothing, remedies or dilatory techniques.

Then from his bed he spotted Rufino, the new fighting fish who lived in his goldfish bowl. He'd been his companion for some ten days, ever since he'd gone hunting for a replacement for the old Rufino, who'd greeted the day face up, fins awry, as if searching for a non-existent wind in the pallid deep purple of the death of a fighting fish. Now young Rufino had stopped, as if exhausted by the effort of swimming in a sea of lava; the Count could almost see the drops of sweat as his eyes stared at the glass and he barely moved his tiny fighting piscatorial entrails: then he entered a slow descent, without a struggle, without fluttering a fin, as if defeated definitively, and the Count assumed that descent as his own, a bitter mirror, the reflection of a free fall from which he didn't want or couldn't escape, like the much heralded decline of the West or the now inevitable collapse of a flaccid, empty penis. Suicidal inclinations?

The Count lit a cigarette and embarked on another slow, pleasant suicide.

"But what the fuck can it be now!" he said, about to go back into the shower, when the telephone rang.

"It's me, Conde."

"Wait a minute, Conde, just a minute, don't go chasing off. No, I really needed to speak to you in the street, you and me and no bother. And a cigarette for me too while you're about it. Wait . . . Look, I don't know what more they want to find out about you, because they know everything and know nothing, and I reckon they're throwing stones at all the dummies to see if they get a hit. I'm not kidding, Conde, just listen, man. Fuck, it's much hotter than yesterday, isn't it? They wanted chapter and verse on you, on me as well, just so you know, but they'd already got all the answers, you bet they had. It's incredible, man: they even know how many cigarettes we smoke a day, but I'm not daft and could see they didn't really have anything to go on. There's a reason why I'm police, I suppose? They wanted to find out what kind of relationship you have with the Boss, if you were friends or not, the whole of Headquarters knows that, whether I thought the Boss favoured you and if he'd ever covered up for you, that kind of thing. They went on and on, and I don't know whether it was because of you or Major Rangel. What do you reckon? They're already investigating him, that you know ... Then they asked me if your fight with Lieutenant Fabricio was related to work or personal gripes, what we think about the investigations they're carrying out, whether I thought you were an alcoholic, why you lived by yourself, just incredible. They also asked me about your informers, and even mentioned Candito's name, whether you gave him protection so you could do clandestine business and such like, as if nobody did that, huh? And, listen to this, they knew you'd had a relationship with Tamara when you were on her husband's case. Who did you tell that to, Conde? Well, they know about it, and that you didn't see each other again afterwards, they know that too. And a thousand stupid little things as well, though nothing important: they asked me why you like going into churches, why you tell people you'd like to live in a house near the sea, if you still think about being a writer and the kind of things you like writing. Well, I just told them you liked writing things that were squalid and moving and so I got them off that kick. But, man, they know everything, you know? The worst fucking thing, Conde, is you suddenly feel like you're living in a glass bowl, or a test-tube, I don't know, that they watch you shitting, pissing and picking your nose, and know if you make little balls to throw or stick under a table. That scared me: they've got us down to a T, know everything we do and everything we don't, and are interested in everything. I'm probably pea-brained, but I didn't imagine it was like that. It really makes you scared, Conde, really. No, there were three of them, I don't know them, a captain and two lieutenants, they said, but they were in field dress and weren't wearing stripes. In a second-floor office, next to the meeting room. They told me to come in, poured me coffee, and it was all very relaxed, a conversation between friends, inquisitive friends who wanted to find out every silly little thing. And they are vicious when it comes to questioning, you should see how cleverly they take you down a side alley, only to lead you back where they want you, but all as if they were quite uninterested, but I beat them at their own game: first because I know their ploys off by heart and I'm like a doughty lion, as you say, and second I don't the fuck know what can be of interest to them. Yes, they say it's necessary work, they've uncovered lots of irregularities, lax discipline, rule-breaking, which can't be allowed, so they've been ordered to come and investigate everyone and anyone who's done wrong will have to assume responsibility. And I can tell you one thing, Conde: they really don't have anything against you or me, but they've got their knives out, doesn't matter who, so tread carefully the next few days, the heat's on. If you don't believe me, well, you know who they told me they'd taken out of Headquarters today? Fatman Contreras . . . No, they didn't tell me why and I didn't stay around to find out, I don't want to get burnt myself just for the fun of it, like some shit-brain, but if they took him out, it's because they've got something on him, you can bet your butt on it, Conde, you bet they've got things on him . . . Poor Fatman, right?"

"It was Afón," Pancho and Rabbit almost whispered, when he saw that the two cans of condensed milk he was keeping as his big treat for a cold, hungry night had gone missing. A vicious anger spread over his face, hammered his temples, dried his throat out, but he thought twice before reaching a decision: I've got no choice but to get angry. If I let this go, they'll end up taking the pants off me, and I'm man enough, for fuck's sake, he thought, then he thought again how he'd lose this argument, black Afón and his weight-lifting biceps would skin him alive, and it didn't make sense to be robbed, and end up split-lipped and black-eyed in front of a disciplinary tribunal, but in that jungle the laws were clearly written on backs of tigers, and the first law admonished that men are men, morning, afternoon and night, and the second said, "Better be dead than humiliated", and if your food was stolen, and you knew who the thief was and decided to keep quiet rather than complain as you must in such cases (fists first), you took the first step on the road to total ignominy: if today they lifted food from your suitcase, tomorrow it would be your money and three days later you'd be washing the dishes for three or four fellows or, like Bertino, making beds for half the dormitory and saying he'd let them stick their fingers up his arse because they did it for fun and he didn't have any complexes. Launched into compulsory communal life, cut off from paternal protection and having to defend their own lives and security, students in those camps were forced to protect themselves and show their primary instincts. It was a constant struggle for food, water, the best bed, a clean bath and the easi-est work in a round of competition which soon gave way to aggression you could only meet with more of the same. A shout for a shout, a theft for a theft, a blow for a blow, was the third fundamental law of this cruel chemistry, without any scope for relativity. He slammed shut the wooden lid on his violated suitcase, and went out into the yard where Afón was peacefully playing volleyball, his weightlifting arms making some unstoppable hits.

The Count entered the playing area, grabbed the ball that flew by him and, carrying it under his arm, to protests from all the players, walked towards Afón, thinking, my voice mustn't fail me, for fuck's sake, and his voice didn't fail him when he said: "I want my two cans of milk." Then the players shut up and got ready to watch the spectacle in the making. Afón looked at the spectators and smiled at his fawning public, confidently and scarily. And he rasped: "What the fuck's got into you, kid?" "You stole my cans of milk, you pansy," the Count shouted and thought – he always thought everything through – he shouldn't say anything else and threw the ball straight at black Afón's mouth and, without thinking, he now threw himself after the ball, at the thief's shocked face. He managed to strike him twice, on the neck, until one of Afón's fists connected with one of his cheeks and knocked him to the ground, for what ought to have been the beginning of the end, when a voice called out from the sideline: "Afón, let the kid be and give him his condensed milk . . ." But, driven by the rage in his blood after receiving the hit to the face, the Count got up and returned to the attack, not thinking of anything or anybody, until four or five players managed to extract him from Afón's lethal arm-lock, as the voice of Red Candito, hands on waist opposite the thief, said again: "Afón, you will give him his condensed milk back, won't you?"

"Afón was going to kill you, Conde," Candito laughed, and finished his cup of coffee.

"Don't bug me, Red, he wasn't going to kill anybody . . . Why did he give me the cans of milk and not fight me?"

"Poor Afón, I don't know how he was so strong, with the hunger that black suffered. Is the coffee good?"

"To die for," the Count pronounced.

"Fact is I'm not too good at fixing coffee. Either it's weak, or sweet, or too strong, or stewed . . ."

"This was really good," the Count ratified, and reckoned he was a good judge of coffee. He lit a cigarette and passed his packet to Red Candito. The mulatto took one and leaned back in his armchair. At that effervescent evening hour, the hall in that building lived its maximum bustle of the day: the voices of children playing, a woman asking Macusa for salt, a radio blaring out Tejedor's voice and another giving news of a train derailed in Matanzas, with dead and injured, as well as a gravel voice which shat on the mother of the owner of the lousy dog which had shat in front of the door to his room.

"Sometimes it makes you feel like going to the moon, Conde . . . You know I was born here, when we didn't have a barbecue or toilet and this room was half what it is now and my parents, grandad, brother and I lived here, and we had to queue up to wash and shit in the communal bathrooms. But it's not true you adapt to everything . . . It's a lie, Conde. I can't stand any more of this, and I sometimes start to wonder when I'll be able to live properly, have a house, be quiet when I want and listen to music when I want and not the whole damned day . . . I'm up to here" – and he touched one of his red hairs. "You know, when I walk down the street, I'm obsessed with looking into other people's houses and thinking which I'd like to have, and I try to work out why some people live in nice houses and the rest of us are born into places that stink of the plague, where we'll live out the rest of our lives . . . When there's a house I like a lot, I even imagine how I'd live there if it were mine . . . Can you understand that? And you know the guy who lives in the second room along, Serafina's son? He's a chemical engineer, Conde, and the cunt's a real know-all, but he's still stuck here . . . That's why I have to accept my lot in this room, you know, and even thank God, because some people don't even have this."

"And that's why you're always in and out of church?"

"Well, at least people don't shout there."

"And what do you ask God for?"

Red took a last drag on his cigarette before crushing it on the clay ashtray and looked at his friend.

"You having me on, Conde?"

"No, I'm serious."

"I ask him to give me good health, peace, patience, to protect me, and I ask him to look after my friends, like you and Carlos . . ."

The Count knew Candito was telling the truth and felt that those prayers, where he also figured, when prayed by his old friend Red, had an accumulated value that moved him. Because Red had not only stopped Afón from doing him over in the training camp, but had been loyal to him ever since, something the Count hadn't always returned with the same sincerity: as a friend who'd never had any time to devote to Candito, and as a policeman who'd put the squeeze on him more than once, mercilessly taking advantage of the knowledge Red had of all the goings-on in the Havana underworld. In a real sense, the Count thought, I'm a selfish cynic.

"If God exists, I hope he's listening to you . . ."

"What a self-interested bugger you are . . . And what are you into now, Conde?"

"I'm after whoever killed a transvestite . . . But it's not easy, I can tell you. It seems the transvestite was a mystic, read the Bible and then right when they killed him he was dressed up like a character from a play. But the best of the story is that they stuck two peso coins up his arse."

128

Candito looked at the ground, while he searched his memory.

"It's a fucker," agreed Candito. "That's something new on the scene. It means something, Conde. I expect they were paying him back . . . So, you want me to help you, I guess?"

"No, not now. I just came to tell you you've got to shut up shop," he said, and lit another cigarette.

"Why, is there some bother?"

"So it seems, but don't ask me, because I really don't know what the problem is and I can't tell you anything anyway. Just do what I say and shut up shop."

Candito ran his hand over his head, as if he had to remove something stuck in his bright red hair.

"It's OK, Conde, you know the whys and wherefores . . . It's a shame though, you know. I'm just trying to save a bit of money . . ."

"And what about the mulatto the other day? The one the fight was over?"

Now Candito smiled, but looked fed up and sad.

"He said he'd come to speak to me so I'd let him in for a piss . . ."

"I told you. You're all mad."

"No, Conde, we're not mad. You know your business and I know mine . . . That guy's a debt-collector."

"What do you mean a debt-collector?"

"What I said. People hire him to collect their debts: he collects money owed or any kind of debt: settling accounts, spying on wives, people wanting to get their own back on someone. And the guy's a pro."

The Count shook his head, refusing to believe all that, though he knew it must be true coming from Candito.

"But was it true the guy wanted a leak?"

"Nobody gets in here just to piss. Everybody knows

that, it was just bullshit. And if it was true he wanted a piss, then the poor guy was fucked, but I wasn't going to get fucked, nor were you. Nor Carlos."

The Count shook his head, denying something words couldn't deny.

"Sure he wasn't after me?"

"He said not, but who knows . . ."

"I'm the one who's never in the know, Red. You know I'm beginning to feel as if I was no longer a player? It's strange, but I understand less by the day. Either everything's changing very quickly, or I'm losing it. I really don't know, but my head feels like a football . . . How about another coffee, go on," he asked, and lit another cigarette. "Let me tell you one thing, Red. After you shut up shop, make yourself scarce, try going to the beach for a week, or the moon, as you put it . . . But if anyone comes after you, the first thing you do is find me wherever I've gone to ground. Because if they put the heat on you, they'll have to burn me too . . . Anyway, go to church tomorrow, and ask God, on my behalf as well, to lend a hand, if he can."

"What a character you've turned into, Conde!"

"Hey, while we're at it. As you're shutting up the office, how about another beer to help the winding-down process?"

The Count contemplated himself in the mirror: head on, in the eyes, observing the shifty rake of his profile, and when he'd finished the self-scrutiny he had to agree: it's true, I've got a policeman's face. And whatever will I do with this policeman's face if they kick me out of the force? To start with, I won't shave today, he told himself, and it was then he decided to call Alberto Marqués and accept his invitation. Nine o'clock? That's fine. On Prado and Malecón . . . Careful you don't get knocked off your feet, my prince . . .

Already by nine fifteen the Count had stood on each street corner three times at the stretch of pavement configured by the crossroads where the Paseo del Prado meets the Malecón, for he'd made the mistake of not specifying an exact spot for his rendezvous with the Marquess. The worst was feeling his hands moistening all the time, as if he was going on a first date with a new woman. This is queer shit of my own making, he reproached himself, but the awareness that he was carrying that terrible burden wasn't enough to mitigate a sweat not warranted by the heat. At that time of day a light but strongish breeze blew in from the sea, refreshing that ancient corner of the city, while intermittent gusts wafted along various women who reeked of the port, who'd flown in like dusky butterflies from some flower in its lunar cycle, perhaps summoned by the penumbra recently installed where their shadowy occupation always prospered. The Count understood his anxiety was down to uncertainty. Where would they go? What would Alberto Marqués propose they should see (or do)? Although he was sure the old dramatist wouldn't try to cross swords with him, the Count had tangibly blushed before leaving home, and reckoned that if he looked like a policeman and was under investigation because he was a policeman, he should take his policeman's pistol with him tonight, the cold weight of which his hands felt for a moment, before he convinced himself that tonight's dangers couldn't be fought off with bullets and opted to consign his weapon to the depths of his desk drawer. When he thought of his pistol, he again thought of his friend Captain Jesús Contreras, the dreadful Fatman, and the news Manolo had brought him. Fuck my mother, he said to himself, surveying the dark expanse of sea he couldn't grasp, like happiness or fear, thought the Count. And then he heard his voice.

"Don't think so hard, Mr Lieutenant Policeman Mario Conde. Please forgive my being so late."

Then he saw him: it was the same man, but was perhaps someone else, as if he'd donned a disguise for an impromptu carnival. A short, thick crop of fair hair now covered his originally bereft head, making him look like a living caricature. He tried to improve things by making constant adjustments to his helmet of hair, while his carefully, abundantly powdered face imitated the yellow pallor of a Japanese mask . . . A pink shirt, open at the neck like a dressing gown, floated over his skinny, sombre skeleton, and he wore the tightest black trousers over his skinny thighs, and sandals but no socks, allowing one sight of his fat toes with nails like gruesome hooks. Then the Count understood: he'd committed a folly, not just made a mistake. That was why he looked at the three meeting-points on the two avenues, looking for possible tails, for if they were watching him, as Manolo said, they'd kick him out not because he was corrupt or inefficient, but for being plain stupid. He tried to imagine the image he and Alberto Marqués must cut from the pavement opposite and was horrified by what he saw.

"Go on then, out with your compass," he finally said, ready to meet his fate.

"Let's go up Prado, for though lots of people won't believe it, the south also has a life."

"You're in charge," nodded the Count, and they crossed over the Malecón, going away from the sea.

The policeman followed in the footsteps of the Marquess, a route he marked out across the old avenue, flanked by oleanders getting more battered by the day, and by the queues which swelled and length-ened at each bus stop. The surviving street-lights lit up the dirty terrain which, for the first time, the Count began to imagine as a boulevard.

"Did you know this road is a tropical replica of the Ramblas in Barcelona? They both peter out in the sea, have almost the same buildings on either side, although the birds they sell in cages in Barcelona once flew free and wild here. The last delight this place lost was its long-beaked *totí* birds that came and slept in the trees. You remember them? I used to enjoy watch-ing their evening flights in bigger and bigger flocks as they got nearer to Prado. I never found out why those black birds chose to sleep in these trees in the centre of Havana every night. It was magic seeing them fly, like black gusts of wind, weren't they? And they disappeared because of an act of witchcraft. Where can those poor *totís* be now? I once heard the sparrows blamed for their departure, but the fact is neither's around now. Were they kicked out or did they go voluntarily?"

"I don't know, but I can ask if you like."

"Well, ask then, because any day now you'll wake up and the bronze lions will have gone too . . . It's pitiful, this place, isn't it? But it still retains some of its magic, as if it had an invincible poetic spirit, right? Look, though the ruins keep spreading and grime's winning, this city still has soul, Mr Count, and not many cities in the world can boast they have soul, bubbling on the surface . . . My friend the poet Eligio Riego says that's why there's such a flowering of poetry here, although I don't think the country deserves it: it's much too frivolous and sun-loving . . ."

The Count nodded silently. He wanted to sidestep that metaphysical turn in the conversation and drift back to levels of concrete reality.

133

"Well then, what are we doing?"

"Well," the Marquess readjusted his blond wig and said: "Didn't you want a close-up of the nocturnal habits of Havana gays?"

"I don't know ... I wanted to get a sense of the scene ..."

The Marquess looked in front, just after they'd walked by a group of youths who'd brazenly eyed them over. "Well, you've just seen a bit ... And what you want to see and know isn't that pleasant, I warn you. It's sordid, alarming, stark and almost always tragic, because it's the result of loneliness, eternal repression, mocking, hostility, contempt, even of monoculture and under-development. Do you understand?"

"I understand, but I still want to take a look," the Count insisted, covering the nostrils of consciousness as a prelude to jumping into that dark, bottomless pit of invert sex.

"Well, let's take a stroll and then go to a little party at Alquimio's place, a mate of mine and an alchemist by any other name ... There'll be people there who knew Alexis, though I did my detective enquiries and he'd not been there for more than a week. You know, I'm beginning to like being a bit of a policeman ..."

Casting off his wig, as if it were plebeian headgear, the Marquess declared: "This man's a noble, like me, though he's only a Count. Sit here, Mr Count," and almost pushed him, so the policeman's bum fell hard on to a cushion on the floor, while his material and spiritual guide yielded himself up to multiple embraces, wet kisses on the cheeks, which the dramatist soaked up, laughing coquettishly, like an insatiably

134

greedy pagan god fond of being worshipped. The reception room in that big house had large balconies open to the mysteries of the night and a high ceiling peopled with friezes, angels blinded by fossilized dust and cornucopias born from the forgotten fruits of the earth, and almost thirty people were gathered there, bent on offering the tribute which the presence of Alberto Marqués apparently deserved, next to whom a Havana chorus had formed, no doubt keen to hear the grisly details of the red death of Alexis Arayán. God, how horrible, exclaimed a girl who had stayed on the periphery, whose thighs the Count inspected from his favourably lower position – he was the only one sitting down – watering at the mouth, thighs visible to within a quarter of an inch of the petite bun of that sparrow fallen from the nest. After two months of manual diet his sexual hunger was stirred and disturbed by a whiff of food, rationed but fresh, distant but tangible.

The praise provoked by the Marquess's presence lasted more than ten minutes, until gradually the chorus deserted and picked up cushions, and the dramatist took his nearest listener by the hand and led him to the Count, signalling to him not to get up.

"Look, Alquimio," he said, and the policeman thus discovered he was his host at that party, "this is my friend, the Count . . . He is a regrettably heterosexual writer and also knew Alexis . . ."

"Pleased to meet you," said Alquimio, extending a gentle hand which slipped on the runaway moisture of the Count's. "If you're a friend of the Marquess, you're a friend of mine and everything in this house is yours. Even me . . . Tell me, what would you like to drink?"

"Give him rum, my boy," interrupted the Marquess. "As he reckons he's a creole macho . . ." and he smiled as he lurched round and swayed towards a corner

135

where a lad with the face of a fresh fish seemed to be expecting him.

"I'll get you a rum right away, Conde. Do you want it in a glass or a goblet?" Alquimio asked, and the Count shrugged his shoulders: in such cases the content, not the container, were what mattered. Then his smiley host also went off, but in the direction of what must be the kitchen. Meanwhile someone had put on some music, and the Count heard Maria Bethania's voice and assumed she must be a regular visitor to the scene. From the metaphysical, objective solitude of his cushion he could concentrate on scrutinizing aspects of the party: there were more men than women and despite the music nobody danced, they conversed in groups or couples, always changing their place or composition, as if perpetual movement were part of the ritual. It was as if they had itchy behinds and couldn't keep still, the Count concluded. On his visual tour the policeman alighted on various oily glances directed his way, dispatched by pansies of the languishing type who seemed to lament his immaculate hetero-sexuality, just proclaimed by the Marquess. The Count surprised himself by taking out a cigarette in would-be Bogartian style, as if he wanted to raise his stock in that pink market: he felt desired, with all the accompanying ambiguity, and was enjoying that fatal attraction. Am I turning into a queer? he wondered, as a green goblet, cheerfully brimming with rum, appeared before his eyes.

Sparrow bun smiled as she gave him his drink, and crossed her legs as she stood there before falling in yoga position on the cushion that had mysteriously appeared in front of the Count.

"So you're hetero?" she asked, examining him like a strange beast on the endangered list.

136

"Nobody is perfect," quoted the Count, and took a long swig that he felt circulate from mouth to stomach and from stomach to blood, like a necessary liberating transfusion.

"I'm Polly, Alquimio's niece," she said, as her fingers combed back the fringe falling over her forehead.

"And I'm the Count, though not of Monte Cristo."

Polly smiled. She must have been in her twenties and wore a purple baby-doll outfit from a sixties movie. She also wore round her neck a cameo brooch tied to a purple ribbon (from which movie did that come?), and though she wasn't pretty or a bundle of visible fleshly charms, she belonged to the category of beddable item of the first order, according to the Count's devalued erotic requirements.

"What do you write?"

"Me? The odd short story."

"How interesting. And are you postmodern?"

The Count looked at the girl, surprised by that unexpected aesthetic interpolation: should he be postmodern?

"More or less," he responded, trusting to post-modernity and hoping she wouldn't ask how much more or less.

"I like painting, you know, and I'm really a mad postmodern queen."

"No kidding," the Count said and finished his rum.

"God, you're terrible, you really gulp it down . . . Give me your glass. I'll get you a refill."

The Marquess waved to him from his corner. He was still there, the fish on his pedestal, and seemed happy with life, in the shadow of the blond locks he'd restored to a sparsely populated pate.

"Here you are," said Polly, and now his glass was full to the brim.

137

"Thanks. And are you hetero?"

She smiled again. Hers were a sparrow's teeth, tiny and sharp.

"Almost always," she confessed and the Count gulped. Could she be a transvestite? With that little bun? "The fact is, if a person wants to reach their potential, all their bodily potential, they must try a homosexual relationship at least once. Hasn't the Marquess told you that?"

"No. He knows I follow a macho-Stalinist line."

"Your choice . . . But you're lacking something very important in life."

"I've managed so far. Don't you worry. Hey, did you know Alexis?"

She stroked her cameo and sighed: "What they did to him was horrible. The poor boy. He never harmed anybody, did he? . . . Others are more violent and go too far with men, the types who go prospecting in lavatories and such like. But he didn't. I'm a would-be painter, as I told you I think? And I liked talking to him, when he came to see my uncle. He knew heaps about painting, particularly Italian painting . . . And when I talked to him he said his problem was that he really fell in love and couldn't stand changing partners every other day."

"But they're into lots of changes, aren't they?"

"Yes, not many have very long relationships, which was what he wanted. He was more a woman than a man, a woman in the head, you know what I mean?"

"No, I don't think I do."

"Well, he'd have liked to live in a house with a man, as if he were his husband, and nobody else's, and just be that man's wife. Do you get me now?"

"More or less. What I don't understand is why he

walked down the street dressed as a woman, as if he'd gone searching for a man."

"Yes, that's very odd, because he was really quite a prude. And I should tell you the real transvestites are scared stiff now because they say this might be the start of a serial lynching. But that must be them being hysterical."

"So they're hysterical?"

"Transvestites? Completely. As they want to be women and there's no woman who isn't hysterical. But Alexis wasn't, I don't think he was hysterical, though he was a champion manic depressive . . ."

"Polly," the Count then took a risk, "you know, I'd like to write about this scene. Tell me a bit about the people here today."

She smiled again, she could always put on a smile and look ingenuous. "Anyone would think you were police."

The Count had recourse to all his powers of bluff: "And you're like a postmodern sparrow."

A gentle titter followed that left Polly's brow resting on the Count's knee. No, of course she's not a transvestite, he tried to persuade himself.

"My God, it's horrible, there's a bit of everything here," she said, looking the policeman in the eye, as if making a confession.

And the Count discovered that in that room in Old Havana, on first evidence, there were men and women who had made their mark because they were: militants on behalf of free love, of nostalgia trips, or of red, green and yellow parties, ex-dramatists with and without oeuvre, writers with ex-libris but never published, queers of every tendency and leaning: queens – drags on full beam and the perverted sort – luckless little duckies, hunters expert at high-flying prey, buggers on their own account who give it in the arse at home and go into the countryside if there's horse on offer, inconsolably disconsolate souls and disconsolate souls in search of consolation, A-I cocksuckers with ass-holes sewn up for fear of Aids, and even freshly matriculated apprentices in the Academy of Pedagogy in Homosexuality, the chief tutor being none other than uncle Alquimio, winners of national and international ballet competitions, prophets of the end of time, history and the ration book; nihilists converted to Marxism and Marxists converted to shit, every kind of chip on the shoulder: sexual, political, economic, psychological, social, cultural, sporting and electronic; practising Zen Buddhists, Catholics, witches, voodoists, Islamists, santería animists, a Mormon and two Jews, a pitcher from the Industriales team who pitches and bats with either hand; fans of Pablo Milanés and enemies of Silvio Rodríguez, expert oracles who know who will be the next Nobel Prize for Literature as well as Gorbachev's secret intentions, the last pretty boy adopted as nephew by the Famous Person in the Higher Echelons, or the price of a pound of coffee in Baracoa; seekers after temporary or permanent visas, dreamers, *femmes* and *hommes*, hyper-realists, abstract artists and socialist realists who'd renegued on their aesthetic past; a Latinist; the repatriated and the patriotic; people expelled from everywhere one can be expelled from; a blind man who saw, disillusioned and deceivers, opportunists and philosophers, feminists and optimists, followers of Lezama (frankly the vast majority), disciples of Virgilio, Carpentier, Martí and one adept of Antón Arrufat; Cubans and foreigners; singers of boleros; breeders of fighting dogs, alcoholics, rheumatics, dogmatists and head-cases; smokers and non-smokers; and one macho-Stalinist heterosexual.

140

"Yours truly . . . And transvestites? Aren't there any transvestites?" he asked, angling his vampire-hunter look at her breasts.

"There by the door to the balcony: that's Victoria, though she prefers to be called Viki and her real name is Víctor Romillo. The prettiest thing, isn't she? And that dark-skinned lass who looks like Annia Linares by day is Esteban and by night Estrella, because she's a bolero singer."

"Tell me one thing: there are about thirty people here . . . How can they do all the jobs you mentioned?"

Polly smiled, inevitably. "They're just multi-occupational and like voluntary work . . . Look over there, the guy next to Wilfredito Insula, he does at least ten of the things I mentioned. God, how horrible, and you're going to write about this?"

"I don't know, I probably will. But I'm really interested in transvestites."

"Then go to a party at Ofelia Belén Pacheco's place, an old queer who lives around the Virgen del Camino, because there they do transvestite parties, live performances, the lot. That's where Estrella sings boleros and a girl called Zarzamora does a striptease and you'll shit yourself laughing."

"The Marquess never mentioned it."

"Of course he didn't: Ofelia Belén Pacheco and the Marquess are sworn enemies, ever since Ofelia bedded one of the Marquess's boyfriends. Although that was in the days when buses were made of wood . . . Well, they have fantastic parties and all the transvestite buddies of Havana go there. Sometimes thirty or more."

In the spacious living room, under the influence of music of a seemingly Barbra Streisand flavour, several couples of diverse make-up had started dancing and the Count stared at Estrella, dancing boleros and cutting an incongruous figure with her dance partner, a titchy black barely five feet tall, whom the Count supposed had bigger dimensions that were momentarily hidden. Viki was still standing by the balcony, and the Count was alarmed when he realized that if he hadn't been warned he'd have thought her a woman who was desirable, if not beautiful.

The atmosphere exuded a ghetto freedom, limited but capacious, as the dancers' hands caressed their partners and muffled voices echoed the song. A distasteful chill ran through the policeman when he spotted a couple kissing shamelessly: two men – according to legal, biological codes – some thirty years old, moustachioed with jet black hair, soldering lips to facilitate a flow of tongues and saliva that injected the Count with a squeamish repugnance he tried to quell by gulping down another glass of rum. He knew then that he'd gone too far on that journey to hell and needed different air if he wasn't going to suffocate or die of shock. A policeman who boasted he'd seen every possible barbarity, he now felt pain-stricken by a vibration born from a tight knot of male hormones, unable to resist that most disturbing negation of nature. He looked at Polly and tried to smile, as he turned his green goblet round, as if to demonstrate that the evaporation was damaging the atmosphere.

"Should I put you on the alcoholics' list?"

"Put me down as an aspiring or discerning drinker . . . Hey, the Marquess says Alexis hadn't been here for days."

"That's right, I hadn't seen him for some time."

"And when you saw him, did he tell you he was in love with somebody?"

Polly looked up, as if seeking her reply in the visible part of her lank fringe.

142

"I don't think so. I think he was still with a painter whose name I've forgotten, one who did things with collages."

"Salvador K."

"Hey, you're really in the know! You sure you're not police?"

"Really I'm not, love . . . And what did Alexis tell you?"

"Nothing much, that he was really fed up and that if he split with the Salvador guy he wasn't going to hitch up with anyone else. And he went off because he was going to mass at the cathedral."

The Count thought how Alexis Arayán must have been carrying his Bible, where perhaps the passage on the Transfiguration was already missing.

"Why did you suddenly shut up?" enquired Polly, pressing one of his legs. "Do you want another drink?"

"That's not a bad idea. I'd like to have a drop with you."

And she smiled, as mischievous as ever.

"Why not have a drink at my place? I live just round the corner."

"Are you a transvestite?"

"Come and find out."

"The walk will warm you up," said the Count, and compared Polly to a St Bernard on a rescue mission in the middle of a snowstorm. Averting his gaze from the kissing moustaches, he looked round for the Marquess. He wasn't in the room, nor was his amphibian friend. Polly's roll-call, he thought, as he stood up, still had a way to go.

The Count let himself be undressed without claiming the promised drink and was pleased to see his best friend on duty, despite the evening's bustle and the worries about sexual fraudulency still torturing him; a whiff of sparrowish behind had woken him up. He took off Polly's baby-doll and wasn't surprised by her small tits, with their ripe nipples, just bursting to be touched and bitten, then he warily checked inside her panties and found no false castrations, but a moist, inverted mine down which half a hand vanished. Awakened abruptly by the discovery of that vein, his travelling companion perked up, stretched, yawned and braced its swollen tissue, before descending, like a bullet winging home, into Polly's mouth, deep like the other cavities he'd already explored.

Polly was a sophisticated lady: unhurried and unfussed, she fellatioed delicately, licking his penis's every cranny, swallowing, then bringing it back into the fresh air only to languish enviously as her sparrow's teeth tightened round his testicles. It was the Count who had to call for a truce, dismayed by the imminent spurt and desirous to deepen his knowledge of her second jousting cleft, and he pushed Polly on her bed, ready to crucify her, just as the girl's hand intervened in her fate.

"Oh, mum, I've always wanted to lay a policeman. Go on, there are some condoms under the pillow," she said, sucking on the Count's nipples as he hooded his anxious friend, annoyed by the lateness of the party.

He penetrated her as if it wasn't a first visit, noticing how much was required to fill a slit worthy of a white whale's rather than a sparrow's, a surprise Moby Dick, but he was happy at the manoeuvrability permitted by Polly's hundred pounds, portable Polly, easily upped and downed the length and breadth of polyethelene which blocked off a good part of that objective, if invisible reality. The Count was surprised by his own energy, which he could only attribute to his systematic

144

lack of such binary practices. He inned and outed like a jack-in-the-box, hooked on a nipple, then offered up an ear for a girlish tongue to explore. Saliva ran like the rivers of life, turned them into slippery, naughty sea snakes. He went back in, conscious the curtain was about to fall, when postmodern Polly snuck away from him, half-turned on the bed and presented her sparrow's bun to his eyes, increased in size by its nearness and pert position.

"Give it me in the arse," she asked, unsmiling.

The Count took one look at his selfless comrade, inelegant but ready for combat, and gripped her buttocks tight to open up the exit door more widely.

"God, how horrible!" she said when he drilled her little hole. Then the Count felt he was the right measure for polyphonic Polly's proportions, and stuck to his task as he heard the girl's anxious lament, which, between push and pull, changed to a smile, a laugh, a guffaw, a cry begging split my arse, split it down the middle, though now there was nothing left to heft and he could only keep up the rubbing which the man tried to do tirelessly. Ay, Polly the prostrate . . .

But everything has an end. The Count was surprised by his own powerful, triumphant macho whoop, as Polly's guffaws faded to a laugh, to a smile before ending on a whimper: "God, how horrible," only to add, with a judgement the Count assumed he fully deserved: "Ay, darling, what a lovely fucker you are, you are!"

There was a face there. He could almost see it, if he stretched out his hand he could almost touch it, but his eyes and hands slipped and slid, entwined by viscous veils and nets that suddenly loosened their knots, let him escape, close in on the face, almost touch it, only to wrap round him again, distance him, refuse him a revelation that evaporated in a luminous heat cloud, swept along by a dirty river, as it finally faded forcing him to wake up, stressed, at the first loud rings of his telephone, his breathing agitated, his body soaked by the sad, sad sweat of doubt. I know him, of course I do, he told himself as he reviewed his passage from dream to a more objective reality, as he tried to find out what was happening. It was a clear, brutal telephone ring, as the sun penetrated the windows to his room, to impose yet another day of aggressive heat.

"You motherfucker," he said, crawling to the receiver, eyes stunned by the brightness. He picked up the phone and asked, "What's the time?"

"Ten past nine, Conde, ten past nine," repeated the voice at the other end of the line, perhaps of the world.

"Shit, Manolo, I didn't hear my alarm clock, or didn't set it. Who knows . . ."

"When did you hit the sack?"

"Around four."

"Alcohol level?"

"Only two glasses."

146

"Just as well, because there's bother: Salvador K. hasn't showed since yesterday afternoon."

The Count finally felt he was awake. "And how come?"

"El Greco and Crespo tailed him. They say he went out yesterday at around five, as if he was going to his studio, and went down the passageway of a house that's on Nineteen and A. They waited for him for more than an hour and then discovered the passageway led to a garage facing Twenty-First Street. He vanished. He's not in the house or his studio."

"Did they talk to his wife?"

"Yes, but only to ask after him, and she just said he was at the studio."

The Count lit a cigarette, trying to cast off the last chains of sleep, and then he remembered.

"Hey, Manolo, I had the strangest of dreams: I could and couldn't see the murderer . . . You know, those funny dreams: when I thought I was going to see him, I didn't, because he also wore this kind of disguise . . . Fuck me if I'm not obsessed with transvestites, the transfiguration, wandering souls and all that shit."

"It wasn't Salvador?"

"I don't know, I really don't, but now I'm convinced I know him, I'm not sure why, but I'm convinced I do. Hey, go and speak to Salvador's wife, put the squeeze on her, though not too tightly, and pick me up at . . . well, when you're finished."

The Count hung up and looked around: there were only traces of more or less distant disasters. Clothes on the ground, a crushed cigarette butt, Rufino the fish swimming in waters murkier by the minute. I must clean the pigsty, he told himself, but forgot this priority as he observed his own nakedness, which sent him back to the previous night's erotic adventure. God, how horrible, she says she's almost always hetero-sexual, what the fuck have I got into? he wondered, smiling as he congratulated himself on having enough coffee for two more breakfasts.

While he was waiting the Count grabbed the newspaper seller who was walking along the pavement with his precious treasure of news under his arm, and, as he wasn't a usual customer, he had to pay double – after the inevitable pleas – to get a copy. Still shirtless, in the doorway to his house, he greeted passing acquaint-ances as he digested headlines and skimmed items to get a round-up that still left him with a few doubts. According to the paper's international pages, the world was in a pretty bad state, though the socialist countries – despite difficulties and continuous external pressures – were intent on not abandoning the uphill, triumphant path of history. The national pages, for their part, made it plain that the island wasn't in bad shape at all, except for the odd episode, like the railway accident which had left several dead (and which naturally wasn't planned). They were planting worms, the sacrosanct CAME, the Council for Mutual Economic Aid, promised it was going to solve the prob-lems of Cuba's telephone system, it would even rain and there'd be an eclipse of the moon in a week's time. That was the bit of news he most liked: the eclipse would be on Skinny's birthday. And when was Dulcita arriving? Moreover, the paper said that this afternoon the famous Eligio Riego would give a poetry reading, and he decided that, as he'd like to talk to him, he'd call Major Rangel so that he'd put him in touch with his friend the poet . . .

The Count breathed in till he filled his lungs, just as

a lorry belched out its unrefined fumes. But he felt reading the newspaper had fortified him so he could face another day of hard labour.

"And where the hell can this guy be?"

The car wove round the potholes left by the last nuclear bomb that stretch of La Calzada must have suffered. After picking him up, Sergeant Manuel Palacios told him about his interview with Salvador K.'s wife: she insisted her husband had gone to the studio and, if he wasn't there, she couldn't imagine where he might be, and she'd asked the policeman rather anxiously: "Should I tell the police?"

"Manolo, you really think she doesn't know?"

"I don't know, Conde, you're the psychologist here. I don't know if she wanted to put us on the wrong track."

"Did you ask her for a photo of him?"

"Of course. Shall we circulate it?"

The Count shut his eyes and let his head fall backwards. "Let's wait a day. He'll probably turn up and we won't need to create a stir."

"If only, but don't pin your hopes on it. If that guy did the little pansy in, he might make a break for it, Conde. Get a boat out of here, or whatever . . ."

"We'll wait a bit longer," the lieutenant decided, as the car stopped at a traffic light. A bus halted next to them and, from his seat, the Count saw the bus driver. He was a man in his fifties and the policeman saw his was a bus-driver's face: he was looking at the street while, bored out of his mind, he hit the steering wheel with the wedding ring he wore on his left hand. He had that slight though visible hump professional drivers get after a few years in the saddle, and something about his face warned: this man could do nothing else with life: he was a bus driver, the Count concluded, and then he saw a girl waving at the driver asking please to open the bus door. From his Olympian height the bus driver seemed to ponder long and hard, before agreeing to her request, one second short of the woman kneeling down in the middle of the street, begging for her ride. Then she smiled, thanked him and put her coin in the collection box, just as Sergeant Manolo Palacios put his foot down and left the bus behind.

"Hey, Manolo, go down Luyanó, I want to see Fatman Contreras."

"Fatman?" asked Sergeant Palacios as if he hadn't understood, though the Count knew that wasn't the sense of his question. Suddenly the vision of the bus driver with a bus-driver's face had helped him grasp the inevitability of certain destinies which were prescribed for ever, and he immediately felt the need to speak to Captain Jesús Contreras as if under orders. About what? Anything. He just had to see him.

"What's up? Did they tell you it was forbidden to speak to him?"

"No, Conde, don't fuck about, you know it's not that, the fact is . . . Remember what I told you yesterday."

"Don't fuck about yourself, Manolo. Are you frightened?"

The sergeant sighed and turned right.

"Okay then," he agreed, shaking his head to underline his disagreement. "Yes, I am frightened. I told you yesterday . . . And why are you doing this? Just to show you're a tough guy and aren't frightened or because you really are?"

Contreras's house was on the corner, a block before the Calzada de Luyanó. It was one of those typical old buildings in the area, with a door directly on to the pavement and very high windows with grilles, covered

150

in pernicious soot from nearby factories. A long, long time ago, when the Count hadn't even dreamt that one day he'd be a policeman and know Captain Jesús Contreras, he'd already decided he didn't like those squat houses or that dingy district which was too grey, too monotonous, without gardens or porches, and for a long time now with very few healthy panes of glass.

"You stay in the car," he told Manolo. He got out and knocked with the wrought-iron knocker.

Fatman Contreras opened the door and beamed a smile the Count feared like death.

"Well, well, well," said the captain, "Look who we have here. Come in."

And he held out his hand. But on that occasion the Count told himself it was time to fight for the lowly and dispossessed on earth: Fatman's greatest pleasure was squeezing hands, whether friendly or hostile, with those five-fingered mechanical diggers, capable of lifting one ton of weight, and making the knees of the ingenuous creature greeted thus buckle from the devastating pressure on their carpals, metacarpals, phalanges, mini-phalanges . . .

"Squeeze your own mother's hand, you fat pansy."

And he exploded. Fatman's second greatest pleasure was laughing, those sonorous guffaws, like a human earthquake, that set dancing the fat neck, tits and ever sweaty, enormous belly of Captain Jesús Contreras, head of the Foreign Exchange Dealing Department at Headquarters.

"You're a sonovabitch, Conde, that's why I like you. And now I see you really like me. Are you after something?" And he laughed again, as if it were inevitable. "You are the first sonovabitch policeman to come and see me . . ."

And he burst out laughing for a whole minute more,

convulsing, obscenely, sweatily, as the Count looked up, expecting to see the first fragments of ceiling crash down.

"It's hard, Conde, hard, real hard, I swear by my mother. You know I'd even put my pyjamas on if that was an option: if they put me on the pyjama game, well I'll obey and put my pyjamas on, but what I'm certainly not going to do is to go begging to anyone. Not to the Major, the investigation team, anyone, because I'm cleaner than the Virgin Mary. And if I smell of shit, it's because I work in shit, wash in shit, like any self-respecting policeman, and I'm not going to let anyone daub me with shit that's not mine. It's not mine, Conde. No, wait a minute. This is rich: they're accusing me of fuck all, but as there are problems in currency black markets they want to implicate me because they say I must be in the know . . . Know what? Know what some police were doing who were fine yesterday and are now into God knows what? My speciality was being on the street, making life difficult for those milking foreigners for their dollars, and I was good at that and you know it. Not a dollar moved in the street I didn't know about, and if I had informers, I gave them protection, if not, who the hell would ever inform? Now if there were accounts in banks in Panama, and people upstairs in dollar deals, and into credit cards and all that jazz, I couldn't touch them, there's no black guy in Old Havana or white wheeler-dealer in Vedado or whore from La Lisa who could take me there. That kind of thing isn't my patch and I don't touch it . . . but don't worry, Condesito, there's no way they can pin things on me. Everything in this house is mine, mine and earned with the sweat of my brow or because someone gave it me as a present, and it's not my fault if that individual's now fallen out of favour, is it? And you know how anyone told to take something took it, right? And now they're talking about my standard of living, about undue privileges, you know. But what do they want, Tibetan monks dressed in a strip of donkey hide? I know I never stole a cent, not a single one. You know me, Conde, don't you? But the hardest thing is seeing how the people who only two days ago practically went on bended knees for me to help them, and did anything to be my friend, and brought coffee beans to my office and said Serpico was shit useless compared to me, they don't want to hear my name because I might harm them, might infect them . . . The only person who has called is Major Rangel, to ask me if I needed anything, and do you know what I told him? That my balls were aching and he shouldn't call me again unless it was to say they wanted to apologize. That's all I can accept now, Conde: apologies, medals and honours . . . No, I'm not shutting the door, but one has one's pride, because if not, what the hell does one have, hey, you tell me? And as I'm clean, my morale is higher than Mount Turquino in the Sierra Maestra, higher than the Himalayas, fucking hell . . . But it's terrible, Conde. I've only been suspended for a day and I'm worse than a tail cut off its dog. I'm up in the air and don't know where to come down. I've been police for twenty years, and the worst bloody thing is that it's all I can do and I even like being a policeman. What the hell am I going to do with my life, Conde, you tell me? Now I've got the plague, I'll tell you one thing: for your own sake, don't come to see me again. I'm the one who doesn't want you back here, because you're my friend, you've shown that today, and I don't want

153

to put you in the shit, Conde. You look after yourself, because this is no joke and when they throw shit at the fan, anyone can get it ... Even a guy like you, a real man and a friend, as they say on the street ... Shake my hand, Conde, don't be a pansy. Shake my hand, I swear by my mother I won't squeeze you ... That's right ... I caught you, you motherfucker ... Ha, ha, ha ... That'll teach you never to trust a policeman, ha, ha, ha."

"Get a move on. We're off again. Off anywhere but Headquarters," said the Count as he got in the car and dropped his cigarette end on the pavement.

"They just called me."

"But I don't feel like going, and I won't, Manolo," the Count interrupted, stamping on the car floor somewhat hysterically. "What they're doing to Fatman is a real bastard ... How can they accuse a policeman like him? I'm not going to Headquarters, Manolo."

"Will you let me get a word in, Conde? ... They called because Alberto Marqués was after you for something urgent. That's all."

The Count felt the angry glare of the August sun come through the windscreen and hit his chest and stomach. He adjusted his sunglasses.

"Come on, let's go and talk to him."

Sergeant Palacios started the car up and looked at the Count. He knew his colleague too well to try to reason with him. He preferred to drive in silence till he stopped in front of number 7 on Milagros, between Delicias and Buenaventura.

"You don't want me to come with you, do you now?" he said, and the Count sensed the sourness in that final twist.

154

"No, I prefer to speak to him alone. I think it's better that way."

The sergeant looked in front: heat haze steamed from the pavement, like phantoms dancing in search of their promised heaven.

"Well, see to the case by yourself, and while you're at it you can have the queer. And much good may it do you. Let's see if rolling over more than a dog with worms you manage to solve it . . . Hey, Conde, you know how I appreciate you and always wanted to work with you, but lately you've changed."

"But what's your problem, Manolo?"

"Everything, Conde. You're chucking all the cases down the pan, you seem ashamed to be a policeman, you do as you please . . . and you just might be getting it wrong."

The Count lit his cigarette before he spoke.

"Don't be a shit-head, Manolo, you're way off . . . It's just that I . . ." and he stopped before completing a self-justification that would ring untrue. Perhaps the sergeant was right and he was relegating him, even excluding him from certain areas of the case, but there was no going back: the dialogue was between the Marquess and himself, and the sergeant's presence might sever his delicate exchanges with the dramatist. It's like a chamber piece for two actors, he thought, and said: "You're right in everything you say and I do apologize, but stick right here."

The bougainvilleas were as lush and petulant as ever in the sun, which seemed enraged that it was almost high noon and ready to kill off any living cell that fell under its red-hot ferrule, except for the defiant bougainvilleas. The Count observed them enviously as he dropped the door-knocker he'd preferred today to the nipple-shaped bell you never heard.

"Well, well, what an efficient policeman you are!" the Marquess commented, opening the door. "Just ring and he comes running."

"Hello," the Count mumbled as he scoured the half-dark for the armchair assigned to him in that stage-set. When he thought how he was there because of the strange death of Alexis Arayán, he felt ill at ease and at a loss, and told himself it was true the case no longer interested him: his only motivation was a morbid curiosity to get further into the world of Alberto Marqués, as shadowy and shocking as last night's party.

"Did you have a good time last night?"

"Yes, really," the Count replied, knowing what was coming next.

"I waited for you till two o'clock at Alquimio's, but my sickly body couldn't resist any longer. It's been a long, long time since I went on a late-night spree like that."

"Sorry if you waited for me. Why did you ring me so early? To scold me?"

The Marquess straightened his dressing gown between his legs before responding: "God spare me giving such a potentate a scolding . . ."

"We are razor-sharp today. Why are you always like that?"

"Oh, I'm so sorry, Mr Count . . . Are you upset with me? I called because something happened that might be of interest to you," and he lowered his voice, to speak confidentially. "This morning María Antonia called again."

"And what's happened now?"

"It's odd, very odd. She asked me if Alexis had left a medallion here which he used to wear. It's a small gold medallion, with a circle around the engraved face of

156

Leonardo the universal man. Was he wearing it round his neck when you found him?"

The Count rewound his tape of memories of the transvestite murdered in the Havana Woods: examined again the dramatic red dress, the silk scarf round his neck, the breastless bosom, and saw no medallion.

"No, I don't think he was."

"Well, I didn't manage to find it here either. Alexis's mother bought two identical medallions several years ago in the museum in Vinci, the village where Leonardo was born. One for her and the other for Alexis. Hers went missing soon after and was never found. And now one has appeared in a trinket-box Alexis had at home. María Antonia says she'd never seen it there, and doesn't know if it's the one Matilde lost or Alexis's."

"But Alexis still used to wear his?"

"Yes, he always wore it. What do you think? That Alexis stole it from his mother and kept it there, or that he left his there for some reason?"

The Count couldn't resist a smile as he pondered the riddle set by the Marquess.

"I really didn't think you liked playing the detective so much. They accuse me of hogging the case but I think you're the one on the hog."

"Oh, don't say that. I'd be incapable of taking anything away from you, Mr Friendly Policeman."

The Count smiled again and lit a cigarette. The Marquess was helping him come to terms with the world.

"Is there no tea on offer today? I think I could do with a cup . . ."

"Delighted to oblige, Mr Friendly Policeman. And I'll add lots of ice cubes," said the Marquess, as he pattered off to the back of the stage, his red Chinese silk dressing gown caressing the sharp edges of his feet.

157

God, how horrible, the Count remembered, seeing the grotesque figure who'd suddenly transformed into his Dr Watson, tea in hand, smiling contentedly.

"You know one thing, Marquess? If Alexis put his own medallion in his jewel box, it's as if he were pointing to suicide. Don't you think? As if he were organizing everything before he left. But he didn't commit suicide. Perhaps they didn't give him time."

"Or perhaps he provoked his own death . . . That's my considered view . . . Look what I found on my bookshelves."

And he handed the Count a page from a Bible: the page cut from the Gospel according to St Matthew, pages 989 and 990, which began with chapter 17: "And after six days Jesus taketh Peter, James and John his brother, and bringeth them up into a high mountain apart. And was transfigured before them." And, written in a margin, in tiny but precise writing, the words: "God the Father, why do you force him to suffer so much?"

"Where was this?"

"Elemental, Lieutenant Conde, it was where it had to be: inside the *Complete Plays* of Virgilio Piñera I have on my shelves. Look," and he touched his temples: "Pure deduction."

"Yes, it had to be there . . . Alexis didn't dress as a transvestite because he liked to. He was either mad, or a mystic as you say, determined to represent an act of transfiguration with which he was aiming to . . ."

"Was aiming to be crucified, Mr Friendly Policeman."

The Count looked at the page from the Bible again, read the whole chapter and felt that the truth of Alexis Arayán's death lay there, but had just eluded him, like the face glimpsed in that dream.

"Yes, you may be right. But why do it like that?"

"It's clear enough to me: because he was afraid of killing himself . . . Remember, Alexis was a Catholic, and Catholicism condemns suicide, but his religion also condemned homosexuality. Thanks to him I learned about the passage in Leviticus which says: 'Thou shalt not lie with mankind, as with womankind: it is abomination: they shall surely be put to death; their blood shall be upon them.' It isn't easy for a believer to live knowing his God called to Moses and pronounced so savagely, you know? But it's only a part of the Tragedy of Life, as one old friend of mine says, who definitely isn't at all homosexual. It's a long time since anyone posed it so Judaically, as it were, but over many centuries that sin known as *contra natura* has condemned the lives of homosexuals, as has the idea that it's a sickness . . . Mortal sin, social aberration, sickness of body and mind: it's not easy to be a queer anywhere in the world, my friendly Mr Policeman, I can tell you. But let me proceed: I've been informed by people expert in the matter that of the ten million Cubans living in our Socialist Republic, between five and six per cent of us are homosexual. Naturally, including our lesbian comrades. Do your sums, do your sums: if there are five million men, and three per cent are homosexual, that gives you one hundred and fifty thousand, or almost a fifth of a million compatriots. Enough to make an army . . . What more can I say? I'm not convinced by this figure, because lots and lots of people are unable to admit to being homosexual, logically enough, because of what I said previously and because of the long national history of homophobia that we've endured between the four walls of this island ever since the Spaniards arrived and deemed dirty and barbaric what our sodomite Indians did while bathing in our peaceful rivers sucking cigars

159

and flinging a yucca ... Your experience of recent history can add other conflicts to the drama, my friendly policeman: don't forget how right here in the 60s there was something called the UMAP, the famous Military Units to Aid Production, where homosexuals were confined, along with other harmful beings, so they would turn into men by cutting sugar cane and picking coffee and then, after 1971, a statute was decreed, also right here, to be enforced by policemen like you, magistrates and judges, which prohibited 'ostensible homosexuality and other socially reprehensible behaviour' ... And you're so ingenuous you wonder why a homosexual still thinks of committing suicide?"

In Paris, in the springtime, you don't usually think of suicide. At least I don't. I felt so free and intelligent I couldn't imagine all that freedom, intellect and revelation in one spring would later lead me to suffer so much and witness my last dramatic act ... Muscles was saying I was a stranger, he'd never seen me so optimistic and happy, as we drove by taxi to Sartre's and Simone's house, where they'd invited me to have supper that night along with those I'd invite formally to come to Cuba to the première of my new version of *Electra Garrigó*. That night, however, destiny had decreed I'd make a decision which might be the possible starting point for everything else. I told Muscles it was perhaps better not to bring the Other Boy, for I reckoned he might get up to his tricks, which included getting drunk and vomiting on the carpet and wanting to kiss Jean-Paul because he'd refused the Nobel ... And Muscles said he agreed, the Other was all right for transvestites and public places, but not so right for

160

Simone's house . . . It was a delightful, even candle-lit supper: we drank Bordeaux, ate platefuls of French and Italian cheeses, and of meat in mushroom sauce, now intoxicating every taste-bud in my mouth and memory, unable to evoke any another taste of that kind. And Dutch ice cream for dessert . . . All night we talked about my project, I discussed how I imagined the set and the costumes, and above all the kind of physical gestures I wanted to impose on the actors, making them up in Greek masks but with very Havanan, white, mulatto and black faces, trying to ensure that the masks showed and didn't hide them, that they revealed their inner life and didn't conceal the tragic and burlesque spirituality I wanted to pinpoint as the essence of a Cubanity which had Virgilio Piñera as chief prophet, because he believed that if anything distinguished us from the rest of the world, it was our possession of Creole wisdom, where nothing is really painful or totally pleasant. My approach, I explained, would be an extreme stylization of nineteenth-century Havana comedy and creole vernacular from the Alhambra Theatre, but distilled with a tragic, philosophical will, until only its artistic essence remained, for at the end of the day that has always been the grand theatre of Cuban idiosyncrasy . . . I added that for a similar reason I had to be sustained by words, and couldn't, like poor Artaud, try to create a stage language dependent only on signs or dynamic, active gestures, because one of the visible traits of our Cubanity is an irrepressible inclination never to shut our mouths. Like Artaud, certainly, I wanted to show how theatre isn't a game, but true reality, truer than reality itself, and I had to resolve the problem which restoring that level to the theatre always entails, how to make each performance a kind of happening to provoke confusion and unleash insights, to go beyond a facile, digestive phase of entertainment, as he said . . . And the facial mask is a vital ingredient in a project wishing to reveal the moral masks many people have worn at some moment of their existence: homosexuals who affect not to be so, the disappointed who smile at the bad weather, wizards with Marxist manuals under their arms, ferocious opportunists dressed as gentle lambs, apathetic ideologues with that most useful party card in their pocket: in a word a very colourful carnival in a country that has often had to renounce its carnivals . . . My intention, pure and simple, was to create a transcendent poetic aura, outside any specific time, but in a precise space, for a tragedy which the author conceived as a family dilemma: to stay or to leave, to respect or disobey, or the old story from Oedipus and Hamlet: to be or not to be . . . As the evening came to an end I told them how Parisian transvestites had given me the final key to that spectral metamorphosis which magnifies the supreme aspiration of performance, when the actor dies beneath the garments of his character and the masquerade ceases to be a passing, carnivalesque act and turns into another life, all the more real for being more desired, consciously chosen and not assumed as mere conjunctural concealment . . . Then Sartre, with the eagle eye he always had, became my oracle: "Isn't what you are suggesting too complex?" he began by asking, telling me to be careful with revelations, for they always suggest diverse readings, a diversity which might be dangerous for me, just like the essential fatalism I wanted to represent through a twentieth-century Cuban Electra: I'd already heard certain insular bureaucrats say that art in Cuba should be different and that difference wasn't like my *Electra Garrigó* and her dilemma of being or not being . . . But it was written that I wasn't to heed him: my decision was irrevocable, and that's how Plimpton told it in the interview with me published in the *Paris Review.*

We went back to our room, and that night, to continue the intellectual and physical intoxication I was experiencing in the middle of that Paris spring, Muscles and I made love for the first and only time, after twenty years of friendship, as his record player poured out languid Strauss waltzes. Everything was possible, everything was permitted, everything was mine, I was thinking the next morning as I lay in bed drinking the Arabica coffee Muscles had percolated, and we heard knocking at the door. I remember recalling how I had forgotten the Other Boy, whom we'd excluded, and I thought it must be him finally returning from his perpetual orgy, but Muscles said the Other had his own key, so he opened the door, and standing there all hieratic and voluminous was an unexpected embassy functionary floating down at us a piece of news from his stoutly arrogant, immaculately diplomatic heights: the Other Boy was behind bars in a Montmartre police station for causing a public uproar, for improper, aggressive behaviour, and the embassy couldn't take on the bail or any legal representation of that personal problem . . .

Once more we had to call Sartre, who luckily was still at home, and he accompanied us to the police station, a horrible place where nobody was like Maigret and which was untouched by a single breath of the spring enveloping the rest of the city: harmony was imprisoned there, if not guillotined. But first Jean-Paul made a couple of calls and, by the time we'd arrived, they handed the Other Boy over to him, all sneers, snot and torn shirt, and it was decided there would be

163

no court case or bail, for everything was down to a slightly frenetic cat-fight between homosexuals of doubtful national origin: the Other and the Albanian transvestite without papers he'd fallen in love with, as he declared, swore and shouted. But the greater evil was already done: the Other had to go to the embassy that afternoon and they told him he must return to Cuba on the plane leaving the next morning. That night Muscles and I spoke to him endlessly, as he cried disconsolately over his lost love, scared about his future as an official writer that he was about to lose, and he asked us to forgive him, as he painfully antici-pated the punishment awaiting him in Havana, where two days later he would appear before the leadership of the National Council for Culture which had financed his trip to Paris, to the very Paris, that very spring when I dreamt everything was possible, that everything was mine, that the theatre was mine.

"Do you want to do the talking?"

"Oh, so now you want me to . . . How do you decide, Mario Conde . . .?"

"Do you or don't you?" the Count asked dismissively, and Sergeant Manuel Palacios nodded: he's too much of a policeman to say no, thought the lieutenant, and opened the wrought-iron gate leading to the Arayán mansion. In the garden, a sprinkler threw tenuous curtains of water over a carpet of recently mown turf, which gave off an aroma that always moved the Count: the scent of damp earth and cut grass, a telluric, simple smell, inevitably bringing back the image of his grand-father Rufino el Conde, a well-chewed, agonic cigar between his teeth, sprinkling water over the layer of sawdust in the cockfight arena, as the radio blared

164

out poetic tirades by peasant poets. The moment he pressed the bell to the house where Alexis Arayán had lived, the Count wanted to be back inside the circular fence which defined the arena, next to Grandad Rufino, on a day when the whole world depended on a rooster's spurs and the skill of the owner in ensuring his bird fought with an advantage. Never play if you're evens, his grandfather had taught him, encapsulating a whole philosophy of life in one sentence.

"Good afternoon," said María Antonia as she opened the door.

The policemen greeted her and the Count told her he wanted to speak to her and Alexis's parents.

"Why?" asked the woman, who'd switched on her alarm lights.

"About the medallions . . ."

"But the fact is," she began and sirens followed lights: imminent danger, the Count registered.

"They don't know you found it?"

The black woman nodded.

"But they have to be told . . . That medallion can tell us a lot about Alexis's death."

She nodded again and beckoned them in.

"Mrs Matilde is the one at home."

"And comrade Faustino?"

"He's at the Foreign Ministry. On Monday he was to leave for Geneva, but the mistress is still so edgy . . ." she added, and the Count and Manolo saw María Antonia, the woman with wingèd feet, skim the floor as she flew into the house, after pointing them towards the big leather armchairs in the ante-room.

"We'll put the screws on her, Conde."

"Don't you worry, this black lady knows more than me and you . . ."

Matilde looked a very sick old woman. In the

three days since the Count had informed her of her son's death, the woman seemed to have lived twenty destructive years, devoted daily to tarnishing the veneer of vitality she'd preserved. She greeted them sleepily, and sat in another of the armchairs while María Antonia stood there, as her status as a submissive maid demanded. The Count again felt he was in the middle of a theatrical performance too much like a pre-packaged reality where everyone had their role and seat assigned. The Great Theatre of the World, what nonsense. The Tragedy of Life, yet more nonsensical. Life is a dream?

"Now then, Matilde," Manolo began, and it was evident he found the conversation difficult, "we've found out something from María Antonia that may be very important for our work, though equally it may be quite irrelevant . . . Do you follow?"

Matilde barely moved her head. Of course she couldn't follow, thought the Count, but he decided to wait. Manuel Palacios had canine instincts and always got back on the trail. Then the sergeant told her about María Antonia's find and added his own conclusion: "If that medallion is yours and Alexis hid it there, well, there's no problem. But if it's your son's, we think it might clear up certain things . . ."

"Which, for example?" asked the woman, apparently awaking from hibernation.

"Well, it's all supposition, but if he put your medallion there, perhaps he was thinking of committing suicide and didn't want it to be lost . . . Although there's another possibility, which is less likely: that someone else put it there . . ."

"When?"

"Perhaps after Alexis's death," Manolo Palacios answered, and the Count looked at him. I shit on your

166

mother, the lieutenant then said to himself, surprised by that strange possibility he hadn't envisaged. Might the murderer have hidden the medallion there? No, of course not, the Count tried to tell himself, although he knew it was an option. But why?

"What's all this about, Toña?" Matilde then asked, barely turning towards the black woman. Striking a dramatic pose, María Antonia recounted her discovery, very early this morning, and her call to Alberto Marqués. Matilde turned to look at her, and finally said, "Please bring me the medallion."

María Antonia glided into the house, while Matilde looked at the two policemen.

"They weren't exactly the same. I differentiated mine from Alexis's. The man on mine had a line etched under his left arm," she said, and sank back into a silence which extended anxiously in the minutes before María Antonia returned. "Give it me," Matilde then told her; she peered at the shiny figure trapped in the circle and said: "This is Alexis's." There wasn't a trace of doubt in her voice.

"Just as well," sighed Sergeant Manuel Palacios, betrayed by the intensity of his desires, and the Count rushed to harness Matilde's burst of vitality.

"We also want to ask if you are sure this is Alexis's writing." And he showed her the page from the Bible.

The woman stretched out her hand mechanically to reach her glasses on the corner table, and María Antonia moved to place them in her hand.

"Yes, I think so. You look, María Antonia."

"It's his," said the servant, without recourse to spectacles, as confident, the Count supposed, as she would be in the art of identifying the creators of renowned Italian Madonnas . . . The lieutenant noted the empty ashtray, and this time held back. He spoke, looking at both women.

"Madame, the medallion, this page Alexis tore out and wrote on, and the dress he wore on the night are very peculiar items. Did Alexis ever mention the word suicide in your presence?"

You cannot imagine what a mother feels when she discovers her son is homosexual . . . You think everything's been in vain, life's come to a halt, it's a trap, but then one begins to think it isn't, it's a passing phase, everything will return to normal, and the son you dreamt of as married and with children of his own will be a man like any other, and then you begin to look at every man, wanting to swap them for your son, that son you think still has time to become what you wanted him to be. But the illusion was short-lived. Alexis was never going to change, and more than once I even wanted him to die, before seeing him transformed into a homosexual, pointed at, execrated, belittled . . . I know if there's a God in heaven he won't forgive me. That's why I'm telling you now, quite calmly. Moreover, I got used to the inevitable and realized that above all, he was my son. But his father didn't. Faustino would never accept him, and converted his disappointment into contempt for Alexis. Then he preferred to stay longer outside Cuba, and leave him here with María Antonia and my mother. And that was very hard on Alexis: can you imagine what it's like to feel different and scorned at school and at home with your own father rejecting and denying you? One day, after the theatre, Faustino and I were chatting to friends, and Alexis left in the company of a boy like himself, a thirteen-year-old, and

Faustino averted his gaze to show he didn't even want to acknowledge him. It was all too cruel. It was giving Alexis a guilt complex, and worst of all I persisted in wanting to cure him, as if it were possible to cure either that or his preference for men. I took him to several psychiatrists, and I now know that that was a mistake. It made him feel unhappier, more scorned, more different, I don't know, as if he were the leper in the family. It was then he began to go to church and apparently nobody humiliated him there, and he also began to chat to Alberto Marqués, when he was working in the library in Marianao, and his life developed in those directions, far from me, from his family . . . He became a stranger. After he had his last row with his father and Faustino kicked him out of the house, he came barely once a week, to speak to his grandmother and María Antonia, and sometimes he would chat to me, but he never gave me space in his world. My son was no longer my son, do you understand now? And I was very much to blame. I helped him to be an unloved person, and he began to say perhaps it would have been better if he had not been born or had even killed himself: he said that to me one day. Is that what you wanted to know? Well, he did say that . . . And now would you be very surprised if I told you I also wish I were dead? If I told you these two hands created Alexis's death? Tell me, can there be a worse punishment than this?

"Well, fuck me, just as well, it looks like rain. Come on, you up there, the one who doesn't want to be the great policeman. Tell me, where are we at now?"

"Well, Conde . . ."

"We now know the medallion is Alexis's and that

opens up two possibilities: he put it there or someone did who must be the murderer. Well, who could have put it there?"

"It wasn't María Antonia, because she wouldn't have rung, or Matilde, because she was the only one who knew the difference between the two."

"Faustino?"

"No, Conde, for fuck's sake. He's his father. They had their problems, but you're prejudiced against the guy. Hey, give me a cigarette."

"Then we must assume the murderer is a stranger who entered the house to put the medallion there."

"Well, that must be it, I guess. The day of the wake and burial the house was left empty."

"Don't be crazy, Manolo. What would be the point?"

"To put us off track. What about that cigarette?"

"Here you are . . . But the murderer didn't know the medallions were different, or even that there were two of them, right?"

"No, I suspect he didn't. But if it wasn't Alexis who put it there, it must have been an acquaintance of his."

"And where does that leave your theory that the murderer didn't throw the corpse into the river because nobody would ever connect him with Alexis?"

"Sure, it doesn't square . . . But what if Alexis, who certainly knew they were different, told Salvador, or another of his lovers? . . . Just as well it's raining, perhaps it will cool down . . . Over the last few days several people have visited the house: the gardener, yesterday; the gas fitter, on Thursday; Matilde's doctor, three times after Alexis died; five, seven, eight people from Matilde and Faustino's families before and after the funeral; Alexis's two poofy friends, Jorge Arcos and Abilio Arango, right . . .? Some thirteen people all told."

"Too many. But a good crew, don't you reckon!"

"Yes, though the doctor had more opportunities than the others, don't you think?"

"Of course, one day he stayed with Matilde until she fell asleep. But why did Salvador K. go into hiding?"

"Yes, he's the jackpot winner so far, don't you think?"

"Conde, the fitter guy was new. Could it have been Salvador?"

"Don't be crazy, Manolo, don't get too far-fetched. Just imagine all the coincidences necessary for Salvador to hear the oven needs fixing, to decide to substitute for the fitter, put the medallion in place, and fix the cooker while he's about it!"

"Conde, you've seen greater coincidences . . . Anyway, if he's scarpered, it's because he's got dirt on his hands."

"Sure enough. And we've got the page of the Bible Alexis annotated and hid in the Piñera book . . . 'God the Father, why do you force him to suffer so much?' . . . What does that mean?"

"I haven't a clue."

"Don't be crazy, Manolo, it's easy: Alexis is suffering and feels solidarity with a fellow sufferer, right?"

"Yes, very touching, but just tell me one thing: why did he put the page in that book?"

"Because he'd already decided to dress up in Electra's gear . . . He wanted to set up his own tragedy . . . That sounds queer enough, doesn't it?"

"If you who know about these things say so . . . And what about the coins? Have you forgotten them?"

"Of course not, but I've not got the slightest fucking clue about them. What say you, Mr Genius?"

"I told you: they were paying him something back."

"But what was it all about . . . Fuck, was it blackmail?"

171

"How the hell do I know? While you're at it, what do you reckon about María Antonia?"

"Toña, black and swift . . . I don't know what to think: that black woman knows much more than she gives away. Why do you think she called the Marquess and set up this complication over the medallion?"

"So we'd find out."

"OK. Then it's because she knows something . . ."

"Shall we bring her in?"

"Don't be crazy, Manolo, your idea is to solve everything by putting the screws on people. If it were that easy, she'd have called us. I think it's going to rain all afternoon, don't you?"

"Yes, look at the sky over your place . . . Well, what are we going to do till Salvador appears and tells us he left home because he couldn't stand his wife any more?"

"What are we going to do? Well think on it, what else can we do? Think like the couple of thinkers we are . . . Now drop me off at home, sharpish!"

He wanted to believe the rain cleaning his window-panes also cleaned his mind and helped him think. That's why he was thinking, with the blurred, slippery image from his dream at the forefront of his mind, trying to get mentally exercised so he could pull away the mask behind which the truth was hiding. It was always truth. Irksome truth always hidden or trans-figured: sometimes behind words, at others behind attitudes and sometimes even behind an entire life simulated and redesigned merely to hide or trans-figure the truth. But he now knew it was there and he only needed an idea, a light like a spotlight able to illuminate his mind and get at the fucking truth. Truth is, he told himself, as he thought more and more, I'd like to see Polly Sparrow-bun again, God, how horrible, he remembered, and though he felt a desire to masturbate he rigorously denied himself that individualist, self-sufficient solution, now that little butt was real and tangible, not tonight, but on Sunday, she'd agreed, because on Saturday I'm going to the ballet, you know, and if it cleared up he'd take the opportunity to go to Eligio Riego's poetry reading, and could perhaps talk to the reader, and he also thought it was a long, long time since he'd seen Skinny and that he must tell him about his first-rate encounter with the mad item who'd extracted all the semen stored in his body, as she said: "God, how horrible!" as if it were all a big mistake. What would Dulcita be like after living so long in Miami? Perhaps she'd put on weight and look like a housewife, or wear those shiny clothes all Miami people wore, or perhaps she wouldn't, and she'd still have those beautiful legs whose distant reaches he'd tried to observe – he knew she had the tightest of butts, Skinny had told him – when his friend wasn't looking. If she was still pretty, perfect and nice, was it right she should see poor Carlos like that? If only everything could be like it was then and Skinny were thin again! If God existed, where the hell had he been the day Skinny was wounded, why Skinny? . . . Who was it? Salvador? The doctor? Faustino? The kitchen fitter? Or perhaps one of the other ten people in the house that day? And why do I never think the Marquess might be implicated? A debt collector hired by the dramatist? Don't get fanciful, Conde, he told himself. I could almost see him, for fuck's sake, but he was all right there, after eating two fried fish and a piece of bread and downing more coffee, not thinking how if he didn't buy some more he wouldn't have any left on

Monday, because everything improved with the cool brought on by rain that didn't look as if it would stop. What would Fatman Contreras be thinking as he watched the rain? Poor Fatman, if I could consult him, he'd surely say he could help. That bastard was a good policeman. Now without Fatman and old Captain Jorrín, whose death the Count still lamented, a policeman's job would be more difficult. Who could he consult when he had doubts? And where had they hidden Maruchi? What can have happened afterwards between the Marquess and the Other Boy with the unmentionable name, deported to Havana for being such a queer? He needed the Marquess to tell him the end of that adventure in which each chapter became more personal and less transvestite. Would he tell me who the Other Boy was and if he'd really peeped the day he peed in his house? What he really needed to know, he thought as he watched the water running down the panes of glass, drank a drop more coffee, lit another cigarette and looked at his watch concluding he had plenty of time to go and ingest a few of Eligio Riego's poems that night, what he really needed to know was the end of the story of Alexis Arayán, so masked and dead in the dirty grass of the Havana Woods, pursuing a death he didn't dare prosecute with his own hands, faking divine retribution, crossing his own Calvary without fame or heaven, a sacrifice made to measure for his sinful homosexuality, wrapped tragically in the clothing of a Havanan Electra. What a good fucker you are, darling . . .! Was it true? Nobody had ever said that before, at least not like that. And how much truth was there in what the Marquess said? In this world only Skinny told the truth, and even he didn't always tell his friend the truth. Would Faustino Arayán tell the truth? And black María Antonia? And could it be true that he, Mario Conde, was befriending pansied, theatrical Alberto Marqués? The truth might be the bus driver with a bus-driver's face he'd seen that morning, hitting the steering wheel with his ring, deciding whether or not to open the door to that girl begging, leaping up and down in front of the bus. What might happen later between those two people who were strangers and perhaps would never have met if the red light hadn't stopped the bus at that exact moment? Was it a chance coincidence? The rain was still falling, streaming softly down the panes like ideas through the Count's mind, as he looked at his hands and thought, after so much thinking, that the only truth was there and in the river sweeping everything along.

He got up and took the typewriter case out from under his bed. He opened it and looked at the ribbon, half covered in rot and good intentions, and went in search of paper. He felt he'd seen a transvestite and that the light of revelation had reached his mind, alarmed by so much thinking. He put the first sheet in the carriage and wrote: "While he waited, José Antonio Morales's eyes followed the extravagant flight of that pigeon." He needed a title, but would look for it later, he reckoned, because his fingertips felt the immediacy of a revelation. He sank his fingers into the keyboard and went on: "He observed how the bird gained height . . ."

It was a perfectly performed act of magic: the rain stopped, the wind swept the clouds towards other pre-cipices and the blazing sun of seven in the evening returned to close the curtain of day. But the smell of rain seemed to have filtered into the city's skin for the night, removing petrol fumes, ammonia from dry

175

urine, ambiguous smells from packed-out pizzerias and even the perfume from the woman walking in front of the Count, perhaps to the very same destination. If only.

Euphoria overflowing because of the eight typed sheets he carried in the back pocket of his trousers, the Count forgot his rush to reach the poetry reading and concentrated, while crossing the Capitolio's ravaged gardens, on completing an exhaustive visual survey. He tried to keep up with the prodigious pace of a no less prodigious woman who enjoyed the confluence of all the benefits of cross-breeding: her long blond hair, swooning it was so lank, fell on the mountable buttocks of a black houri, an arse of strictly African proportions, finely flexed rotundities descending two compact thighs to wild animal ankles. Her face – an even greater shock for the Count – didn't betray her all-conquering rearguard: ripe papaya lips dominated by elusively spare, definitively devious Asiatic eyes which, by the theatre where his pursuit and optical frisking ended, looked at the Count in a moment of oriental arrogance and ditched him without right of appeal. The right bitch knows she's hot and is flaunting it. She's so hot I could kill her, the Count told himself, pleased to quote himself, as he climbed the imposing stairs where at other times all the city's money, wrapped in silk gowns, linen suits, fox and ermine, went up and down from the nation's most exclusive drawing rooms, unthinkable in that torrid town where, nevertheless, it was possible to think anything.

He found the lecture theatre on the second floor and peered in; the poetry reading was apparently over and the poet, from behind an exhaustingly huge table, where his papers, spectacles and half glass of water lay, communed with the faithful who'd responded to his lyrical summons. Eligio Riego was in his seventies and his tepid, lethargic voice had a modulated rhythm that belonged to poetry rather than old age or exhaustion.

From the margins the Count furtively observed him in inquisitive, emotional mode: he knew that many people thought the gentle man with the dusty absent-minded *guayabera* was one of the most important poets the island had ever given birth to, and that, in his movement through poetry and time, he had bequeathed a unique view of the strange, awkward country they inhabited. The poetic grandeur, invisible to many, hidden behind a physique nobody would ever have pursued admiringly through the streets of Havana, had, however, an essential, permanent value because of the enviable range of its power, made only from the magic substance of words.

Now, as he sucked on his blackened pipe, like an anxious smoker with emphysema, Eligio Riego's small eyes ranged over his audience, and he allowed himself a smile, before continuing: "We Catholics are too serious when it comes to the divine. We lack the vital, primitive happiness of the Greeks, Yorubas or Hindus who dialogue with their Gods and sit them at their table. I've always thought it wrong, for example, to ignore the humour that exists in the Holy Scriptures, to scorn the holy smile that God gave and communicated to us, and forget how Jesus's first great miracle was to convert wine into water . . . A very clear sign from on high."

"And what about devils, Eligio?" asked a know-all in the front row.

"Look, young man, the existence of devils attests to the existence of God, and vice versa. They need each other as Good needs Evil to exist. And that's why evil is also everywhere: in hell, on earth, inside and outside.

177

Moreover, if we follow the tradition of the Talmud, the angels appeared on the second day of creation. Hence Lucifer, the most beautiful of all these angels, has existed from that early date, do you see? Then the fall of Lucifer and his dissident band took place, and so I've heard, the devil has been characterized ever since by the fact that every third time he blinks, he blinks upwards, he cannot walk backwards or blow his nose; he never sleeps and is impatient, ambitious and never creates a shadow; his favourite food is flies, but he eats other things, which are always highly spiced, though he has an aversion to salt ... But what most interests me about devils is their real artistic prowess: they say the malign one is an excellent musician and prefers stringed instruments. I always remember as an example how Juan Horozco y Covarrubias in his *Treatise on True and False Prophecy*, published in Segovia in 1588, states that he possesses proof of the devil's artistic vocation. In his book the father recounts how he saw Lucifer, after the latter had taken on the body of a rather thick village girl, compose some beautiful profane verse and, as they say now, put them to music, so they could be sung to the accompaniment of a lute which, with a woman's hands and arms, he played 'like the most expert in the world'. Now, young man, I'm more interested in demons on earth than in hell, like Max Beerbohm, the English novelist who wrote *Zuleika Dobson*, that fascinating story of the planet's most beautiful woman, who caused a love-sickness able to provoke the suicide en masse of all Oxford students in love with her devilish charms and, as one gleans from the novel's final pages, also loved by those in Cambridge, where she was bound. It is one of the most diabolical stories I've read ..." Eligio was emphatic, with his eyes receding when the Count opted to guarantee peace and quiet for his conversation with the poet and went out to reserve a table at the Louvre Café. Do you have any vintage rum? Yes, and Gold Medal. No, two vintage rums, without ice. No, not now, I'll be back, keep the table, he warned the waiter, and went out to find Eligio Riego who, pipe in hand, was chatting at the exit from the lecture theatre to a young woman apparently melting under the heat from his words. Could he be the devil himself? I've no option but to interrupt, old friend, the Count told himself, and accosted him thus: "Forgive me, maestro ... I'm your friend Rangel's friend."

"Young man, it's a fabulous story about the tranvestite murdered wearing Electra Garrigó's costume. Almost half demoniacal, you know? Like nearly everything involving Alberto Marqués, who's more shocking than Max Beerbohm ... Look, young man, he and I have known each other and been friends from the forties, when we used to meet to prepare the issues of the magazine, often in Fat Lezama's house, and I've always thought it was lucky this fellow was there to turn everything into a joke and puncture the atmosphere of poetic solemnity imposed by Lezama. We held poetry to be something entirely serious, transcendent, telluric, as they say now, and for him it was always a way to show off his cleverness, brilliance and talent. Because Alberto is one of the most intelligent men I've known, although I've always criticized the fact that he could sacrifice everything for a good joke, for the erotic chase, as he calls it, or one of his diabolically evil deeds, naturally. His break with Lezama and the whole magazine group in the fifties was one of his most shockingly evil deeds, but then I also understood him:

179

he needed to be himself and shine alone. He was always like that, a loose cannon searching restlessly, and that was why I lamented the excesses committed against him, when they isolated him completely, just because they wanted to punish his irreverence and artistic rebelliousness. It was intensely sad, young man, and the ten years they delayed before trying to right this wrong was too long for him. But what was most extraordinary about Alberto's dramatic character flourished in those difficult years: he displayed a dignity that was frankly enviable, and stopped writing and thinking about the theatre, which was all the more surprising in someone like him who lived for the world's stages ... Did I say he is an exhibitionist? ... Careful with him. Alberto's a born actor, one of the best actors I've ever seen, and he likes to invent his own comedies and tragedies. He exaggerates what he is or explains what he isn't, so you really don't know what goes ... He says it is a form of self-defence. Perhaps this character of his is the reason why our friendship improves at a distance: we prefer to respect rather than engage with each other. I think he may understand me. No, my situation was different: I've always been a Catholic, though I'm not a mystic like your transvestite and in no way sanctimonious: as you can see, I drink large quantities of rum, smoke my pipes, and have never been able to deny myself the sometimes desperate contemplation of a girl coming into flower, because I'm convinced there's no beauty on earth to surpass the heat which comes from youth. In a word, we are children of time and dust, and no poetry can spare us that. Other things perhaps, but the time allotted to each of us, no chance. That's why I think life should be enjoyed on one's own terms, provided the enjoyment doesn't prejudice one's neighbour, do you see? But there was a phase when it was thought that the vision of the world and life propounded by Catholic writers was inappropriate, that our fidelity was blemished by irrevocable spiritual fidelities and consequently we couldn't be trusted, apart from being retrograde and philosophically idealist, you know? So we were discreetly sidelined. Nothing like what happened to Alberto and other people. The fact was, social commitment was confused with individual mind-sets and then extremists put us on the list of targets to be dealt with: we were ideologically impure and, for some, pernicious if not reactionary, when the preponderance of matter seemed clearly demonstrated, as they say out there. Someone with a Muscovite mentality thought uniformity was possible in this hot, heterodox country where nothing's ever been pure, and then they unleashed a wave of hysteria against literature which left several corpses abandoned on the roadside and several walking wounded covered in scars . . . But I left the stage voluntarily: I couldn't renounce something I'd always believed in (a lovely trait, as Alberto would say) or mistake the circumstantial for the essential. In any case I'd have betrayed myself if I'd let myself be defeated by what was transitory or, worse, if I'd pretended to change, as many people did . . . That's why I trusted to silence but didn't stop writing. The Marquess is different, as you'll know if you've had a couple of conversations with him: his extreme sacrifice has the ingredients, many would say, of theatrical tragedy. But, I repeat, don't be put off by what he says, try to see the truth in what he has done: he resisted all the insults, but stayed here, although only, as he says, to see the final fate of those who harassed him . . . The fact is he calls for the right to revenge, though he'd be incapable of transforming

181

it into physical acts or public outrages. Look, young man, I'd also advise you, if at all possible, not to be misled by the many unpleasant incidents and stories you've heard about any of us: writers and artists aren't as diabolical as is sometimes thought or alleged. Did they never tell you about the wrong-doings and hassles that occur among bank employees or workers in innocent canning factories or dozy members of a diplomatic mission? Don't such things happen among you policemen? What I mean is that we don't have an exclusive on back-biting, opportunism and ambition. Like everywhere, Good and Evil blend in each and every one of us. Young man: what more can I say, except to thank you for this vintage rum nobody could classify as diabolical which has warmed our conversation in a place that is so delightful? . . . Perhaps, as a result of some professional defect, you got the wrong person, and expected to hear a different opinion from me, but I profess two unchanging fidelities in my life: friendship and poetry. As long as I live I'll write poetry, whether it's published or not, whether it wins a poetry festival or not, whether they give me recognition for it or not. And friendship is a voluntary commitment one enters into, and if one does, it has to be respected: although we don't agree on many things, Alberto Marqués is my friend and when someone, you or anyone else, asks about him, the first thing I say is that he is my friend, and I think that says it all. Don't you agree, young man?"

While he waited, José Antonio Morales's eyes followed the extravagant flight of that pigeon. He observed how the bird soared dizzily, then tucked in its wings and performed strange pirouettes, as if discovering for the first time the vertiginous sensation of plunging into the void. It soared again, then disappeared behind the building, to return to the patch of sky visible from the corner of the yard where José Antonio awaited the accounts inspector. He thought how in his twenty-eight years as a bus driver he'd never seen pigeons while waiting for the results of the day's takings and he felt more strongly than ever he would kill that woman.

José Antonio had till that day behaved like a balanced, responsible person, who'd never thought of killing anyone, at least coldly, with premeditation. Sometimes when he was driving his bus and suffered careless knocks from other drivers, he'd felt so under attack he even imagined he was carrying a sawn-off shotgun, seen in some Sicilian film, and that from his bus window he'd executed the dastardly violator of his rights on the road. But even those summary judgements of imagination had become less frequent over the years, as José Antonio got used to tolerating insouciant drivers whose existence now seemed as commonplace as ants in the sugar or roses on a rose bush. Or could it be he was growing old?

That was why he was surprised by this sudden command from his consciousness: he would kill that woman, and nothing in the world would stop him. The imperative appeared so clear-cut José Antonio feared it was all a snare set by love at first sight. It couldn't be anything else, he told himself, as he signed the card for his daily takings and calculated he'd collected 47 pesos 35 cents, which meant 947 people had passed by the bus cashbox, not counting the firm's employees who'd shown their pass and the inevitable bastards who always performed acts of magic to avoid paying or put in tokens rather than coins. In round figures: a thousand people, and only the face of that woman, someone in her early thirties, pleasant enough, a little on the thin side perhaps, dressed carefully though inelegantly, wearing next to no make-up, had imprinted itself on his memory and, into the bargain, with an order that again seemed irrevocable: namely, to kill her.

When he got home, José Antonio rehearsed a routine which complemented his routine on the bus: he went down the side passage, towards the terrace, left his seat cushion on a chair and washed his hands, soaping himself up to his elbows, as meticulously as a surgeon. He thought it the only way to get rid of the dangerous dirt from the buses, where everybody gets on, the sick and infirm, the dirty and healthy, the infected and the newly born smelling of eau-de-cologne. He picked up his cushion, whistled as he went through the back door, and met his wife, as always at this time of day, between laundry sink and kitchen. He kissed her on the cheek, was kissed by her, asked whether Tonito had come back from school and greeted the smell of fried onion and garlic, while she asked him how it had gone and he said all right. They ate, talked about the usual – the money that was never enough, the bad state of public transport, the unrelenting heat, the possibility she might go back to work in the factory – then he slept his two hours of siesta. He got up, put on his rubber sandals, drank the coffee his wife had just prepared and sat on the terrace to read the newspaper, and thought about that damned woman once again and tried to forget he would definitely kill her.

The following morning the woman didn't appear. José Antonio Morales remembered he'd picked her up on his third round (left garage: 8.16 a.m.) at the stop on San Leonardo and 10 de Octubre (8.29 a.m.). However, he wasn't relieved or too worried by her absence, for he knew he wouldn't forget her and was determined to kill her. The woman didn't show for another six days, until Tuesday – the same day he'd seen her the week before – she appeared, inelegant, without make-up,

184

*carrying a folder brimming with books and papers which José
Antonio hadn't seen on their previous encounter, and she
threw her coin in the box, didn't even glance at the driver
who'd decided he was going to kill her. He looked at her, as he
looked at all his passengers, shut the door and drove off,
entering the huge, rather dirty thoroughfare of 10 de Octubre,
previously dubbed Jesús del Monte.*

*That night, as he was watching the television news, José
Antonio told himself that the idea he'd met her before, which
was why he wanted to kill her, made no sense. In fact, until
last Tuesday he'd never seen her, and perhaps he'd have lived
his whole life without seeing her if, three weeks earlier, in the
last settlement of routes for the second half of the year, he
hadn't taken the unexpected decision – for him, his wife, and
the rest of the bus drivers – to change his route 4 for route 68,
which began two minutes before his usual shift, and finished
three minutes later, at 1.27 p.m. The decision was as spontaneous as it was irrevocable, and José Antonio then sought
out explanations: he would earn thirty-two cents a day more,
perhaps he was bored by the roads on route 4, the people who
travelled on the 68 were slightly different, the minutes spent
crossing the Apollo building estate were very pleasant . . .
Perhaps on the day of decisions it had been very hot in the
meeting-room and he'd felt very uncomfortable with his dirty
hands. Or could it be he was growing old? Yes, he was now
forty-seven and when he'd begun as a bus driver, just out of
military service, he'd been barely nineteen, and all that time
he'd been driving on route 4: ever since, every day five drives
round Havana for eleven months in succession, driving
through the same streets, at the same times, with the same
stops and even picking up the same people who came to be his
friends over the months and years, and he went to weddings,
hospitalizations, some birthday parties and even several
burials of his usual passengers, and he'd never thought of
killing any of them. Nothing had interfered with the predict-*

able routine and much less with what was logical for such a period: at twenty-one he'd got married, had a son whom he'd given his name, his own mother died peacefully, in her sleep, just after her sixty-second birthday, and they never called on him to fight in Angola, despite the fact that one day in 1975 he'd been summoned and, because of his military aptitudes, been told he belonged to the artillery reserve for unit 2154 and been asked if he was ready to fight as an internationalist soldier wherever the Revolution sent him, and he'd said he was. That night José Antonio slept peacefully, after making love with his wife, in the position they always adopted: she mounted him, put his penis in and her vagina rode the length of his member, José Antonio's spine, mistreated by years of driving, resting flat on the mattress. The remainder of the week he also slept peacefully, although on Monday night he thought he felt a certain anxiety over the encounter he expected to have the following morning. But he shut his eyes and in four minutes fell, like the extravagant pigeon, into a dizzy sleep.

When you work for twenty-eight years as a bus driver you master, almost unthinkingly, all the tricks necessary to survive in the job: the lies you can tell the inspector when he catches you running several minutes ahead of time; the way to respond to irritable passengers, knowing when you can take the offensive or when you need to apologize or even pretend you didn't hear the insult, how to ask for a coffee at some point on the route without having to join the queue: or begin a relationship with someone, according to your own sex, age and interests.

José Antonio saw her under the sign for the stop, carrying her folder, next to three other passengers. He stopped the bus ten yards before reaching the group and forced them to walk towards him. She was the last to get in and, when she went to put her money in, no doubt annoyed by him braking before the stop, he said: "I think we're going to have to change buses." If he'd said something concrete like: "The brakes are in a bad state," or, "There was a pothole," or something like that, the conversation would have taken off, if she'd been a very talkative person. But the riddle he'd set was unassailable. She stopped next to him, supported herself on a vertical bar and asked: "Why?" As he explained that the front right wheel brakes weren't working properly, he asked her for her folder so he could place it on the bus rack and finally discovered she was an English teacher in an elementary secondary school in Luyanó and that day she started her classes on the second shift at 8.55, and the bus left her there at 8.42, giving her just enough time to arrive and get to her classroom, and if he switched buses . . .

The rest of September and the whole of October, she got on his bus on a Tuesday; he asked her for her folder, and they chatted thirteen minutes, which enabled him to find out she was Isabel María Fajardo, thirty-three years old, divorced, childless, and had been a teacher for some time, and considered herself a boring individual. What's more, she gave him her address, and the third Tuesday in October invited him to drop by some day for a coffee. I'm always there after six, she said.

Although he'd thought of going to a psychiatrist, José Antonio discarded the idea straight away: he wasn't in the least mad, and his decision to kill Isabel María wasn't even a sentence he'd personally adopted, but a mandate he'd received. The only problem was that he thought himself a complete atheist, with no expectations of a life beyond. What most worried him, nevertheless, was grasping why it had to be Isabel María and nobody else. Really, if it was necessary to kill someone, he could perhaps choose someone better, a person he hated or disliked, or someone infirm who'd even be

187

grateful for his act of mercy or, better still, someone harmful to society whom society would be overjoyed to see executed by a voluntary, anonymous avenger. He knew several undesirables of that kind. So why her? After seven Tuesdays and approximately ninety-one minutes of conversation that woman hadn't managed to arouse any special feeling in him: hatred, love, desire, repulsion, anything to justify the need (the mandate?) to kill her. Like him, she was one of those millions of anodyne beings peopling the earth, who lived in the country, right now, spent their days honourably, without excessive euphoria or ill-feeling, not in major dispute with society or the times, without well-defined political ideas or ambitious individual projects. She worked, ate, slept, suffered slightly from loneliness but wasn't visibly tormented and, as she'd already confessed, loved spending hours listening to classical or popular music. Why? Perhaps that was it, he thought: because she represented nothing . . . But did he know that before meeting her?

What was even stranger, he told himself when he thought how he must kill her, is that he was in no hurry to do so, nor did he have a clear plan, and he was almost on the point of persuading himself it wouldn't be a murder premeditated or with malice aforethought, but a fatal accident while he drove his bus. But then he realized that wasn't right: he would kill her, with his own hands, some day, perhaps soon.

José Antonio was a good reader of the newspaper: every day he'd read for more than an hour, and dwell on each piece of news or comment, so he wouldn't forget: so many things happened in the world every day, his memory recall barely lasted twenty-four hours before it gave way to fresh news and events. That Thursday afternoon he read a very interesting item on Aids and the scant immediate hopes of finding an antidote, despite the efforts of thousands of scientists through-

out the world. He thought: if God existed, this would be a divine punishment. But if he doesn't exist, why do such things happen in the world? He wasn't usually so thoughtful, and concluded that wherever the plague came from, it was a punishment against love. He liked the idea so much that, while taking a shower, he mentioned it to his wife and later told her, "I'm going to take a spin Aunt Angelina's way," knowing full well he was going to drink the coffee Isabel María had offered him on the last two Tuesdays.

He knocked on the door and waited, thinking about how he felt: I'm not nervous, not anxious, I don't know whether I shall kill her today, he'd just told himself when she opened up. She was still thin, unmade-up, yet more dressed up than usual; her hair was damp, just washed, and she didn't seem too surprised to be inviting him in. She wore a dressing gown that was quite modest, and melancholy music was coming from some part of the house, the kind José Antonio could never have identified, and she'd later inform him: "It's Mozart's Requiem." They went to the kitchen, because he said he'd come to drink the coffee she'd promised. She prepared the coffee pot, and they sat at the table. It was a clean, well-lit place, where José Antonio felt at ease, as if he'd been there before. As he savoured his coffee, he knew that he didn't know what would happen in the minutes to follow. Would he try to make love to her? Would he leave when he'd drunk his coffee? Would he even tell her he was going to kill her? Then he looked her in the eye: Isabel María also looked at him, an adult woman's look, ready for anything, and he heard her say: "Did you come so you could go to bed with me?" And he said: "Yes."

Isabel María was naked under the dressing gown and, when they dropped on the bed, she climbed on top of him, put his penis in, and her vagina started to ride the length of his member, as if she knew that position allowed José Antonio's spine, mistreated by years of driving, to rest flat on the mattress. It was a good session, well synchronized, satisfying for both.

189

Then she said: "From the first time I saw you, two weeks before we started talking, I knew we would make love. I don't know where the idea came from, or why. But I knew you were going to talk to me and that one day you'd come here for a coffee . . . It was all very strange because when I looked at you I didn't see too much I liked and besides, I thought I was still in love with Fabián, the headmaster. But it was like a very strong presentiment, like an imperative, a mandate, what do I know," she said, and kissed him on the lips, the nipples, his paunchy belly and purple-headed member. "And now you're here. What most worried me," she continued, "was why it had to be you . . ." "I experienced something similar," he confessed, and felt the need to drink more coffee. "I'll go get some more coffee," he said.

He abandoned the bed, and before leaving to go to the kitchen, looked at Isabel María's nakedness for a minute; two small breasts, two red, sore nipples and a little triangle of quite lank, uncombed dark hair. He poured himself some coffee, lit a cigarette, and went back to the bedroom smoking and carrying a knife. He sank it into her chest, under her left breast, and she barely flinched. Why? he wondered again, before putting his cigarette out in the ashtray next to the bed and deciding he should dress her so they didn't find her naked. Then, as he moved Isabel María's pillow, he felt the cold weight of the knife she had hidden there, perhaps to fulfil her own mandate. Just then José Antonio remembered he had to get a move on, for his wife hated eating without him.

Mario Conde, 9 August 1989

"You bastard, now you need a title . . ."

"Forget that. Just tell me what you made of the story?"

190

"A real scream."

"Is that all?"

"Well, squalid."

"And moving?"

"As well."

"Do you like it?"

"Terribly."

"But terribly good or terribly bad?"

"Good, you idiot, good. Let me give you a hug, you pansy. Fuck, you've finally got back to writing."

The Count bent over the wheelchair between the open arms of Skinny Carlos and let himself be squeezed against his friend's greasy, sweaty chest. Knowing he could write and that what he'd written appealed to Skinny Carlos was a combination too explosive for the Count's emotions and he felt he was about to cry, not only for his own sake, but for a future that was impossible to imagine without a man who'd been his best-only friend for over twenty years, whose goodness, intelligence, optimism and desire to live life had been rewarded by a bullet in the back, shot from some still unknown rifle, hidden behind a dune in the Namibian desert.

"Congratulations, you bastard. But bring me a photocopy tomorrow or never look me in the face again. I know you, you'll wake up one day saying it's a load of shit and tear it up."

"It's a deal, pal."

"Hey, but this is cause for celebration, right? Take the twenty pesos in the drawer. Add ten of your own and buy two bottles of that Legendario they've put out in the bar in Santa Catalina today."

"Two?"

"Yes, one each, right?"

"God, how horrible!" said the Count.

"Hey, what horrible god? My lovely lad, all this consorting with queers doesn't do you much good, just listen to you."

"Yes, something sticks. A sparrow's butt, for instance."

"Tell me more."

"No, later. I'm going to fetch the two bottles. Stay right there, OK?"

"Hey, wait a minute. I'll read the story to the old girl and, if she likes it, expect to eat well."

"And if not?"

"Rice and tortilla."

Josefina blew her nose on her handkerchief, and said: "Ay, the poor girl, my boy, being killed like that just for fun. The things you think of. And that poor bus driver . . . But I was moved, and this son of mine says it's the best Cuban story in the world, and if that's what he says, well, I got a bit inspired and started to think what kind of meal I could get for you so you don't drink your rum on an empty stomach, and what I did was real silly, the first thing I thought of, though I reckon it will taste real good: turkey stuffed with rice and black beans."

"A turkey?"

"Stuffed?"

"Yes, and it's very easy to make. Look, I bought the turkey yesterday and defrosted the fridge today, it was still soft, so I took it out and basted it while it was thawing. I made garlic, pepper, cumin, oregano, bay, basil and parsley leaves into a paste and, naturally, bitter orange and salt, and basted it well inside and out with that paste. Then I threw in plenty of big slices of onion. The best would be to leave it a couple of hours basted, but as I can see you look starved . . . Then, as

192

I'd already got black beans on the boil, I started to prepare a tasty sauce: I took two strips of bacon I cut into small pieces and fried, and put more onion in the fat, but cut tiny, with ground garlic and plenty of chilli, and there you go, I poured the sauce on the beans when they were almost cooked and added a cup of dry wine, so they taste a bit sour, the way you like them, right?"

"Yes, that's how I love them."

"Me too."

"And what else?"

"Well, I poured in the white rice to make the *congrí*, a bit more oregano, and for good measure a pinch of salt, and a handful of finely chopped onion. Then I waited for the rice to dry out, before the grains went soft, of course, and switched it off and stuffed the turkey with the *congrí*, so it cooks inside the bird, right? You know what I didn't have? Toothpicks to close it up . . . So I used a few stems from the bitter oranges, which are pretty hard . . . Then put it in the oven, so don't despair, it will soon be ready. Have your drinks in peace, and it will be on the table at nine thirty. And pour me a drop of rum . . . That's it, just a drop, Condesito, or I'll get drunk . . ."

"And how many are going to eat this, Jose?"

"As the bird was about eight pounds, there'll be enough for ten or twelve helpings . . . but with you two . . . Well, I hope something will be left for lunch tomorrow. I'll just go and have a look."

"Did you hear that, you bastard? The old dear's mad."

"What I'd like to know is where the fuck she gets it all . . . The only thing she didn't have were the toothpicks."

"Don't be such a nosy policeman. Pour me some . . . This rum is good for getting a skinful and taking a running jump."

"What's the matter, Skinny?"

Carlos downed more rum and didn't answer.

"Is it still the business with Dulcita?" the Count asked, and his friend looked at him for a moment.

"Smell that, the bird's really cooking," he said, going off at an opportune tangent. "Hey, do you know what should come after a feast like this? A decent cigar. A Montecristo or something of the sort, right?"

"Fuck, of course, a Montecristo," the Count replied, downing his rum in one gulp. "It has to be a Montecristo," he said, as he finally saw the face he'd sensed in his dream, where a dirty, raging river suddenly precipitated the fall of the mask, a mask made of a thousand lies which had hidden the truth from him. Yes, that had to be the truth!

Nothing can justify such a crime, was the most sophisticated philosophical conclusion he could reach as he felt the cold water on his back. The vivid memory of the whole bottle of pale Legendario rum still coursed rich and bitter round his mouth, though he was surprised to discover he was hungry and hadn't much of a headache. How could it be? In the kitchen, after swallowing a couple of analgesics, he looked alarmed as the funnel to his coffee pot swallowed his last stocks of coffee and waited for it to strain and for Sergeant Manuel Palacios to arrive, pulled on his old blue jeans – you're dead thirsty, he told himself, observing the remains of an evil liverish stain on the cloth at thigh level and on his pockets – and went out on to the porch, as he did every Sunday, to savour a whiff of nostalgia for life in the neighbourhood that was also transvested, metamorphosed, definitively different, where he'd felt happy or miserable, in like doses, on many other Sundays in his life, ever since he'd been conscious of life. The church bells had tolled for no one for many a year, and that invigorating smell of freshly baked bread had never again floated from the nearby bakery, what's bread made of now, if it doesn't smell like it used to? But he resisted; despite these absences, it was a simply wonderful day: the previous evening's heavy downpour had swept away the filth from heaven and earth, and the sun's brightness triumphed over any darkening doubts. A good day to play baseball (but was there also the will?), the Count thought, and he went back in for his coffee and drank a big cupful, a bitter swill round to clear out the last phantoms of sleep, alcohol and hangover. As he lit his cigarette, he heard the car horn calling him from the street. Shirt unbuttoned, he went out on to the pavement, and as he opened the car door, greeted Sergeant Manuel Palacios.

"Well, tell me where," Manuel Palacios mumbled, making it clear he was ready to obey.

"I've fucked up your Sunday?"

"No, of course not."

The Count smiled. That's all I need, he told himself, thinking he too would have preferred not to work on Sunday and to stay at home, sleeping, reading, or even writing, now he'd started to write again. But he said: "Let's go to Headquarters, the Boss is there . . . Hey, did you find Salvador?"

"No, not yet."

Manuel Palacios started up the car, without looking at his boss, and when they reached the church the Count decided to show his hand.

"Look, Manolo, I've thought of something to wind up this case. That's why I called you."

He waited in vain for a response from his colleague and continued: "Do you remember there was a bit of a Montecristo cigar among the things they found in the place where Alexis was killed?" And he waited. He didn't wait long.

"Fuck, you're right, Conde! Do you think . . .? No, it can't be. His father . . .?"

"Let's see if we can find the butt of the Montecristo I gave the Boss and if the lab can tell us if they're similar. Even if they're only distant relations, I think Faustino Arayán has hit the jackpot with a single ticket."

Manuel Palacios, conclusively persuaded by Conde's reasoning, put his foot down and the car lurched off fearfully.

"Easy does it, we've got time."

"No, the quicker this is sorted, the quicker I'm on the razzle ... If you'd seen the girl I picked up yesterday ..."

While Manuel Palacios told him of the virtues of his newly promised – he sometimes called them that, though there was never a single promise, even in the realm of fantasy, and according to the lieutenant's tally he was on number sixteen for the year – the Count tried to imagine what had happened in the Havana Woods the night of the day of the Transfiguration, but was thwarted by an inability to fable: what had happened? A father who kills his son? What about the two coins? he wondered as Sergeant Palacios turned into the Headquarters parking lot, as tranquil and sunny as everything else that August.

Determined to take advantage of the peace and quiet of the Sabbath, the Count waited for the lift to arrive empty, to avoid for once the climb to the top floor. But when the metal doors slid open, he felt a thump in his chest: there were three men in the lift, dressed in combat gear, without stripes on their shoulders, staring at him hard. His mind, which had to decide what to do in the scant seconds the open door allowed, finally signalled that he should say good-day and get in the metal box, rather than run to the stairs, as he wanted to do. The men returned his greeting and the Count turned his back on them and looked at the panel which indicated floor levels. His skin smarted from the inspection he'd been subjected to: perhaps those same three were the ones who'd questioned Sergeant Manuel Palacios, revealing they knew chapter and verse about the life of Mario Conde. Perhaps these three were the ones who decreed his friend Fatman Contreras should be suspended and even took poor Maruchi out of Central Station. Perhaps they were the emissaries of a new Apocalypse: the Count imagined them in the long robes of Inquisitors, ready to burn pyres and use the rack. The anti-natural law of police who spy on other police had put there three of its undesirable but unavoidable executors, whom the Count regretted giving anything, even as basic as a good-day, when he felt the lift brake on the third floor and the men excused themselves and departed the cage, saying: See you, lieutenant, while he held out his hand and pressed number four, and denied them an answer, stood on his dignity.

When he entered the deserted ante-room to Major Rangel's office, the Count found his face was burning the way it does when somebody hits you and homicidal furies are unleashed and you become a blind bull only fit to attack. He decided to wait till the malign vapours dissolved in his blood, then walked towards the glass door and heard the voice of the Boss, on the phone, he concluded, when he didn't get a reply, and knocked gently on the door.

"Come in, Mario," said the Boss. How the hell does the bastard always know when I'm around?

The Count waved at him and waited for his boss to finish his call. The Boss said "yes" two or three times, and hung up the receiver as if afraid he'd break it. The Count observed that, though it was Sunday, the Major was wearing his uniform. Something bad was brewing.

"There's no peace, Conde, no peace," he said and looked though the windows. "And what are you doing here? Did you get to see Eligio yesterday? Have you solved your case?"

198

"I think I'm well on the way."

"How many days you've been on this wretched case?"

"Four."

"Four days and you think you're well on the way?"

"I need something from you . . ." And he saw his boss's lips smile sceptically. "Don't worry, it's very simple. Have you smoked the Montecristo I gave you the other day?"

"Yes, why?" asked Rangel startled, finally turning to look at the Count.

"Where's the butt?"

"Now what's got into you, Mario?"

"I need that butt. I've got an idea . . ."

"You've got an idea. How strange . . . Look, it must be in the basket, they didn't empty the rubbish yesterday," said the Major, picking the wastepaper basket from the floor and exclaiming, "Here it is. Its thickness gave it away . . . Why do you need this, Conde?"

The lieutenant took the piece of cigar, which had been consumed as far as the Major took things. He observed how the end was chewed, half broken, and concluded that the Boss had enjoyed it, though while he was smoking he must have been anxious or upset to bite it like that.

"Give me half an hour, Major," he pledged, and left the office, imitating Rangel holding a cigar.

"Don't play games with me, Mario," he heard as he left.

"Well, Conde, this is not definitive, but you could say the two cigars have the same origin. Steady on, that only means they're made from a similar leaf, though it's obvious they weren't twisted by the same person.

The one from the Woods is bigger, has a slightly tighter twist to it and appears to have been lit only once, because it's accumulated less tar and nicotine round the mouth end, apart from being only half smoked, and that's probably why it's still got its band. No other clues. A little earth, that's all. But remember, cigars made by more than one person may go into the same box, because they pack them as they come. But what I am sure of is that they're a similar quality tobacco, the same harvest, I mean, though that means nothing."

"Then I can't say the two bastard cigars are brothers?"

The laboratory man looked at the Count and smiled: "But why make them relatives like that? They originated from the same place, period. But don't ask me to say they're brothers from the same leaf or plant."

"And if I were to bring you more cigars from the same box, do you think you could be any surer?"

The laboratory man looked at the remains of the two cigars, their guts opened up as if for an autopsy.

"That could be really helpful."

"Well, I'll get some. When will you work till today?"

"Don't worry, I'll be here till four, but if necessary, I can wait. Or what are friends for?"

The Count went into the corridor and walked down a flight of stairs to his cubbyhole. His prejudices kept digging at him and he wanted to make them reality as soon as possible. He entered his small office and found Manuel Palacios brandishing a piece of paper.

"Look at this, Conde: we've tracked down Salvador K."

"I'd forgotten all about that insect. Where might he be?"

"He turned up in El Cerro. Living a new romance."

"With a woman?"

"Almost, but not quite a woman. El Greco says he went and talked to him after they'd tracked him down; the rooster told him that since everybody knew about his thing with Alexis, he wasn't going to hide any more and would live life as it should be lived. He says the guy seemed as happy as anything now he'd come out a swashbuckling queer. What do you reckon?"

"I think he's the only one to have got something out of this mess, don't you?"

"What shall we do? Bring him in?"

"Let him enjoy himself for the moment . . . Then we'll see if we need to speak to him. But they should keep an eye on him."

"That's what I thought," said Manolo, and he put the paper and the address away in a folder on the table on which was written in red, irregular letters: *Alexis Arayán/Homicide/Open.*

"Now let's play our last card. Give me the telephone."

The sergeant pushed the receiver over to the corner of the desk where the Count was and watched him dial, as he lit a cigarette.

"María Antonia? . . . Yes, Lieutenant Mario Conde here. How are you? Look, María Antonia, we need you to do us a favour . . . No, it's very simple . . . We want to talk to you . . . No, no. I said talk, talk over a few things to do with Alexis, because we know you and he were very fond of each other and that you saw much more of him than Faustino or Matilde, right? . . . Yes, I'd also prefer it to be here . . . OK? I'll send a car . . . Where? Uhuh, on the corner of Thirty-Second, of course . . . And, oh, María Antonia, I'd like to ask you another favour. Could you bring me a cigar from the box of Montecristos on the coffee table?"

"Thanks, María Antonia," said the Count when the black woman opened her bag and gave him the cigar. He looked at it lingeringly, as if spellbound by the pale, polished beauty of an excellent cigar grown in Vueltabajo, and smiled as he handed it to Manuel Palacios. "Come in, please," and he opened the door to his cubicle. María Antonia's feet didn't seem as light as usual; she had rather the wary tread of a hunted animal, and the Count imagined the doubts raining down on the woman's consciousness, as she turned round to see if the door was closed. He felt pity for her again as he pointed her to a chair, talked to her about the heat in the street, the tranquil view he enjoyed from his cubicle window and how that was why he preferred it to the big offices that faced the other wing of the building, and finally asked her if she was married.

"No, single," she replied; wearing a flowery Sunday dress, her bag on her knees, her hair gathered beneath an imitation silk scarf and lips painted blood-red, she seemed like an escapee from a scene in *The Color Purple*, thought the Count.

"And how long have you known the Arayán family?"

"From '56, when I started to work for them. Matilde and Faustino had just married and at the time lived in Santos Suárez with Matilde's mother, who was widowed. After the Revolution I decided to leave the house, I wanted to make a life for myself, quite away from them, and intended looking for another job, but the child was born and I developed an affection for him and kept postponing and postponing my depart- ure, until four days ago, when this happened . . . Now I think I will leave, though I don't know where I'll go. As I've always lived with them, I don't have a home, or a right to a pension . . . I'd have to go and live with my

202

brother and that's a real hell, with his wife, three children and who knows how many grandchildren."

"Did you get on well with the Arayáns?"

"Yes, Fabiola, Matilde's mum, behaved very well towards me, and I loved the kid as if he were my own. For many years we three lived alone in the house, especially here in Miramar, when they began to give Faustino work outside Cuba. The boy spent more time with me and his grandmother than with his parents, and we went out a lot, to the cinema, the theatre, museums, because Fabiola had been a university teacher and was very cultured. Faustino says it's our fault the way he turned out, well, you know how, but I swear I brought him up like my own child. The fact he was such a loving, helpless child, and that Faustino put so much pressure on him, threatened him a lot, even hit him more than once, I think it was Alexis's way of taking his revenge on him. They had a very difficult relationship, for a father and son. They didn't speak to each other for several years . . ."

"What do you think of Faustino?"

María Antonia looked for a pocket handkerchief in her bag and wiped the sweat from her top lip. The air in the cubicle was perfumed by a wave of that handkerchief, which made the Count feel even sorrier for her: the woman had assumed a perfectly aristocratic manner that seemed out of kilter with her submissive attitude in the Arayán household. How many of her real aspirations and aptitudes had she hidden for years, as she deferred her own life to be close to the child of another she'd adopted as her own?

"I don't think it's my place . . ." was her response, finally.

"Tell me something," the lieutenant continued. "Nothing will go beyond these walls."

"Well, what is there to tell? He's somebody in high favour with the government, you know, that's why he travels so much, has been an ambassador and the like. He's always behaved well towards me, although never like Fabiola or Matilde, you understand. And I never forgave him for the way he acted towards his son. The poor boy got to be afraid of his father. That's why he left home. I was very, very happy, and we decided if he ever got his own house, I'd go and live with him."

As he saw the tears running down María Antonia's black cheeks, the Count thought the end of this soap would more than consume his Sunday quota of pity. He reproached himself for mistaking, in a flash judgement, the face of love for the mask of submission and tried to imagine the woman's stellar solitude, her life lived at the wrong time and place, whose only reason to live was the strangled transvestite she'd reared and cared for like her own son. The Count stood up and let her cry: he supposed her pain to be as deep as her boundless solitude. Then he heard her asking him to forgive her, just as he looked at his watch and calculated that Manuel Palacios must be about to arrive, and he wanted to see a victory "V" on the sergeant's hand more than ever. For the sake of María Antonia, hapless Alexis, even the Marquess and himself and his blessed prejudices. He wanted it so badly that his cubicle door swung to let in the skeletal form of Manuel Palacios, right hand signalling a "V".

"María Antonia," he said, and returned to his seat opposite the woman, now putting her small handkerchief back in her small bag. "For some days I've been under the impression you wanted to tell us something which perhaps had to do with Alexis's death. Or did I get it wrong?"

The woman looked him in the eye.

204

"I don't know why you imagine that."

"Rather than imagine it, I'm sure, particularly after yesterday when you phoned Alberto Marqués and told him you'd found the medallion in Alexis's trinket-box. I don't know why, but I'm also convinced you knew it was Alexis's and that you called the Marquess so he'd call us. Or have I got it all wrong?"

"Well, I wasn't sure . . ."

"Let me help you, for you're the only one who can help us now, if you know something, which I think you . . . Listen carefully: next to Alexis's corpse they found a piece of Montecristo cigar which, according to the laboratory, belongs very probably to the box Faustino Arayán has in his lounge . . . That and Alexis's medallion placed in his trinket-box don't prove anything, but they might mean a lot. Do you understand?"

At each of the Count's words the woman's head sank a little lower, as if the world had deposited the burden of truth on her neck and all she wanted to contemplate, as she suffered her punishment, was the bag her two gnarled hands were fingering nervously. The Count waited, feeling his hopes fading, defeated by fear, until he saw the burden disappear and María Antonia's face look up, and meet his beseeching gaze. The woman's eyes now gleamed, though she didn't look about to cry.

"There were two threads of red silk on the trousers he wore that night. He put them in the washing machine, but I took them out because it was a blue dye that might have stained other clothes. I was surprised because the turn-ups were muddied and that's why I inspected them closely . . . Let him fucking rot," she said, and the Count was surprised by the power in her voice, the evil glint in her eye and the way her hands twitched murderously, oh, María Antonia, so fleet of foot. "The son of a whore," she said, pronouncing every syllable, and she burst into an aristocratic, disconsolate flood of tears.

"I've brought you a present, but it's not to smoke," the Count warned, placing on Major Rangel's desk the tray with three transparent envelopes where the massacred cigars were visible.

"What the fuck's that?"

"It's the second piece of evidence in the case against Faustino Arayán for murdering his son, Alexis Arayán."

Major Rangel slapped the palm of his hand down on his desk.

"What the hell do you mean?"

"Don't play deaf . . . The great Faustino killed his son in the Havana Woods. Get it now?"

But before Major Rangel really got it, the Count had to relate the results of his conversations with María Antonia Galarraga, the fact that Faustino was AB blood group, the story about the medallion with a line etched under the arm and the two threads of red silk on mud-stained trousers which belonged to that same Faustino Arayán.

"But what I still don't understand is why he killed him," the ever sceptical Major Rangel insisted.

"The only people who know are Alexis himself, who can talk no more, and God, who gets less of a look in now but was involved in this affair . . . For what it's worth, Major, I suppose Alexis did, said, demanded or reminded his father of something so terrible that Faustino decided to kill him. It seems the boy was beside himself and suicidal, and blamed Faustino for all his personal tragedy. Look what he wrote in this page from his Bible . . . Then he dressed as a woman,

206

went to meet him, they had a row and Faustino killed him. That simple."

"Has this country gone mad?" the Major asked, and the Count thought that was his moment.

"It seems to be the case. Must be the heat. Look what they did to Maruchi and Fatman Contreras . . ."

The Old Man stood up.

"Don't start, Conde, don't start," and now his voice floated in the air, exhausted and bitter. "What they did to Fatman? Do you know why I'm here now? Well, because of Captain Contreras . . . because Captain Contreras shat outside the pan, Mario Conde, and they caught it all sides."

The Count tried to smile. The Boss was bad at jokes, that's why he never told any. But this just had to be a joke.

"Are you mad, Major?"

"This is no madness, Conde. For starters, foreign currency trafficking, bribes and cooked investigations. For seconds, extortion and smuggling. And they've got loads of proof. What do you reckon now?"

Lieutenant Mario Conde felt in his pocket for a cigarette and, though his fingers touched the packet, he couldn't take it out. His friend, Captain Contreras, one of the best policemen he'd known. No, he thought, it can't be.

"This is shit those guys want to smear him with," he said, still resisting the idea.

"He did the shit and smeared me as well. It's his fault they're investigating even my hair . . . Wait, let me calm down." But he didn't shut up, only changed his tone: ever more exhausted and bitter. "He fucked it, Conde, fucked it, and there's no excuse . . . This morning the Chief Attorney put out the arrest warrant and they went after Contreras. That's how things stand . . . I think you know me: I trusted Captain Contreras, like I trust you, and got my fingers burnt for him, in fact up to my shoulder, and twice I stopped them investigating him, and put my rank, my position, even my rocks on this table to prevent them even suspecting him . . . But they were right all along, Conde, and I wasn't. Now I have to explain why I put my trust in Contreras. Do you know what that means? It's the end for me . . ."

"I'm off home, Boss," replied the Count, as he half turned round.

"You just stay there, you're not going anywhere. You finish your case. What the hell's up with you? Aren't you a policeman? Behave like a man, and then like police. Understood?"

The Count finally managed to extract the cigarette, light it and taste shit. He decided to sit down, as infinite exhaustion invaded his muscles and mind. The Boss was still the man he admired and respected, and didn't deserve him acting like a child. Would they screw the Major as well? No, I don't want even to imagine that, he thought.

"And since you're so interested in Maruchi's final destination, listen to this: she too worked for Internal Investigations and was the agent they planted here to trigger off this investigation, from that bastard desk out there, in front of my office door. How do you like that bit of news?"

"It's squalid and moving," he opted to say and nodded: another mask had dropped. "Well, Boss, let's finish this off: how shall we resolve the case? Should I bring him in and kick Faustino up the backside till he tells us his thousand and one nights, or do you have to call in someone and review all this?"

The Major eyed covetously the remnants of cigar in the envelopes. Then he looked in his desk drawer and took out another of those short, sinewy items he'd been smoking over the last few days.

"I've got to make a call, Mario. This is a bombshell, and you know it. This will resonate as far as Geneva when Arayán doesn't go to that conference on human rights . . . Yes, this country has gone mad. Look, they're now making cigars in Holguín and putting a Select label on them . . . A plague on Fatman Contreras's mother . . ."

The only thing Lieutenant Mario Conde would regret as investigator in charge of the Homicide Department at Headquarters would be not seeing Faustino Arayán's face the moment they arrested him, on the charge of murdering his son, and sentenced him, long before his trial, to lose all his perks and trips, all his immaculate affairs and dazzling *guayaberas*, an embassy close to heaven and his exquisite cigars, a mansion in Miramar with two cars in the garage, the taste of caviar and whisky – and I like whisky and can never drink any – his powerful friendships and the servant who, much to his chagrin, washed his clothes and always inspected them to gather more evidence on his sly sexual adventures which had become shakier and shakier, the same servant who on this occasion hadn't done her housework properly and had decided to keep to one side those trousers stained with river-mud from which hung two threads of red silk rotted by damp and years of censorship . . . The Count wondered whether they'd put him in a prison for common prisoners. Surely not. He was Faustino Arayán and, much to the Count's disgust, they wouldn't shut him inside a jail with murderers of every kind and type, capable of forcing him to clean out their cells and their sexual backwardness, making his arse as pink as a bunch of carnations without even paying him two copper pesos. Apart from that, he was glad he'd concluded the investigation and could return to his isle of melancholy and longing for coffee which never came, to think about Polly and the next story he was going to write, about Skinny's birthday in four days' time, to observe the disorder reigning at home and to think how it might always have turned out differently: even Fatman Contreras might have turned out differently. What would happen to the Boss? he wondered, and refused even to contemplate the response he could imagine.

Two captains, dressed in plainclothes, had arrived around midday and the Count explained the details of the case and handed over the paltry incriminating evidence: three gutted cigars, a medallion with the engraved figure of the Universal Man, two yellow coins and a page with a couple of chapters from the Bible which revealed to mankind the divine essence of Joseph the carpenter's putative son and the nature of his huge sacrifice in the Kingdom of This World. He then pointed them in the direction of the laboratory, where they were still analysing the silk threads and mud from the river Almendares. The officers congratulated him on the speed and efficiency with which he'd brought the investigation to a conclusion and assured him they'd revisit his temporary suspension, because Cuba needed people like him. And explained – although you don't need these explanations, you're a policeman and know about these things – it was a case surrounded by special circumstances and required special treatment. The Count agreed, and they couldn't imagine that, opening the door and going into the corridor, he only regretted not seeing Faustino Arayán's face when they severed the ties of the mask which had finally become his face. Would he cry? Beg for forgiveness? Would he kneel down, stoop petulantly? Yes, he'd like to be there to witness the scene, the downfall of a man capable of judging and condemning, classifying, casting out and crushing people and lives like pesky flies in line with his rigid political and moral criteria. Human rights? Screw him, he finally regretted, yet again, he would miss out on that final performance after labouring so much time on the job . . . And then he thought there were additional regrets: he would like to know what Alexis had said to his father, what words provoked his homicidal anger, and also to know what was going on in Alexis Arayán's mind when he donned the unbecoming gown of Electra Garrigó, on that suicidal night when he went out to manufacture his death, though he knew the truth had been lost, had departed for ever with the fears, hates and life of that part-time transvestite. And he'd also like to know – and naturally regretted not knowing – why such terrible events happened in the world where his trade obliged him to get enveloped, as in a tragic mantle . . . And Fatman Contreras? A corrupt policeman, who used his position, uniform and badge to screw everyone else? No, he still said, refusing to accept what apparently could no longer be denied.

When he went out into the car park at Head-quarters, the Count felt all the heat in the city descend on him, as must happen when you cross the black waters of the Styx, before the sulphurous doors of a world from which there was no return.

"Did you take María Antonia back?" he asked Manuel Palacios, as he got in the car.

"Yes, she told me to take her to Miramar. She wanted to collect up her things. She says she'll go to her brother's tonight."

211

"At least she'll see the unmasking. I hope she enjoys it ... Take me home, I need to sleep. Perchance to dream," he quoted, lit a cigarette and spat into the street. "What a load of shit, right?"

"Yes, Conde, and what shit ... Hey, does it seem stupid if I ask you to forgive me for the silly things I said the other day?"

The sweat woke him up, his skin as slimy as an eel. He looked for the red figures on his electronic clock and found a blank screen. The fan had also stopped turning. But how can the power go at this time of day, he protested, when he finally found his wristwatch and saw it was barely four o'clock. Penetrating the thickness of his curtains, the reflection from the sun drifted rudely into his room, like a favour imposed which he couldn't refuse. He'd intended waking when it was dark. He got up and went after the mortal remains of the coffee he'd made that morning. As he drank, he looked through the window at the perspectives for his most immediate future and for the first time in several months they seemed vaguely promising. He smoked quietly and, when he was about to take a shower, the telephone rang.

"It's me, Mario."

"Yes, Major, what's the matter?"

"The man's here, he's confessed already."

"And how did he perform?"

"Well, he says it must have been a moment of madness, that he never planned to do it, and puts all the blame on Alexis. He says he left the Hotel Riviera, where he had an appointment with an Italian deputy who is a personal friend, and bumped into a woman at the side of his car. He says he didn't recognize her to

212

begin with, but looked at her because there was something odd about her, then realized it was Alexis." Major
Rangel's intentionally monotone voice continued
the story while Conde's mind, already racing on
ahead, visualized one scene after another, to the tragic
dénouement: the character of the tall man, who'd
been faceless till that morning, now wore the face of a
Faustino Arayán shocked to see his son, dressed as a
woman, waiting for him by the exit from a hotel.

"What are you doing here in that woman's clothing?"

"Nothing. I was waiting for you to take me home.
Toña told me you'd be here. Can you drive me or does
it make you very embarrassed to see me like this?"

Alexis doesn't get a reply, but his father gets into his
car and opens the far side door. Annoyed, Faustino
lights one of the Montecristos he's carrying in a pocket
and the inside of the car is flooded with smoke that
disappears as soon as the car sets off.

"And what will you do at home in that dress? Have
you gone mad? Doesn't it upset you walking the streets
like that? Where've you been dressed up like that?"

"I got dressed in the hotel bathroom and I'm not
upset at all . . . Today I felt my life would change. I saw
a light, which gave me an order: do what you must do
and go to see your father."

"You are mad."

"I couldn't be more lucid."

"Tell me what you want for God's sake and don't
fuck around any more."

"Let's go into the Woods, where we can speak more
calmly."

Once again Faustino thought his son had gone
mad, that he was provoking him and that perhaps it
was better to resolve everything before they reached
home. He turns left and the car goes down to the

Havana Woods, where at that time of night a breeze contrasts with the heat in the rest of the city.

"Let's go towards the river. I want to see the river."

"Fine, fine. Well, what was it you wanted to tell me?"

And Alexis told him he hated him, had only contempt for him, that he was an opportunist and hypocrite, and suddenly launched an attack on his face. Faustino dropped his cigar and pushed Alexis, who fell to his knees on the grass, but only to spring back up and attack him, and Faustino, not realizing what he was doing, went into action with the swathe of silk he'd taken from the waist of that equivocal, enraged woman who in turn was putting him in a rage, attacking him, making him mad, and by the time he realized what he was doing, Alexis had collapsed, his lungs without oxygen . . . What do you reckon?"

"Sounds pretty good, but you missed out half the story. Alexis said something else, which is what drove him mad: he threatened to do or reveal something, whatever . . . And I think that's why he paid him with two coins."

"You're inventing now, Conde."

"I'm inventing nothing, Boss. Alexis had already called him an opportunist, a hypocrite and hateful person a thousand times. They must find out what Alexis knew that might be very dangerous for his father . . . Alexis told him because he knew he'd react like that. Let them dig out the whole story and they'll see some horrible things crawl out, or my name's not Mario Conde. But they've got to put the screws on, Boss, like with any criminal."

"I can imagine . . ."

"And what about the coins?"

"He says he was very scared and suddenly thought of

214

that to put people off track, so they'd think it was a homosexual scrap."

"What a bastard! And what does he say about the medallion?"

"He says he thought maybe nobody would identify Alexis, and that's why he took it. But he forgot he might be carrying his identity card."

"Yes, I didn't think that a woman carrying his identity card was very elegant either. So we're both agreed on that. I'm sorry for my part."

"He says he put the medallion in the trinket-box that same evening . . . Now all he does is to put all the blame on Alexis and say he doesn't know how it all happened. You know what it's like."

"Yes, Boss, I know what it's like, but don't forget one thing: that guy's a bastard with real pedigree and comes with a guarantee . . . You must have a really twisted mind to think about taking a medallion from a strangled man who is your own son in order to try to save your own skin and then put two coins up his arse for good measure. And why does he reckon he didn't throw him in the river?"

"He says a motorbike drove by and he took fright. That was when he removed the medallion."

"Well, the guy's sick . . . Hey, Boss, don't start feeling sorry for him . . ."

"No, don't be like that, Mario, everything will be done by the book."

The Major's voice now sounded mellow and peaceful, and the Count thought it was better that way: everything should be mellow and peaceful, and he decided he'd start lifting the red ghost of Alexis Arayán from his shoulders.

"Well, good luck to you and him . . . Boss, how about giving me a week's holidays?"

"What's up? Don't tell me you want to do some writing?"

"No, of course not. That's history. I'm just exhausted and fed up. What about you?"

The silence floated down the line more than it usually did with Major Rangel.

"I'm fed up, Conde. And disappointed . . . I think I'm going to hang up the sword. But forget it. Take a week and, if you can, start writing. Learn to help yourself and quit the self-pity . . . Come back next Monday. If I need you I'll call you before, OK?"

"OK, Boss, look after yourself. And you know, I'll get you some real good cigars," he said, as he hung up.

While he showered, he thought he'd more than enough time to tell the Marquess the last chapter of that sordid story the whole truth about which would never be known. But he owed him that version. He tried to imagine how he'd tell it to the dramatist, and realized that all he was doing was concealing the real anxiety he felt at the prospect of the visit: he'd take his manuscript to the old dramatist. Will he like it? he wondered as he washed, when he got dressed, as he went into the street, and was still wondering when he let the door knocker fall for a third time and waited for the curtains to open on the theatrical world of Alberto Marqués.

"You're a surprising man, Mr Friendly Policeman. So much so that I now think you're a fake policeman. It's like another form of transvesting, right? The difference being that you've stripped off . . . and everything's out in the open," said the Marquess, waving the pages of the story like a fan.

"But . . . what do you think?" implored the Count, shy at his perceived nudity.

The dramatist smiled but tittered not. That Sunday evening he wore a towelling dressing gown, a degree less decrepit than his silk one, and in order to read he'd opened all the windows in the room and lifted the pages up close to his eyes, and at last the Count managed to construct a precise idea of the set where they'd been meeting recently. It was the image one always forms of an attic or one of those dusty, cobwebby places, ripe for a horror film, which don't exist in Cuban houses, even less so in those with such lofty ceilings. As the Marquess read, the Count smoked two cigars and concentrated on creating an inventory of what might be useful from that surrealist accumulation of objects that one never usually saw: apart from the two armchairs where they sat, the lieutenant thought that a very grainy wooden table, a bronze leg which must have sustained an Art Nouveau lamp and a few plates that looked healthy, perhaps even bone china, were just salvageable. The rest reeked of exquisite corpses, without the option of resurrection: they must be the final remains of the autophagy the Marquess had surely practised on his own house.

"I'll tell you what I think later. First tell me something. Have you recently read Camus or Sartre?"

The Count looked for a cigarette.

"No, I've hardly had time to read. Why?"

"Are you familiar with *The Outsider*?" The Count nodded and his host smiled again. "Well, your bus driver really reminds me of Mr Meursault in *The Outsider* . . . That metaphorical possibility is beautiful, isn't it? French existentialism and Cuban buses bonded by the glare of the sun." And he smiled again

217

and the Count felt like grabbing him by the neck. The bastard's making fun of me.

"So you think it's silly."

"But it doesn't have a title," proceeded the Marquess, as if he'd not heard the lament of the Count, who was now shaking his head. "Well, I've thought of one, seeing these people are dead before they've died physically: 'Iron in the Soul'. What do you reckon?"

"I'm not sure, I think I like it."

"Well, if you want, I'll make you a present of it. After all, it's Sartre's . . ."

"Thank you," the Count had to respond, as he thought it made no sense to ask for his final opinion on the already devalued quality of that story from his soul.

"It's funny reading stories like that again . . . In another era you'd certainly have been accused of adopting aesthetic postures of a bourgeois, anti-Marxist character. Just imagine this reading of the story: there's no logical or dialectical explanation of your characters' irrational behaviour or their anec-dotes; it's obvious these creatures cannot explain the chaos in human life, while the narrator's naturalist detail only reinforces the desolation of the man who received, God knows from where, an illumination in his existence. Such an aesthetic could then have been said (as was often said) to be a simple reflection of the spiritual degeneration of the modern bourgeoisie. Besides, your work offers no solutions to the social situations you pinpoint, just to state what's most obvi-ous: you communicate a sordid image of man in a society like ours . . . How do you like that interpret-ation? Poor existentialism . . . And what should we do then with those ever so horribly beautiful works by Camus and Sartre and Simone? . . . And poor Scott

Fitzgerald and eschatological Henry Miller and the good characters in Carpentier and the dark world of Onetti? Decapitate the history of culture and of man's uncertainties? . . . But you know what surprised me most: it's your ability to create a fable. You don't write like a fledgling, friendly policeman, but like a writer, although I'd have preferred a different ending: she should have killed the bus driver . . . And, tell me, where did you get the idea to write this story? The mystery of creation has always fascinated me."

"I don't know, I think because I saw a bus driver with a bus-driver's face, and recently people have said I've got a policeman's face."

The Marquess's smile dissolved into a string of titters which seemed bent on disarming him once and for all, and the Count was on the point of standing up and leaving the house.

"And you believed me, Mr Friendly Policeman? I was only joking. Or it was self-defence, I'm not sure. I wanted to create a distance, you know. Fear and suspicion? The fact is when you've been beaten once, you learn to raise your arms before they try to beat you again. Like Pavlov's dog. But I think I went too far with you, really: I'm not as perverse, ironic, or . . . or as pansied as I make out. No way. So please forgive me if I showed a lack of respect. I'd like you to forgive all my ironies."

"So you said you liked my story?" insisted the Count wanting a simple declaration bereft of equivocal verbal whirls.

"But didn't you hear me? I told you . . . I'll go even further: I admire you as a policeman. The cigar thing was a mark of genius, right? I'd never have thought of that dramatic solution as catalyst to the tragedy which had been woven . . . Because I don't know if you noticed how it was all like a Greek tragedy, in the best style of Sophocles, full of ambiguity, parallel stories that began twenty years ago and which come together on the same day and characters who aren't who they say they are, or who hide what they are, or have changed so much nobody now knows who they are, and at an unexpected moment there is tragic recognition. But they all confront a destiny that goes beyond them, that forces, drives them to make dramatic acts: only here Laius kills Oedipus, or Aegisthus anticipates Orestes . . . Should it be dubbed filicide? . . . And all is unleashed because of the *hubris* committed. There are excesses of passion, of ambition for power, of pent-up hatred, and that's usually severely punished . . . What is really regrettable in this almost theatrical game is that the gods chose Alexis to sacrifice his destiny morbidly. What that poor boy did has grieved me sorely. At my age I've seen too many people die, dozens of friends, all my family, and each close death is an alarm bell warning that mine may be next, and the older I get, the greater my fear of death. But now I'm very pleased you've unmasked this gentleman and that he's been jailed . . . Because I'll tell you something else: do you want to know where the lines of this tragedy began to cross? In Paris, that spring of 1969: Faustino Arayán was the embassy functionary who rang Muscles' place that day to say the Other Boy was at the police station. And he was the one who decided the Other should go back to Cuba, and sent him back wrapped in papers where he'd wiped all the shit he could find, about the Other and about me, naturally. And, obviously, Alexis was also fully aware . . ."

The feast was finally over and I left Paris in the rain. Because springtime in Paris is so fragile: winter's

220

deathbed rattle can launch an attack with an impunity that is simply an awful revenge. The bad weather started without warning and the windows we left open during the day to the season's pleasant noises and smells had suddenly to be shut, so we could see through the glass how the icy rain abused the virgin shoots on the trees in the nearby square. Two days before, I'd finished my research in the Artaud papers and also my course of master classes at the Théâtre des Nations, where I'd expounded for the first time in public my new idea for a production of *Electra Garrigó* based on what I called a transvestite aesthetic. It was a success, in fact, my last great public success ... From Sartre to Grotowski, by way of Truffaut, Néstor Almendros, Julio Cortázar and Simone Signoret, I was praised publicly and privately and was invited there and then to present the work the following season, with performances in six French cities. I was at the height of my dreams when it began to rain in Paris, as if it had never rained before, and I decided to return to the sure but merciless sun of Havana, in a feverish haste to get on with my work. Muscles accompanied me to Orly, and we could never have imagined that that embrace and kiss on my neck would be last carnal contact I'd have with him. We'd never see each other again.

As soon as I arrived I started work. I let the other directors get on with the year's repertory and shut myself up in my house with Virgilio's text, and began to elaborate my idea for the production. By December I had the first libretto ready, with all the sketches for the sets and costumes, the staging of scenes and acts, and a tentative cast in which actors from various groups participated, because I had to engage the best from Cuban theatre. But the sugar harvest had begun

221

and the entire country was cutting and grinding sugar cane: even actors and theatre technicians, and I had to wait till July to have the chance to work with the actors I wanted. I wrote to Paris and explained the reasons behind the delay and they very kindly postponed the tour to the *annus horribilis* of 1971, and then I used the time to prepare the best ever Spanish edition of *The Theatre and Its Double* . . .

Finally, on 6 September I gathered in the theatre all those who were going to work on the project and made a first reading of the script, and explained the requirements for the stage, lighting, costumes and acting. The applause at the end, a standing ovation, convinced me beyond doubt I'd reached the gates of heaven: I only had to knock and Saint Peter would welcome me with open arms . . . And we started work. Although everything turned very difficult (the material for the costumes, the making of the thirty-two masks, the immaculate costume for the Centaur-Pedagogue, the scenery design), we gradually got the necessary and in January moved on from plain rehearsals to dress rehearsals on stage. What the actors had to do was really complicated and I demanded nothing short of perfection. They had to handle the masks as if they were their own faces and that meant special training, lots and lots of practice, and we spent long hours watching films of Japanese theatre. I then began to invite very specific people to see the rehearsals and they all left on cloud nine. Only Virgilio said something which, in my euphoria, I failed to register: Marqués, this is better than what I wrote, more intense, more provocative, and you've quite thrown me arse over tit, that is, my arse is all over the place . . . But, my friend, it's too turbulent and cruel and I'm afraid it'll upset . . . In fact, the air was already murky, but I failed to see the danger signals coming from every direction. I've always had a problem believing weather forecasts. I let passion take over and shut ears and eyes to anything that's not my single goal . . . And so we finally set the première in Havana for April and the start of the tour in France for May. And then began the last act in the affair which ended with the performance the four bureaucrats put on behind the dissecting table on the set . . . One day I got a call to say there were problems with the Paris trip. They'd received reports about the fairly serious moral problems during my last stay in France, and they even knew I'd lodged at Muscles' place, that I had an ambiguous attitude to the revolutionary process and suspiciously cordial relationships with certain pseudo-revolutionary and revisionist French intellectual circles . . . That I'd met up with Néstor Almendros and other people who held critical attitudes, including even loyal Julio Cortázar, and it was then they started to tell me things which only two people knew, Muscles and the Other Boy. I was told the Paris embassy was fully informed about all the goings-on, and I discovered they'd lumped together lies and truth in surprising fashion: the events were real and only the Other could have told them that way, because his vulgar stamp was obvious on all they recounted, but their conclusions would have made you piss yourself with laughter if it hadn't been so serious. There they could say anything they liked about my character, my work, my morality, my attitude, my ideology and even the way I breathed . . . But I still didn't give up . . . I wrote to Muscles to ask him to use his influence in Paris to activate the invitations and send them the most official way possible, and I kept the April première date in Cuba. Then the master stroke: in one week my production said goodbye to Orestes,

223

the Pedagogue, Clytemnestra Pla and even Electra Garrigó . . . I thought I'd die, but I still didn't give up and I started to look for other actors, to the very day they summoned us all to the theatre and it was decided, in my absence, to expel me from the group by twenty-four votes for and two abstentions.

Two months later the Other Boy published an article on Cuban theatre which didn't mention my name or work, as if I'd never existed or it were impossible I might ever exist again . . . I then understood there was nothing doing, or that I could do nothing but retreat into my shell, like a persecuted snail. And I let the curtain fall. I gave in and took every punishment: first, factory work, then library work, forgot theatre and publishing, trips and interviews, was transformed into a nobody. And I assumed my role as a live ghost, performed with mask and all for so long, that what you see as a white mask is now my very own face.

"Really?" the Marquess said and added, "Come with me," and the Count followed him through the living-room, across the bedroom and down the passage to the room which reeked of damp, ancient dust and old papers. The dramatist switched on the light and the policeman found himself surrounded by books, from the floor to the highest point of the ceiling, books the number and quality of which was incalculable, in dissimilar bindings and volumes, in various sizes and colours: books.

"Take a good look, what can you see?"

"Well, books."

"Yes, books, but as a writer you must know when you are seeing something more. Look, that one there is the edition of *Paradise Lost* which I stole with illustrations by Gustave Doré. Now I'll ask you something: who would know the name of Milton's neighbour, a very wealthy man, much feared in his time, and one who perhaps one day accused him of some barbarity or other? You don't know? Of course: nobody knows or should know, but everyone remembers who the poet was. And was Dante a Guelph or a Ghibeline? You don't know that either, do you, but you do know he wrote *The Divine Comedy* and that his reputation is greater than that of any politician of his time. For that is what is invincible ... And now I'll tell you why I brought you here!"

And he walked over to one of the shelves and took down a red folder tied with ribbons which one day had been white and now lay under several layers of dust.

"I'll tell you this, Friendly Policeman, because I think I owe it to you, as I owe you an apology for my excesses with you ... Herein are eight plays written in my silent years, and the other folder you can see contains a 300-page essay on the re-creation of Greek myths in Western theatre in the twentieth century. What do you reckon?"

The Count gestured: shook his head.

"And why is all this hidden away? Why don't you try to publish it?"

"Because of what I said before: my character must endure silence till the end. But that's the character: the actor did what he had to do, and that's why I keep writing, because, one day, as with Milton, they'll remember the writer and nobody will even recall the sad functionary who repressed him. They wouldn't allow me to publish or direct, but no one could prevent me writing and thinking. These two folders are my best revenge, do you understand me now?"

"I think so," replied the Count, and caressed the

typed pages of his story and realized right then that he didn't know where he should take it. Perhaps it was only a story for three readers: himself, Skinny Carlos and Alberto Marqués, and yet that was enough for him. No, he didn't feel a need to expose himself further, or have pretensions to literature: just do it, for the Marquess was right: those pages contained what was invincible.

"I also want to apologize, Alberto. At times I must have been too rough with you."

"Oh, my honey chil'! You're an angel! You don't know what it is to be rough with me. Look, if I tell you . . . Better not, forget it."

The Count smiled, remembering the stories he'd heard about the Marquess's erotic adventures, in that very house. Well, whatever they say, he is a pansy, that's no lie, but I like the man, he concluded.

"Come on, let's sit down," the Marquess suggested and they went back to the sitting room, as the Count lit a cigarette.

"I must admit I'm the one who's now arse over tit," the policeman said as he returned to his seat and position on that stage set. "But all these confessions have reinforced an idea I've been harbouring for two or three days: you know something you've not told me and which could help explain Alexis's death. Will you tell me now or must I interrogate you?"

"Ah, so you think there's more to it . . . I get the full bloodhound treatment now, do I? So you want to know more?" the Marquess persisted and, not waiting for a reply, he raised one of his arms so his dressing gown sleeve created a space where, like a spectacular magician, he could put in a hand and pluck something out to show the Count. "You want me to tell you what Alexis said to Faustino to cause him to react that way? But I shouldn't tell you, because when Alexis told me, and he did tell me, he made me swear on the Bible that, whatever happened, I wouldn't tell anybody. And I never have . . . That's why I've gone silent, right?"

The Count smiled.

"So now you believe in sacred oaths? Even though the secrecy may save Alexis's murderer or attenuate his guilt?"

The Marquess wiped a hand over his sparsely populated head and smiled devilishly.

"True, if I don't believe in anything and that gentleman is . . . But I should tell you I also kept silent because I didn't think the man capable of doing what he did . . . For what Alexis said to him was that he'd found out about the fraud his father committed in 1959, when he falsified documents and got himself a couple of false witnesses to swear he'd fought clandestinely against Batista . . . That was how Faustino climbed on the chariot of the Revolution, with a past to guarantee he could be considered a trustworthy man who deserved his reward . . . Can you imagine what would happen if this got out? Well, you know: his feast would be at an end."

The Count tried to smile but couldn't. Another of this bastard's tall stories, he thought.

"That's why he paid him with two coins . . . And how did Alexis find out about this business? Who could have told him?"

"María Antonia told him . . ."

"And why did she tell him?"

"I don't know, perhaps she thought Alexis should have that card in his hand, you know?"

The Count finally smiled.

"So it was María Antonia. The things María Antonia knew; and I thought . . ."

227

"Yes, you're naive, my policeman friend. But it's better that way: better naive than cynical. That's why I'll make one more confession to you: many of the accusations made against me are true: I am self-sufficient, proud, an experimentalist and ever since my twelfth birthday when I saw I was in love with my sister's boyfriend, I've known the only antidote was to frolic wherever with men, which I've been doing ever since. Because I'm that way, yesterday, today and tomorrow as the saying goes . . ."

The Count never thought he'd listen to something like that and find it appealing and wouldn't want to get up and kick such an exultant little poof. But anyway he did decide it was time to beat a timely retreat and try to tie up the last loose ends to his case.

"Did Arayán write that report?"

"Who did, if he didn't? He was always a sly, insidious cunt on the make."

"And what's the latest on Muscles?"

"This is all awful, isn't it? I discovered he's very ill, really ill. They say he's got a few months . . . My poor friend. He suffered a lot from what they did to me. Perhaps even more than I did."

"Right," the Count responded, standing up. "I've got to go. But I must ask you two last questions . . ."

"It never changes: always two last questions."

"Who is the Other Boy?"

"Haven't you guessed? Ah, you're not such a good policeman after all. I gave you all the clues. So find out for yourself and don't get into deep water. And what's the other one?"

"The day I went for a pee in your bathroom, did you take a peek?"

The Marquess rehearsed that gesture of amazement the Count was already familiar with: his mouth formed a huge silent O and he put his right hand on his chest, as if about to swear an oath.

"Me? Do you think I'd do that kind of thing, Mr Friendly Policeman?"

"Yes."

Then he laughed, but tittered not.

"Well, your mind has an evil bent . . ."

"If you say so."

"Of course I do . . . Hey, I'd like to ask you a little favour: keep my secret. I've become fond of you and when I get fond of someone, I love to go confessional. But only three people know what's in those folders and you're one of them."

"Don't worry. I won't even ask who the other one is, apart from Muscles . . . OK, I'm off. Thanks for everything."

"When will you be back?"

"When I write another story or they kill another transvestite. Here's the book by Muscles you lent me, so I don't owe you anything, do I? Well, next to nothing . . ." he said, and stretched his hand out to the Marquess, who placed his squalid bony structure on the Count's palm. If Fatman Contreras grabs you . . . the lieutenant thought, and lightly pressed the dramatist's hand, but dropped it immediately, for he thought he glimpsed a dangerous advance light up on the Marquess's face. Does he want to kiss me? No, that's not on, he thought, and went into the street, where a magenta sun was putting its final delicate purple touches to the languid, velvety death agony of a Sunday afternoon more pansied than Alberto Marqués himself.

As he dived into the old part of the city, the Count's eyes interrogated every woman who crossed his path:

could she be a transvestite, he wondered, looking for a revealing detail in her make-up, hands, the shape of her breasts and curve of her buttocks. Two young women who were walking along, swinging their hips, arm-in-arm, struck him as slightly suspect of transform-ism, but the half-dark in the street didn't allow him to reach a verdict. He then understood that he wanted to meet a transvestite. Why? he wondered, unable to find an answer, and, as he walked up to Polly's flat, he thought how he should rid his head of all that ballast if he wanted to lift himself up and enjoy the spectacle of seeing a female, especially a Cuban female on a street in Havana, and think those dancing breasts, unattain-able buttocks and juicy lips might be just for him.

Polly welcomed him in her doorway, barely covered by a white dressing gown which revealed the reddish dark of her nipples and the black of her nether hair. She didn't given him a chance to speak but leapt on him and shot her tongue between his lips, like an anxious snake.

"Oh God, how wonderful, my heterosexual police-man," she cried when she'd finished her frisking by mouth, and her hand pressed the perky tumescence of a Count who asked her, bursting with pride: "Were you expecting me?"

"What do you think, you macho Stalinist? And what have you got in that bag?" was what she then asked as she turned to look inside his pack, but the Count stopped her.

"Wait, first I've got to ask you something . . . Can I stay here for three days, without going out or seeing the sun?"

She smiled and showed a row of sharp little sparrow teeth.

"Doing what?"

230

"Something you never tire of . . ."

"I think so."

"Well, take my bag and put it in the sideboard. I've brought ten eggs, a can of sardines, two bottles of rum, five boxes of cigars, a chunk of bread and a packet of macaroni. That will make us strong enough to resist the siege . . . You got any coffee? Good, then we're invincible, like Milton."

"Which Milton?"

"The Brazilian musician . . . Now I need to make a telephone call," he said finally, as he stripped his shirt off.

"Boss, listen to me and prepare to fall off your chair," he said as he smiled and told him the last possible revelation on the masquerade of Faustino Arayán. "Well, what do you reckon?"

"What I said before: this country has gone mad." And his voice sounded neutral, neither astonished nor exhausted: it was simply an empty voice, and the Count thought what he'd thought on other occasions: his voice was the mirror of his soul.

"OK, I've earned my week off, haven't I?"

"Yes, you certainly have. I hope one day you'll decide to be a good policeman . . . Talking of which, will you tell me some time why you ever joined the police, eh, Conde?"

"Well, I'll try to find out and then I'll tell you . . . Oh, I can tell you one thing I do know: you're the best police chief in the world, whatever they say or do."

"Thanks, Mario, it's always good to know such things, though they sometimes don't help one little bit."

"Yes, they do help, Boss, and you know it. Look after yourself and I'll see you Monday," he said as he hung up to ring Skinny's number. It only needed three rings.

"Skinny, it's me."

"Go on, wild man. You going to drop by?"

"No, I can't tomorrow or the day after . . . I'm with little sparrow butt. I asked her for asylum for three days."

"Hey, have you fallen for that little madcap?"

"I don't know, Skinny. I think my thinking head isn't thinking so much, and it's just as well."

"Sure . . . But watch the other head, for when it fancies an idea . . ."

"Note down my number. Six, one, three, four, five, six. That's for you and old Josefina, but don't give it out even to death if she makes a call. Or the Guggenheim Foundation, or Salinger if he comes to Havana to see me, right? Oh, give it to Red Candito if he needs me for something . . ."

"And what if those investigators want to see you?"

"Let them go to hell. Skinny, to hell, or they can set their sniffer dogs after me. We're going to mount the Cuban version of *The Fugitive* . . . Oh, and I was forgetting the most important thing with all this shit I'm pouring out: buy two bottles of rum for Wednesday, and I'll give you the money. It's my birthday present. I'll call Andrés and the Rabbit to see what we can think up for the day, all right?"

"No problem. Do you know what the old woman wants to do on my birthday? She says an Argentine roast-up, with best beef, porterhouse, fillet, chitterlings . . . Hey, and remember you didn't bring me a photocopy of your story, right?"

"But I'll bring it on Wednesday . . . What's happening about Dulcita?"

The Count knew he would have to wait and he waited with all the patience he could muster.

"Nothing, Conde, what the fuck can I do? If she

comes, well, let her come, and I'll see her and tell her: 'It's life, my love.' "

"Yes, it's life, a fuck-up. Well, let's speak later. A big hug for my brother," and he hung up.

Polly was waiting for him on the edge of her bed, a glass of rum in each hand, and the Count thought it wasn't right to feel happy while Skinny, who was no longer skinny, a victim of a geopolitical war in which he'd been a pawn destroyed, had had shut off any avenue to that necessary satisfaction and he anguished over the idea that one of his old flames might see him at the bottom of the void. He caressed Polly's fringe, chose the fullest glass and went out shirtless on to the small balcony wanting to relieve his physical and mental heat, and observed, as night began to fall, the roof terraces of Old Havana, spiky with aerials, desire to collapse and stories impossible to contain. Why the hell did it have to be like that? Because life is like that and not any other way. Was it possible to retrace steps and right wrongdoings, mistakes, errors? Impossible, Conde, though you can still be invincible, he told himself, when, in the heart of that darkness, he spotted the extravagant flight of that white pigeon, which sprang from a dream and mocked her habits as a daytime animal, defied the torrid night and soared high, relentlessly vertical, and then opened her wings and pirouetted strangely, as if at that moment she had discovered the dizzy sensation of plunging into the void, till he lost sight of her, behind a building worm-eaten by time. I'm that pigeon, he thought, and thought that, like her, he could do nothing else: only soar high till he disappeared into the night-time sky.

Mantilla, 1994–5

FEVER

Friedrich Glauser

"With good reason, the German language prize for detective fiction is named after Glauser. . . He has Simenon's ability to turn a stereotype into a person, and the moral complexity to appeal to justice over the head of police procedure."
Times Literary Supplement

When two women are "accidentally" killed by gas leaks, Sergeant Studer investigates the thinly disguised double murder in Bern and Basel. The trail leads to a geologist dead from a tropical fever in a Moroccan Foreign Legion post and a murky oil deal involving rapacious politicians and their henchmen. With the help of a hashish-induced dream and the common sense of his stay-at-home wife, Studer solves the multiple riddles on offer. But assigning guilt remains an elusive affair.

Fever, a European crime classic, was first published in 1936 and is the third in the Sergeant Studer series published by Bitter Lemon Press.

Praise for Glauser's other Sergeant Studer novels

"*Thumbprint* is a fine example of the craft of detective writing in a period which fans will regard as the golden age of crime fiction." *Sunday Telegraph*

"*Thumbprint* is a genuine curiosity that compares to the dank poetry of Simenon and reveals the enormous debt owed by Dürenmatt, Switzerland's most famous crime writer, for whom this should be seen as a template." *Guardian*

"A despairing plot about the reality of madness and life, leavened at regular intervals with strong doses of bittersweet irony. The idiosyncratic investigation of *In Matto's Realm* and its laconic detective have not aged one iota." *Guardian*

"Glauser was among the best European crime writers of the inter-war years. The detail, place and sinister characters are so intelligently sculpted that the sense of foreboding is palpable." *Glasgow Herald*

£9.99/$14.95
Crime paperback original
ISBN 1–904738–14–1/978–1904738–14–5
www.bitterlemonpress.com

FRAMED

Tonino Benacquista

"One of France's leading crime and mystery authors."
Guardian

Antoine's life is good. During the day he hangs pictures for the most fashionable art galleries in Paris. Evenings he dedicates to the silky moves and subtle tactics of billiards, his true passion. But when Antoine is attacked by an art thief in a gallery his world begins to fall apart. His maverick investigation triggers two murders – he finds himself the prime suspect for one of them – as he uncovers a cesspool of art fraud. A game of billiards decides the outcome of this violently funny tale, laced with brilliant riffs about the world of modern art and the parasites that infest it.

In 2004 Bitter Lemon Press introduced Tonino Benacquista to English-speaking readers with the critically acclaimed novel *Holy Smoke*.

PRAISE FOR *FRAMED*

"Screenwriter for the award-winning French crime movie *The Beat That My Heart Skipped*, Tonino Benacquista is also a wonderful observer of everyday life, petty evil and the ordinariness of crime. The pace never falters as personal grief collides with outrageous humour and a biting running commentary on the crooked world of modern art."
Guardian

"Edgy, offbeat black comedy." *The Times*

"Flip and frantic foray into art galleries and billiards halls of modern Paris." *Evening Standard*

"A black comedy that is set in Paris but reflects its author's boisterous Italian sensibility. The manic tale is told by an apprentice picture-hanger who encounters a thief in a fashionable art gallery and becomes so caught up in a case of art fraud that he himself 'touches up' a Kandinsky."
New York Times

£9.99/$14.95
Crime paperback original
ISBN 1–904738–16–8/978–1904738–16–9
www.bitterlemonpress.com

HAVANA BLACK

Leonardo Padura

A MARIO CONDE MYSTERY

"The mission of that enterprising Bitter Lemon Press is to publish English translations of the best foreign crime fiction. The newest addition to its list is the prize-winning Cuban novelist Leonardo Padura" *The Telegraph*

The brutally mutilated body of Miguel Forcade is discovered washed up on a Havana beach. Head smashed in by a baseball bat, genitals cut off with a blunt knife. Forcade was once responsible for confiscating art works from the bourgeoisie fleeing the revolution. Had he really returned from exile just to visit his ailing father?

Lieutenant Mario Conde immerses himself in Cuba's dark history, expropriations of priceless paintings now vanished without trace, corruption and old families who appear to have lost much, but not everything.

Padura evokes the disillusionment of a generation, yet this novel is a eulogy to Cuba, and to the great friendships of those who chose to stay and fight for survival.

PRAISE FOR *HAVANA BLACK*

"A great plot, perfectly executed with huge atmosphere. You can almost smell the cigar smoke, rum and cheap women."
Daily Mirror

"This is a strong tasting book. A rich feast of wit and feeling." *The Independent*

"Well-plotted second volume of Padura's seething, steamy Havana Quartet. This densely packed mystery should attract readers outside the genre." *Publishers Weekly*

"Lt. Mario Conde, known on the street as 'the Count,' is prone to metaphysical reflection on the history of his melancholy land but the city of Havana keeps bursting through his meditations, looking very much alive."
New York Times

£9.99/$14.95
Crime paperback original
ISBN 1–904738–15–X/978–1904738–15–2
www.bitterlemonpress.com

THE MANNEQUIN MAN

Luca Di Fulvio

Shortlisted for the European Crime Writing Prize

"Di Fulvio exposes souls with the skills of a surgeon, It's like turning the pages of something forbidden – seduction, elegant and dangerous." *Alan Rickman*

"Know why she's smiling?" he asked, pointing a small torch at the corpse. "Fish hooks. Two fish hooks at the corners of her mouth, a bit of nylon, pull it round the back of the head and tie a knot. Pretty straightforward, right?" Amaldi noticed the metallic glint at the corners of the taut mouth.

Inspector Amaldi has enough problems. A city choked by a pestilent rubbish strike, a beautiful student harassed by a telephone stalker, a colleague dying of cancer and the mysterious disappearance of arson files concerning the city's orphanage. Then the bodies begin to appear.

This novel of violence and decay, with its vividly portrayed characters, takes place over a few oppressive weeks in an unnamed Italian city that strongly evokes Genoa.

The Italian press refers to Di Fulvio as a grittier, Italian Thomas Harris, and *Eyes of Crystal*, the film of the novel, was launched at the 2004 Venice Film Festival.

" A novel that caresses and kisses in order to violate the reader with greater ease." *Rolling Stone*

"A powerful psycho-thriller of spine-shivering intensity . . . written with immense intelligence and passionate menace. Not to be read alone at night." *The Times*

"A wonderful first novel that will seduce the fans of deranged murderers in the style of Hannibal Lecter. And beautifully written to boot." *RTL*

£9.99/$14.95
Crime paperback original
ISBN 1–904738–13–3/978–1904738–13–8
www.bitterlemonpress.com

THE SNOWMAN

Jörg Fauser

"A gritty and slyly funny story. About the life of the underdog, the petty criminal, the fixer, the prostitute and the junkie. With a healthy dose of wit." *Cath Staincliffe, author of the Sal Kilkenny series*

Blum's found five pounds of top-quality Peruvian cocaine in a suitcase. His adventure started in Malta, where he was trying to sell porn magazines, the latest in a string of dodgy deals that never seem to come off. A left-luggage ticket from the Munich train station leads him to the cocaine. Now his problems begin in earnest. Pursued by the police and drug traffickers, the luckless Blum falls prey to the frenzied paranoia of the cocaine addict and dealer. His desperate and clumsy search for a buyer takes him from Munich to Frankfurt, and finally to Ostend. This is a fast-paced thriller written with acerbic humour, a hardboiled evocation of drug-fuelled existence and a penetrating observation of those at the edge of German society.

Jörg Fauser, born in Germany in 1944, was a novelist, essayist and journalist. Having broken his dependency on heroin at the age of thirty, he spent much of the rest of his working life dependent on alcohol. He nevertheless produced three successful novels, including *The Snowman*. On 16 July 1987 he had been out celebrating his forty-third birthday. At dawn, instead of going home, he wandered on to a stretch of motorway, by chance or by choice, and was struck down by a heavy-goods lorry. He died instantly.

"Prose that penentrates the reader's mind like speed, fast paced, without an ounce of fat." *Weltwoche*

"A wonderful crime novel. If justice prevailed, Fauser would be world-famous overnight." *Frankfurt Allgemeine*

£8.99/$13.95
Crime paperback original, ISBN 1–904738–05–2
www.bitterlemonpress.com

SOMEONE ELSE

Tonino Benacquista

"A great read from one of France's best crime writers.
A tale peppered with humour, unpredictable twists and a
healthy dose of suspense. It all makes for a cracking read,
with witty insights into the vagaries of human nature."
Guardian

Who hasn't wanted to become "someone else"? The person
you've always wanted to be . . . the person who won't give up
half way to your dreams and desires?

One evening two men who have just met at a Paris tennis
club make a bet: they give each other exactly three years to
radically alter their lives. Thierry, a picture framer with a
steady clientele, has always wanted to be a private investigator. Nicolas is a shy, teetotal executive trying not to fall off
the corporate ladder. But becoming someone else is not
without risk; at the very least, the risk of finding yourself.

"Benacquista writes with humor and verve. This novel is less
a mystery than a deftly constructed diptych of existential
escapism: each story offers a unique map to new possibilities
in the midst of suffocating lives." *Rain Taxi*

"This has been a big hit in France, and it is easy to see why –
Thierry's attempts to slip into a story by Simenon and
Nicolas's explosive encounter with vodka make for
unexpected, cynical comedy." *The Times*

"Exuberantly written, Benacquista's book is another triumph
for the genre-bending approach to crime fiction."
Tangled Web

Winner of the RTL-LIRE Prize.

£9.99/$14.95
Crime paperback original
ISBN 1–904738–12–5/978–1904738–12–1
www.bitterlemonpress.com

TEQUILA BLUE

Rolo Diez

**"Like a Peckinpah movie: violent, funny, sad, as
hot as salsa, as tasty as tacos and twice as enjoyable."**
Independent on Sunday

It's not easy being a cop in Mexico City.

Meet Carlos Hernandez, Carlito to his women. He's a police
detective with a complicated life. A wife, a mistress, children
by both and a paycheck that never seems to arrive. This
being Mexico, he resorts to money laundering and arms
dealing to finance his police activity. The money for justice
must be found somewhere.

The corpse in the hotel room is that of a gringo with a weak-
ness for blue movies. Carlito's maverick investigation leads
him into a labyrinth of gang wars, murdered prostitutes and
corrupt politicians. A savagely funny, sexy crime adventure
that is a biting satire of life in Mexico.

Rolo Diez, born in Argentina in 1940, was imprisoned for
two years during the military dictatorship and forced into
exile. He now lives in Mexico City, where he works as a
novelist, screenwriter and journalist.

**Both a scathing and picaresque comedy, a biting and spicy
concoction. Just like tequila."** *Le Monde*

£8.99/$13.95
Crime paperback original, ISBN 1–904738–04–4
www.bitterlemonpress.com

A WALK IN THE DARK

Gianrico Carofiglio

"Carofiglio writes crisp, ironical novels that are as much love stories and philosophical treatises as they are legal thrillers."
New Yorker

When Martina accuses her ex-boyfriend – the son of a powerful local judge – of assault and battery, no witnesses can be persuaded to testify on her behalf and one lawyer after another refuses to represent her. Guido Guerrieri knows the case could bring his legal career to a premature and messy end but he cannot resist the appeal of a hopeless cause. Nor deny an attraction to Sister Claudia, the young woman in charge of the shelter where Martina is living, who shares his love of martial arts and his virulent hatred of injustice.

Gianrico Carofiglio is an anti-Mafia prosecutor in southern Italy. *A Walk in the Dark,* his second novel featuring defence counsel Guerrieri, follows on from the success of *Involuntary Witness.*

PRAISE FOR *A WALK IN THE DARK*

"This novel raises the standard for crime fiction. Carofiglio's deft touch has given us a story that is both literary and gritty – and one that speeds along like the best legal thrillers. His insights into human nature – good and bad – are breathtaking." *Jeffery Deaver*

"*A Walk in the Dark*, features an engagingly complex, emotional and moody defence lawyer, Guido Guerrieri, who takes on cases shunned by his colleagues. In passing, Carofiglio provides a fascinating insight into the workings of the Italian criminal justice system." *Observer*

"Part legal thriller, part insight into a man fighting his own demons. Every character in Carofiglio's fiction has a story to tell and they are always worth hearing . . . this powerfully affecting novel benefits from veracity as well as tight writing." *Daily Mail*

£9.99/$14.95
Crime paperback original
ISBN 1–904738–17–6/978–1904738–17–6
www.bitterlemonpress.com